No Time Talking

A Novel

Jon Shirota

TotalRecall Publications, Inc.
1103 Middlecreek
Friendswood, Texas 77546
281-992-3131 281-482-5390 Fax
www.totalrecallpress.com

ISBN: 978-1-64883-104-1
UPC: 6-43977-41041-2

Library of Congress Control Number: 2021946333

FIRST EDITION
1   2   3   4   5   6   7   8   9   10

In fond memory of Mitchell, a jockey and a race horse trainer, for the tons of thrills and excitement he brought me.

To Lauren Reiko an aspiring writer

Author Bio

Jon Hiroshi Shirota was born on Maui, Hawaii. After serving two years in the U.S. Army, he graduated from Brigham Young University and became an Internal Revenue Agent. He quit his job when he was invited to the Handy Writers Colony in Marshall, Illinois (*From Here To Eternity* fame) where he finished his first novel *Lucky Come Hawaii*. Jon also authored *The Chronicles of Ojii-Chan* and *A Navajo Love Story*.

Jon is the recipient of several awards: The John F. Kennedy Center Award; The Rockefeller Center Award; The American College Theater Festival for New Plays; The Best Stage Scenes of 1992 by Smith and Kraus Books; and a grant by the Japan/USA Friendship Commission and the National Endowment for the Arts to spend six months in Okinawa doing research of its immigrants to the United States.

About the Book

The *No Time Talking* Story follows an unlikely pair as they discover that good friends, though hard to come by, are forever, first appearances can be deceiving and the designs of fate are hard to circumvent.

The Friends

George Tsukayama hates his job as an IRS Agent. So, while he is auditing stuffy, prejudiced, old haoles, he dreams of becoming the next great American novelist. He finds inspiration in his friends; a fellow gruff World War II Nisei (Japanese-American) vet who runs a laundromat, and the Mexican college student who sells discarded flowers and parks cars to pay for classes. When he is assigned to audit a beautiful haole woman, who speaks his ancestral language better than he, he is warily captivated by her warmth and love of all things Japanese.

Christine Barrington misses Kobe, Japan. That's why her garden is the style of the Japanese gardens she grew up with, and maintains her Japanese language by cajoling her best friend Carole, a Japanese American, to practice with her. She paints to ease the pain of the death of her parents and the loss of her childhood friend in Kobe. She longs to paint a portrait of the striking young man who parks her car and sells flowers to her. Above all, she wants desperately to befriend the IRS agent sent to audit her, a handsome nihonjin from Hawaii who reminds her of her first love, Shoichi.

Acknowledgement

Grateful acknowledgement is made to the memories of James Jones and Lowney Handy, founders of the Handy Writers Colony, without whose spiritual and material guidance this novel would never have been written.

To Professor Marie Yamazato, for her wonderful translation and her insightful understanding of the Japanese-American experience.

To Patricia McFall, a teacher and a writer, for her devotion, perception and suggestions in editing this novel.

CONTENTS

CHAPTER 1:

The IRS Agent

George Hiroshi Tsukayama hated his job.

He was an Internal Revenue Agent for the U.S. Treasury Department.

He was still angry at himself for majoring in accounting. He should have majored in journalism or creative writing. Accounting, on the other hand, offered a safe and secure career. He could always find a job.

That's what he had thought. After graduating from Cal State Los Angeles four years ago in 1951 he couldn't find a job. No one was hiring a Japanese accountant.

Being an ex-GI, he had preferences over non-veterans applying for federal jobs. The only civil service opening for him then was an Internal Revenue Agent's position. A title he did not especially relish. But it was a job. A job he could not turn down.

And so for the past four years he had been investigating and auditing people's tax returns, mostly white Americans, who were suspicious of a slant-eyed IRS auditor.

He was now driving his five-year-old two-door Ford through spacious Amber Street in Remington Park. The wide streets were shaded by sky-reaching palms and oak trees, the mid-morning Southern California sunlight peering through the branches. The huge windows of the upscale homes were glaring brightly, the sprawling green lawns stretched out to the edge of the street.

It was only a twenty-minute drive from George's packed and crowded office on Sunset and Cahuenga in Hollywood, but the drive was taking him farther and farther away into unfamiliar ground where only the rich and elite lived. As he got closer to the taxpayer's address on 1566 Amber Street, he began picturing the taxpayer.

Christine Barrington. A classy name. No doubt, a rich old widow or a well-heeled divorcee. Thousands of dollars of charitable contributions, sizable capital gains and losses, and a pretty big income from an office rental in downtown LA and another one in Mid-Wilshire.

Yeah. A tax return could sure tell you a lot about a taxpayer--age; education; even personality. And, of course, nationality and religion. This one was undoubtedly a haole, a wasp, who probably stayed home and counted her money every morning and spoke to her affectionate and devoted dog.

The mail box at the front yard said, 1566.

He drove into the wide semi-circle driveway that curved around a four-car garage and led to a huge two-story home with a wide front porch flanked by a couple of grand old columns. One of those old-money homes, he thought, parking and feeling out of place. Picking up his briefcase, he checked himself in the rear-view mirror, making sure his hair was in place, his tie straight, his smile nice and wide. He slid out and took a deep breath. You just didn't know who you'd encounter on an audit. Some were polite; some defensive; some belligerent; almost all resentful. Damnit! He wished this was his last audit. Gettahell away from it all, away from people who hated him but were forced to respect him because of the badge he carried. It won't be too long now when he would be able to tear off his suit and tie and be himself again, a happy, easy-going barefoot boy from Maui, smiling and laughing when he felt like it; not when he had to.

He stepped up to the door, hoping no one was home and he could return to the sanctity of his office. He pressed the door bell and could hear the delicate chimes inside. Then footsteps.

The door finally opened.

A rather tall, slim, reddish-blonde woman stood there. Blue-eyed, she was about his age, late twenties, in a casual white blouse and Levis, and barefoot. Her glasses were perched above her forehead.

"Hello," she said, pleasantly.

"Hello," he returned. He showed her his badge. She was about an inch above his five-eight. "Is Christine Barrington in?"

"I'm Christine," she said. "You must be the IRS agent I spoke to."

"Yes," he said, concealing his surprise. She certainly was not the old maid or old widow he had expected. And she didn't have a German police dog to protect her as in the last audit in Glendale where the old lady held her dog close to her throughout the audit.

"Come in," she opened the door wider. "Please. Come in."

He stepped into the huge front room, noting the high ceiling, the well-preserved furniture arranged precisely where it should be, the wall-to-wall grayish carpeting stretched to all four corners. Near the long winding stairway that led to the second floor was a grand piano with music sheets on a stand. The French doors directly ahead were wide open, letting fresh air into the home, unlike some of the old-money, stale-aired homes in Beverly Hills where he had visited on other audits. Beyond the French doors were a kidney-shaped swimming pool, the blue water glittering in the mid-morning sun, and farther back, beyond the swimming pool, a Japanese garden with a traditional bridge over a fish pond flanked by green bonsai pine trees. Surrounding the palatial backyard were tall California pines, their branches dancing in the morning breeze.

"I have all the records in my office," Christine said, leading him upstairs.

"*Nihonjin?*" she asked.

He looked at her, almost missing a step. "Yeah. Japanese-American."

"Tsukayama," she went on. "Not a common Nihonjin name."

He looked at her again. She had pronounced "Tsukayama," without a haole accent.

"Well," he said, "it's actually an Okinawan name."

"Ah, so, Okinawan," she said. "Are you from there?"

"My parents," he said, slightly annoyed. If he were from Okinawa how would he be speaking English?

"I detected a slight accent over the phone," she said.

"I'm from Hawaii," he said. "Born and raised there."

"Really," she said. "Wonderful place, Hawaii."

They were now at the top of the stairway, approaching the doorway of her studio.

"Ever been there?" he asked, feeling she expected him to ask.

"Yes. Several times," she said. "Oahu, Maui and the Big Island."

"You picked up *nihongo* while there?"

"I grew up speaking nihongo long before then," she said.

"Oh?"

"I was born in Nihon."

"You?"

"Hai," she said. "Nihongo ga hanase masuka?" *Do you speak Japanese?*

"Well," he said, hesitating at the studio door, "I haven't spoken it for so long I'm afraid I'm out of practice."

She laughed pleasantly and opened the door.

"My studio," she said. "Please excuse the mess. I'm the only one who comes into this room."

Looking around, he immediately caught the flood of oil paintings and sketches hanging on the four walls. Some were finished; some unfinished; some were framed; others not. There also were a few sculptures on the floor, some finished; some works-in-progress.

The most noticeable painting was hanging on the near wall before him. It was a painting of an Asian girl in her 20s with long, jet-black hair and glasses. It looked so real he had to study it to be sure it wasn't a photograph.

"That's my best friend, Carole," she said, "Carole Ikeda.

"Born and raised here in California--well, except for those awful camp days."

"Manzanar?"

"Heart Mountain, Wyoming."

He knew a little about the camps from Nisei classmates at LA State and some of the fellow interpreters he had met in the Army. This was the first time he'd heard a haole mentioning it.

He kept studying the painting of the Asian girl. "How did you get to know her?" he asked.

"At SC. We were taking art classes together. She spoke pretty good Nihongo and we'd practice speaking to each other every chance we had. She spent many nights here."

"A nice painting," he said. "Yours?"

She nodded. "Took a while. I finished it just before she got her Masters and went to San Diego State to teach there.

"Ever posed for a portrait?" she asked.

"Me?"

"You'd make a good subject.

"Not me."

"Why are you men so reluctant to pose?"

"Me, I'm no model."

"Like Carole you have interesting features," she said, examining his face a little closer. "I can tell by your eyes you've gone through a lot."

"Just by looking at my eyes?"

"All eyes tell a story."

"Not mine."

"Another man I mentioned it to said the same thing you just said when I told him I'd like to do a portrait of him. And his eyes most definitely told a lot about him."

"He refused to pose?"

"I haven't given up. I'll keep asking him until he gives in. — Oh, I'm sorry," she said. "I almost forgot why you're here."

She stepped over to an old desk, opened the rare folding top cover and revealed a neat stack of bills and receipts, an accounting record of income and expenses, and other items backing up her tax return for 1954 filed in 1955.

"Would you like to sit here?" she said, sliding back a chair and offering it to him.

"Thank you," he said politely, sitting and opening his briefcase.

"Coffee?" she asked. "Nice and hot. Just put it on."

"No thanks. I had a cup before coming here'" he said.

"If you change your mind…"

"Thanks."

He reached into his brief case and brought out the original copy of her 1954 tax return which her CPA, Tom Hoffkins, had filed. He knew Tom had advised her what to expect in the audit and not to volunteer any information. He had teased Tom about it the last time he was at his office in Beverly Hills. "Provide information only when asked," was Tom's motto to his clients.

"How long have you been an IRS agent?" Christine asked, watching him opening her tax return.

"Four years," he replied. "Going on five."

"Career?"

He nodded.

He began checking the larger contributions.

"The Buick," he now said, "you contributed it to the City of Hope, too?"

"It was my mom's favorite charity," Christine said.

"It was her car?"

"Yes. A 1952 Buick. Hardly any miles on it. And Mom kept it well maintained."

"If it were her car what made Tom Hoffkins deduct it on your return?"

"I inherited it from her."

He looked at her. "She gave it to you?"

"I got it when she died."

"Oh," he uttered, feeling foolish for thinking that Tom would make that mistake.

Studying the contributions, he realized that the dresses, coats, shoes and personal woman's items must have once belonged to her mother, and had been passed on to her.

He kept studying the list.

What about the man's suit, tie, shoes, etc? he thought. Were they passed on to her, too?

"They belonged to my Dad," Christine volunteered.

He looked at her. Her eyes had turned misty, her pleasant smile evaporated.

"They died together," she now said. "In an accident. Three years ago."

Jeesus! Now, he's got to ask about the accident. Find out if all the contributions to City of Hope were actually hers and not her parents'.

"You might have read about it," she said. "Sunset Boulevard, near UCLA."

Oh, Christ! So they were her father and mother! A kid crossing over the divider at hairpine bend and driving head on into a car with a couple going the opposite direction. All three. Gone!

"Yes," he finally said. "Yes, I read about it. I'm sorry I didn't make the connection."

She forced a smile.

"It changed my life," she said. "I had to quit teaching and go through psychological therapy."

"All your paintings," he said, indicating all the paintings in the room, "they've helped?"

She nodded. "I've always painted, but these past years, I've really kept myself busy.

"What about you?" she asked. "Your mom and dad still live in Hawaii?"

He shook his head.

"Back in Okinawa?"

"They're gone, too."

"In an accident!"

He shook his head again. "My father, cerebral hemorrhage; my mother shortly afterward, pneumonia.   The year I graduated," he added.

Oh, jeesus, now he's telling her about himself. It wasn't nearly as tragic as hers; nevertheless, just as traumatic. His father, gone in the beginning of the month back 1950; his mother at the end of the month. He went back home for the funerals, but it was Kimiko, his sister, who made all the necessary funeral arrangements, and later, the settlement of the farmland in Kapuna. It was now rented to a family friend who was raising pigs, chickens and vegetables on the land.

"Look," he said, "if you want to, I can come back and continue the audit some other time.   Or, better, I could talk to Tom Hoffkins about it."

"If you don't mind, "she said, "I'd rather you finish it here. Tom is a wonderful CPA, but I hate to keep burdening him."

"If that's what you want," he said.

"How about a cup of coffee now?" she said. "I can bring it up in a second."

"Yes," he said. "Yes, I think I can use a cup."

"Good." She headed out the door and down the stairway.

He sure had this woman wrong, he told himself. Her tax return revealed nothing about her. She's young, not old; she's friendly, not resentful; she's a genuinely cheerful person; not bitchy and suspicious. And, to top it all, she's like a classy, yasashii Japanese woman.

She's most likely the only heir to the estate. This house alone must be worth a couple of million and the rental office properties even more. And all she's interested in is her paintings.

Well, she can afford it. No mortgages; no back bills; no IOUs.
A steady income coming in every month. It sure would be great
if it were happening to him, too. Hey, he said to himself, don't
complain. Your father and mother left you something, too. The
income from the farmland you and Kimiko are sharing is not
nearly as great as this woman's, but you can't complain.
Someday, when you devote yourself completely to your writing
the farm income would surely help.

For now, you just gotta keep hanging in there. Until Lowney
Handy invites you to her writers' colony. Then, goodbye tax
returns, goodbye conniving tax attorneys and sayonara
Hollywood CPAs and their egotistical actor clients. Kiss my
okole.

Christine returned with a tray containing a shiny silver pot, a
couple of delicate cups, and milk and sugar in tiny dishes.

She moved the tax records aside, laid the tray on the desk, and
poured coffee from the shiny silver pot. "Milk? Sugar?"

"No. No thanks. Black's okay."

"I think both of us need a break," she said.

"Yeah," he agreed. "Yeah. Good idea."

He took a sip, then another. "Great coffee," he said. "Nice
and hot.

"You said you were born in Nihon?" he asked, curiously. He
had wanted to ask much earlier, but was anxious to get the audit
going.

"Kobe," she said. And, very candidly, "1927. Ever been
there?"

He shook his head. "Just Yokohama and Tokyo. Late 1945.
Except for the Emperor's palace grounds and MacArthur's GHQ

building, nothing was left standing."

"Kobe was destroyed, too," she said, sadly.

"Came back after the war?"

"Before," she said. "1938. When Dad and Mom decided they should --Oh, I forgot to mention. Dad and Mom went there before I was born. 1925. Christian missionaries."

"Oh," he said. "They were missionaries."

She nodded again. "Before that, Dad's mom and dad, my paternal grandparents, were missionaries there."

"Wow," he said, not knowing what else to say.

"For several years after we returned," she said, "I kept up a correspondence with a dear friend of mine, Shoichi Murata. Actually," she went on laughing, "he was my grade-school boyfriend."

He chuckled.

"We were both eleven. Someday, when we're grown-ups," she continued, "we would get married and live happily ever after in Kobe." She laughed again.

He joined her in laughter.

"Then the war, huh?" he said.

She nodded. "We lost touch with each other. No letters after Pearl Harbor."

"And after the war?"

She shook her head. "I prayed he and his family were spared during the bombings."

He could say nothing. All the big cities in Japan were annihilated, Tokyo, Yokohama, Osaka, Kobe... There was nothing standing when he went there on his pass. Like people in Naha, Okinawa, everyone in Japan seemed in a daze, barely making a go of it.

He took another sip.

"What about you?" she asked. "Any children?"

None that I know of, he was tempted to say. He thought better of it. She wouldn't find it funny.

"I'm...not married," he finally said.

"Haven't met the right girl yet?"

"I'm still looking," he said, bringing the cup up to his lips and shutting up.

"You should meet my friend, Carole," she said. "Very attractive, a talented painter, smart, a dedicated schoolteacher."

"I would disappoint her," he said.

"Oh, I wouldn't say that," she said. "You seem very stable, a dedicated IRS man, knows what you want in life."

He choked back a laughter. If she only knew, he thought. A dedicated IRS man! Did he really seem like one?!

"That painting," he said, pointing to Carole Ikeda's portrait, "you ever exhibited it?"

"Exhibited it?"

'In one of those exhibits we have in LA."

She shook her head emphatically. "I'll never do that."

"It's a beautiful piece of work," he said, still admiring the portrait. "I'm not a painter, but I've studied some pretty good paintings during my audits. You know, taxpayers taking deductions for paintings they've donated to galleries, schools, churches, local governments..."

"Donate Carole's portrait?!" she protested. "I wouldn't think of it."

"Not donate it," he said. "See what the experts think about it."

"Why would I want to do that?"

"Don't you want to know how good that painting is?"

"I know it is good. And that's all that matters."

He chastised himself for opening his mouth. The portrait he nevertheless thought was really beautiful. Much better than some of the donated portraits he had checked on his audits.

"I paint because I enjoy painting," Christine said. "It's not only a pleasure, but a challenge. To create something on a bare canvass."

"And not show it?"

She shook her head. "What matters is what I think of them."

Can't argue against that, he told himself. Painting is not like writing. In writing you've got to impress the reader; in painting it's a personal observation, a personal evaluation. Whodahell cares what others think. Especially if you're not trying to make a living selling them.

He sipped the last drop. Better lay off talking about her paintings, he told himself. Very independent woman. Don't give a damn what others think of them.

"Want another cup?" she asked.

"No thanks," he said.

He returned to her tax return, once more going through the list of donations.

"You really enjoy your work?" she questioned, not sarcastically but genuinely curious.

"It's a living," he said. He almost said, "Not all of us have a great big inheritance…" He bit his tongue.

He came to a coat, obviously once belonging to her mother. "How did you arrive at the value of this coat?" he questioned.

She leaned over and studied the list. "Oh, that coat," she said. "It was Mom's. A beautiful fur coat she had bought many years ago in Japan."

"How much did it cost?"

"I...really don't know."

"You deducted $1,000 for it."

"That's what Tom believed was the fair market value. Isn't that how much you deduct, its fair market value?"

He nodded. 'Yeah," he said. "How much you're willing to sell it for; how much someone is willing to pay fot it."

"That's what Tom said."

"I'll have to check it with City of Hope," he said.

"Whatever you say," she said. "You're the IRS man."

He looked up at her. Was she getting bitchy?

"Are you checking all of the clothing deductions?"

"No," he said. "Not all. I'm sure most of them are reasonable."

"What about Dad's suits, shoes, ties? Are they reasonable?"

"They look okay."

"And the Buick?"

"I'll check the blue book value."

"It was hard for me to decide what to do with all the clothing," she said. "They were the last of Mom's and Dad's belongings. I...guess I did not want to part with them."

He avoided her eyes. Christ! Whydahell are you getting so hard-nosed with her, he told himself. After what she went through, losing her father and mother the way she did.

He was tempted to give her a no-change audit, accept the return as filed, then warned himself, the downtown office would go through the audit and want to know on what basis he had allowed the deductions. Also, there was still the loss on a stock transaction he hadn't questioned yet.

"This loss you took on your investment…" he began.

"Oh, yes," she said. "Tom said you'd ask about that. Actually, it was an investment in a film that a friend was producing."

"A movie?"

"A documentary. Hal, Hal Bolden, a classmate in films, had several of us invest in his project. It seemed a wise investment then. An environmental document. How to get rid of smog around the world."

"You were all students?"

"Just me. Hal was…well, he could have been more than just a friend. I discovered he was seeing one of those wannabe actresses."

"Didn't you get your money back?" he questioned.

She shook her head. "He declared bankruptcy. Would you like to see the stock certificate? The bankruptcy court order?"

He shook his head. "As long as Tom saw them…"

"He said something about not being able to take the entire film loss, but I could offset most of it against a stock gain."

"That's what he did."

"Besides, I needed some money to rebuild the Japanese garden," she said, pointing out the window at the garden. "I needed a new bridge and the pond needed repairs."

"Your father built it?"

"Grandpa. Then Dad expanded it. That was many years ago. Would you like to see the garden?"

Well, why not? How many chances would he have walking through a spectacular backyard with a kidney-shaped swimming pool and a colorful Japanese garden. Right in the heart of exclusive Remington Park. Besides, he wanted to get away from the paper work and get some fresh air.

He gathered his notes, placed them and the tax return into his briefcase, and followed Christine out the door, the briefcase in his hand.

Outside, he walked around the swimming pool with Christine, then approached the bridge of the Japanese garden. Below, in the water, were countless, multi-colored koi fish, red, orange, blue, gliding effortlessly, peacefully, oblivious to the not-too-far away fast life of raucous Hollywood Boulevard and Vine. The koi, every conceivable size, from a few inches to a foot-and-a-half, stuck their snozzles up in the air, apparently waiting to be fed.

Christine reached into a bag tied to the rail of the bridge, took out a handful of feed, and tossed them into the water. In a second, the koi, dozens of them, all scrambled to get their share of the food.

"Want to try?" Christine asked, pushing the bag of feed to him. "Not too much; just enough to get their attention."

He had never fed a bunch of koi. He saw a lot of them in Narita, Japan, on a sightseeing excursion, but never this close. They seemed tame enough to be petted.

He tossed the feed into the water and watched the koi splash together for their food.

"That's Mamoru," Christine pointed to the largest koi. "The one with a red streak from its head to its tail.

"Now, Mamoru," she said to the koi, "don't be so greedy. Share the food with your friends."

"You have names for all of them?"

"Just my favorites," she said, "Mamoru, Sachiko, Hitoshi..."

"No Shoichi?"

She looked at him. Her eyes returned to the koi. "He was my favorite," she said.

"Was?"

"He expired."

"Oh."

"The day I got my letter back from Japan."

Now don't tell me she believes in those Japanese tell-tale signs? he told himself.

"I'm more Nihonjin than you think," she said.

He could say nothing. He, too, was influenced by old Japanese myths growing up in superstitious Japanese neighborhoods. Obake ghost stories, reincarnation of dead foxes in human forms, communications between a fish and humans... But to connect a returned letter to the death of a koi!

"You think it's just a coincidence?" she tested him.

She's way ahead of me in these matters, he told himself. Don't argue.

"I gave Shoichi a decent burial," she said, nodding toward the tall pine near the concrete wall. There actually was a headstone there, small but unmistakable.

Wow! He thought. Is she weird or what?

"Did you notice my koi painting?"

He retraced the paintings on the wall. Yeah. There was a painting of a koi.

"That's Shoichi," she said.

All he could do was to nod.

"They've both found peace," she went on.

There was serenity on her face when she said it.

This audit's turned out to be far more than he had expected.

"Look," he said, "I'll have to go down to City of Hope and

verify your contributions."

"You're leaving? I thought you'd have lunch here with me."

"I'd like to, but…"

"Next time?"

"Yeah, next time! I'll give you a call for another appointment."

"Whatever you say. You're the IRS man."

Damnit! He wished she'd stop saying that. The briefcase firmly in his hand, he stepped away from the bridge.

They walked back across the bridge, around the swimming pool, into the living room, and finally came back out into the front porch.

She extended her hand. "It was nice meeting you," she said, bowing.

He shook her hand, also bowing.

"I hope you'll be able to close the examination the next time you're here," she said.

"I'm sure I will," he said.

"Sayonara."

"Sayonara."

CHAPTER 2:

The Painter

Christine always felt a warm natsukashi feeling sweeping through her whenever she spoke or heard Nihongo. Even just a few words. They would always bring back nostalgic scenes of Kobe, Japan. Scenes of yasashii childhood friends with whom she sang sweet Japanese songs.

After waving good-bye to George Tsukayama, she stepped back into the front door and climbed up the stairway into her studio. She decided to leave all the tax paperwork on her desk until he came back. Once the audit was over, she'd be able to concentrate on her next project, a colorful impressionistic scene of her Japanese garden.

Although she already had a degree from prestigious USC in education and art, she was now a student at LA State. She was there because her favorite art teacher at SC was now teaching an advanced art class at LA State.

Painting sceneries was always relaxing and rewarding. It was so unlike the daunting task of doing a portrait with its demanding, uncompromising rigidity. Not that portraits weren't rewarding and satisfying when the result was nearly photographic.

The advantage of doing sceneries was the isolation and seclusion they provided, away from the mundane surroundings and endless conversations. There were drawbacks, however.

She would lose contact with people and have no sense of what was happening to the rest of the world.

Maybe that was the problem with her and Hal Bolden. She preferred to be alone or to be with only a handful of select friends while Hal enjoyed the company of many. Especially beautiful would-be actresses.

The bigger complication with Hal was her investment in his production company. It wasn't much, $25,000, a trifle when considering the total cost of a movie production. Her near-relationship with Hal was over by then. She had felt painfully betrayed when she discovered, along with the other investors, that Hal was spending their money on himself: trips to Hawaii with girlfriends, luxury car leases, parties in Beverly Hills restaurants and gifts for hanger-on friends.

When she tried to withdraw her investment, Hal had spent it all.

She had been taken, and the sooner she admitted it, the less anger she had felt for Hal. Movie production was a risky, hazardous business. Investors were always losing money in their quest to make a fast buck. And she had been one of them.

She looked over at the portrait of Carole on the near wall. It was one of her favorites, and she was glad George Tsukayama had admired it. What was missing was a companion piece. Maybe George would go for it. That is, if she could persuade him to pose for her.

And there was the young Mexican man who also refused to have his portrait done.

Armando Fuentes was a tall and trim Latino in early twenties with dark brown hair and the dark brown eyes. He was an attractive man. Actually, very handsome in a rugged way, with a deep, severe scar running from the corner of his right eye down to his jaw. Undoubtedly, a mystery behind that and his artificial leg.

She was always tempted to ask him about the scar and his leg. But would always back off. The brief moments she spoke to him were at the parking lot he managed in the mornings at the corner of Vermont and Santa Monica. He also sold flowers from the back of his pickup truck parked at the first space, and attended City College nearby as a part-time student.

She started to park her late-model Chrysler at Ray's Parking when the semester began, and would walk down to the campus. Armando always reserved a space for her on her school days: Monday, Wednesday and Friday mornings. She would buy a bouquet of roses from him on Mondays, and he would place it in a vase and leave it in her car. When her car was dirty, he would wash it, and she paid him generously.

It had been going on for several weeks. She still could not fathom the cause of the conspicuous scar on his cheek nor about his missing leg. Once, for a brief moment, after she told him about her art class and he told her that he was attending City College, which shared its campus with LA State, she was tempted to inquire about the scar and his leg. She just couldn't do it.

Then, last Monday morning, when she was quite early for her class, she bought her usual bouquet of roses, and stood at Armando's pickup truck striking up a conversation. Nothing special. More about their classes. All the while tempted to ask the pressing question. And feeling a little guilty for trying to maneuver him. She told him about her parents' accident, which he had heard about and was surprised they had been her parents. She had hoped he would tell her about his own misfortune. But he maneuvered clearly off the subject and instead began asking questions of his own. Her license plate showed USC. Was she really a graduate of USC? If so, why was she taking a class at a state college? Or was she a professor there?

That left an opening. She told him about her professor at LA State and her interest in doing portraits. Would he be willing to pose for her?

The opening quickly closed. "I'm no model," he said.

She tried coaxing. She would pay him for his time. By the hour. All he had to do was sit and relax.

"No way!"

And that was as close as she could get.

First him, then George. They would be good subjects for her private collection. They would be different from the Caucasian models in class, the usual blue-eyed, blond-haired, young egotistical aspiring actors from Hollywood.

Christine stepped over to the window and surveyed the Japanese garden shaded by the tall pines bordering the backyard.

She had always yearned to go back to Kobe, but the war had ruled that out, and then the post-war restrictions. Then the accident. She could go back now, stay a few months or even a year. She could learn Japanese painting, sculpture and sumi sketching. And get to speak Nihongo and feel at home again.

There was always something missing in her life, she thought. When Carole was around she could confide in her. When Carole left for San Diego she realized that Carole had been filling that gap. And now it was widening.

After the accident, she found herself deliberately staying away from church services. Why didn't God prevent the accident? Why didn't He warn Dad about the erratic, drunken driver approaching him?

Her life has been filled with more unanswered questions the past three years. And she was certain there would be no immediate answers, if there ever would be one.

Thank heaven, she had her paintings!

She stepped back from the window, went over to the phone, and dialed Carole's number.

It rang. And rang.

Of course! Carole wouldn't be home. Today was Thursday. She'd be lecturing at her English class.

CHAPTER 3

The Orphanage

While Christine was obsessed trying to learn about his mysterious scar and his prosthetic leg, Armando Fuentes was in his pickup at Ray's Parking Lot studying for his mid-term English exam. The parking lot was filled and he had put up a sign "FULL" at the entrance. He had also sold all the flowers in the back of his pickup which netted him $15.00.

Every school-day morning, he'd direct the incoming traffic at the corner of Santa Monica and Vermont and would remind the customers of the fresh flowers in his pickup. Earlier in the morning he'd be in downtown LA picking up flowers the whole sellers had discarded. He would return to the parking lot, clean and trim the flowers and place them in buckets of fresh water. His customers, mostly ladies, loved the roses. Some the gingers, others the gardenias, and a few the chrysanthemums.

He'd often wonder what the ladies would think if they knew they were buying unwanted flowers. On the other hand, they seemed happy to be buying the flowers at a huge discount.

One of the patrons, a tall, slim lady, her reddish-blonde hair fallen casually over her forehead, always bought a bouquet of roses. And would pay the full price for it. Never bargaining. Every now then, when she was a little early for her class at LA State she would talk to him about her art classes or would ask him about his own classes. He caught her staring at his scar once or twice, but never inquiring about it.

She was a classy lady, he thought, the way she spoke, the way she dressed, the car she drove. He knew she wanted to ask him about his scar, but—how do you say it? she was too sophisticated—to ask him about it. She probably wanted to know about his leg, too.

He got back to his mid-term exam. He had to make an "A" in his English class. At worse a "B." He wanted to maintain a 3.5 average so he could be accepted at UCLA after LACC. He was taking just the minimum classes until he was accustomed to college life. After another semester, he hoped to be a full-time student, and be able to maintain a B-plus average.

He was saving his GI Bill for his future at UCLA. His rent was cheap, his second-hand pickup with nothing special for a handicap was not too expensive to run and his steady disability checks from the VA and his earnings selling flowers and parking cars were enough to keep him going.

His major would be physical therapy. He had been a patient for almost two years and had received the best treatment the VA hospital could offer. Highly impressed by the dedication and care of the therapists, he decided he'd become one of them. He had received encouragements from the therapists and assurances from the doctors that they would give him strong recommendations so he could be accepted by most universities in the country.

He had never thought he would one day go to college. A mechanic's or a carpenter's or even a truck driver's school, but never college. And here he was attending Los Angeles City College with kids five years younger than he who seemed to think going to college was no big deal.

His high school grades weren't really bad. They weren't good either. Just average. Which was expected of kids at Valley Orphanage in San Fernando Valley. There was no one there pressing them to make good grades. The main goal was to attend school every day.

Even Aunty Wilkins, his orphanage mother, did not expect him to go on to college. Aunty, however, insisted that he finish high school.

A middle-aged negro lady, Aunty was as close to a mother as he ever had. She worked at Valley Orphanage where she had multiple duties. She was always a kind, gentle woman all the kids looked up to. She had no children of her own. And Armando had come into her life when he was left at the orphanage at three. According to her, Armando's mother had died a few weeks before and his father had brought him to the orphanage. No one knew what happened to his father who, according to rumors, returned to Mexico.

Aunty was partial to him because he was the youngest in the orphanage and he had taken to her right away. They became inseparable. Every now and then, after receiving permission from the administration, Aunty would take Armando to her home for the weekend and she and her husband, Jason, a janitor at a high school, would take him to the movie, zoo or to the beach.

One of the assignments for his college English class had been to write about the closest person in his life. Armando, of course, had no one closer than Aunty Wilkins. His paper was about someone who was not his real mother, but had become more than a real mother. A real mother, he wrote, had no choice but to be a mother because she gave birth to her child. A mother, who was not a birth mother, becomes a mother by choice. A choice led by true love and affection.

He knew his writing was very simple, which was the only way he knew how to write. It did, however, express his deep love and devotion to Aunty Wilkins.

The story could have gone on and on, but the teacher had limited the assignment to three pages. After revealing briefly his life at the orphanage, he ended it with his volunteering in the Army. He was 18 going on to 19 in a few months, and had always wanted to see the world outside of the orphanage surroundings. The Korean War was at its peak and Aunty was afraid what could happen to him, but she gave her blessings and, in a way, was glad he was now a man able to serve his country.

He and Aunty wrote each other once a week from his basic training days to his overseas assignment. Then, one day, while in combat, he received a letter from Jason saying that Aunty had a heart attack and had passed away at the General Hospital.

He concluded his story that his real mother had died when he was a child and hardly knew her, and now the only mother he really knew was gone. He said he was glad that he was wounded after, not before, Aunty was gone.

Going through physical therapy at the VA Hospital was a tough road. Fortunately, he was always in top shape. The exercises he went through to rebuild his left leg was painful at first. Then gradually felt as though he had not lost it. He sometimes even had an urge to reach down to his phantom leg and scratch it.

Then came the adjustment to the prosthetic addition to his knee. It was terribly uncomfortable, if not painful in the beginning, but with the help of the therapists, eventually adjusted to it. Before long, he was able to walk without any help. And the limping became less and less.

The gym exercises had helped rebuild his arms and his right leg to what they were before he was wounded. The workouts brought back the many days he had spent in the boxing gym in San Fernando Valley during his high school days. He had started as a 160-pound middleweight, then as a 175-pound light heavyweight, and during his senior year as a 190-pound heavyweight. Except for losing a couple of fights during his earlier bouts, he was undefeated and his trainer took a special interest in him. The trainer thought he was a great pro prospect. Especially after he knocked out his last two opponents in the Golden Gloves tournaments.

His urge to join the Army, however, put away all thoughts of turning pro. The trainer was disappointed. He encouraged Armando to keep fighting in the Army, and when he was discharged, to come back to his gym and talk about a pro career.

Again, going back to his English book and memorizing some of the rules of grammar in his pickup, Armando wished he had studied harder in high school and had learned what he was now studying, nouns, pronouns, adverbs, adjectives and proper sentence structures. Thank heaven he had always enjoyed reading novels, magazines and newspapers. They had helped him to improve his vocabulary and had made him realize that every sentence and every paragraph in the novels, magazines and newspapers were written by writers who had studied the basic rules of writing.

He was now catching up with the younger students in his class and hoped he would soon be their equal or better. He had an advantage over the kids. He was older, more matured, and knew why he was in college. He was not interested in college social life. Nor did he care to associate with the kids after school hours. They were all nice friendly kids and showed respect for him, if not sympathy, for what had happened to him in the war, but that was the past; he now had his future to consider.

Basic training in the Army had not been as rough and tough as it had been cracked up to be. He actually loved the calisthenics, the long hikes, the rifle and machine gun practices, the grenade throwing techniques and the long-range artillery shelling.

What he enjoyed most was training for the Fort Ord boxing matches. He had turned out for the company boxing team with Rudy Diaz, a great welterweight he had met during the LA tournaments. Rudy, weighing less than 150 lbs, could hit like a heavyweight. He won all his five fights by KO's.

Rudy had a year of college before he volunteered in the Army. After his discharge he planned to continue college on the GI Bill. He was promoted to Pfc then to corporal in Korea. Shortly afterward, because of the heavy casualties in the front lines, he got his sergeant's stripes and became a squad leader.

Armando, too, eventually got promoted. First as a Pfc then a corporal.

Like Rudy, Armando fought GI fighters from all over the country. He won two by KO's, another by a technical knockout when his opponent was unable to answer the bell in the second round, and the last one against a well-known Golden Glove heavyweight champ, Ernie Campbell, from Chicago.

Campbell, a Negro, knocked Armando down in the first round with a vicious right and for a moment Armando did not know where he was. He had never been down on the canvas before. He looked up and Campbell was grinning at him, daring him to get up. At the count of seven, after the referee pushed

Campbell to a neutral corner, Armando forced himself to get up, his legs wobbling. He gazed over at Campbell's corner. Campbell still had a triumphant grin on his face. Armando shook his head to clear the cobwebs, and waited for Campbell to come charging.

In a few seconds, his head cleared and he was able to resort to the lessons he learned from his trainer in San Fernando Valley. He backed away, circling the champ, ducking blows, holding on, refusing to give Campbell an opening.

Armando was now able to flick jabs at Campbell who was beginning to be frustrated. Armando would maneuver closer, hit Campbell several quick blows, then back away before Campbell could retaliate. The round ended, and Armando was grateful.

In the second round, Campbell began cursing at Armando whenever Armando gripped his arms and refused to let go. Armando's confidence was building up. He had lasted the vicious first round and was now well into the second round.

In the third round, Campbell kept waving Armando to start fighting. Armando grinned at him and stuck to his strategy, flicking jabs, moving right to left, feeling Campbell's heavy blows missing by inches. Campbell now left himself open. Armando timed a hook to his head and Campbell went down. The crowd jumped up to their feet, yelling and screaming for Armando to finish off the champ.

Campbell rose to his knees, shook his head, jumped up and came charging in a rage with blows from every direction. Armando, knowing that he could not afford to trade blows with Campbell, kept dancing away, jabbing, throwing an occasional right, hanging on to the champ's arm refusing to let go.

And Armando won the fight on points.

Next day, when the Stars and Stripes wrote about the

spectacular heavyweight fight and showed a picture of the champ down on his knees, Armando clipped the article and sent it to his trainer. The trainer, very happy and excited, urged him to continue training. He warned, however, not to start drinking or smoking as most GIs do.

And he did not. Not until he was wounded.

His boxing days were, of course, over. He never bothered to look up his trainer after coming home. Their dream of his pro career remained a dream. He had to start a new life now. A roadwork, not in boxing, but a journey on a new untested career.

Even before his discharge from the hospital, he began learning to drive with one foot. Fortunately, the therapist who used his own car to help him, had a car with an automatic shift, and he learned to drive it after only a few tries.

He would have looked up Rudy's family in East LA had he not been confined in Army hospitals in San Francisco, Seattle and finally at the Vets hospital in LA. He was sure Rudy understood why he had not kept his promise yet.

His therapist friend helped him buy a used car from a salesman who was also a wounded vet and understood what he, Armando, would have to go through adjusting to a new life. The salesman gave Armando a big discount on a second-hand Chevy pickup with an automatic shift that the original owner had kept in pretty good shape.

His next move was to find an apartment. His therapist friend, a white, suggested that Armando find an apartment in the safe Hollywood area near LA City College. The therapist, never having experienced racial discrimination, did not expect Armando to be turned down by landlords. At times subtly, at times abruptly.

Always having a roof over his head at the orphanage and not knowing the ways of landlords, Armando believed if he could afford to pay the rent landlords would welcome him with open arms.

He soon learned that the white landlords were no different from the white kids at school who looked down on people like him from the orphanage. The lesson came gradually. He believed the first rejection and then the second, "The apartment has just been rented out." When he came to the third "Apartment For Rent" sign and was told by the landlord that he had forgotten to take the sign down, he became suspicious. Coming to another "Vacant" apartment, he was out of patience. He asked the landlord if the "Vacant" sign meant for whites only. The landlord stammered for a moment, then said he was not the landlord. He was just a manager.

Pissed and wanting to retaliate against the damn Hollywood landlords, he drove to the less attractive neighborhood near the stores, shops and bars. Parking his car in a lot on Santa Monica near Vermont, he walked into the back door of a bar adjoining the parking lot. He needed a beer to cool him off.

Sitting at the partially empty semi-dark bar, he paid for a Bud and sat there stretching his prosthetic leg. Is this what he had fought for? Almost got killed? So a bunch of money-grabbing sonsofbitches could stay home count their money while stupid GIs like him was out there fighting for 'em?

The thirtyish bartender, a burly white, had watched him limping into the bar. The bartender had tried not to notice the scar on his face. "Your leg bothering you?" he asked.

"Yeah," Armando said, not really wanting to speak to anyone. "One of them days."

He kept stretching his prosthetic leg.

"Just back from the war over there?" the bartender asked.

Armando nodded.

"Me, I was in the other war," the bartender said. "Normandy."

The last thing Armando wanted to do right now was to talk about wars.

"Going to City College?" the bartender asked.

Armando nodded. "Right now, I'm looking for an apartment."

"Yeah?" the bartender said. "There's a three-story building on Madison. Coupla blocks down and another block to the left. Cheap rent. Nice place."

Armando studied the man. "They rent to Mexicans?"

The bartender grinned. "Gave you a bunch of bullshit over there in Hollywood, huh?"

"Yeah."

"It was Italians yesterday," the bartender said. "Today, it's Mexicans."

"And negroes."

"You don't see none of them even trying around here."

It occurred to Armando that he had not noticed negroes looking for an apartment in Hollywood.

"Some day, maybe," the bartender said.

"Yeah," Armando said. "Maybe some day."

The bartender extended his hand across the bar. "Ray. Ray Giacamo."

Armando shook the man's hand. "Armando. Armando Fuentes."

"Hey, man," Ray now said, "you good at parking cars?"

"I used to be."

"Want a job takin' care of my lot next door, you got it."

"Parking cars?"

"It'll get you lunch money. The last kid workin' for me got through LACC and went on to UCLA."

"Got to find a place first," Armando said.

"That place I just told you. Go on over."

"You know the landlord?"

"Not the landlord. One of the guys livin' there. He comes here for a few now and then. George... --There I go 'gain. Keep forgettin' his last name. A Japanese. A vet like you and me."

"If they rent to a Japanese they'd rent to a Mexican, huh?"

"Hey, man," Ray said. "I've got not'ing to do with the damn rules people make. Don' like it no more than you."

Armando took a sip. Rules, he thought. Damn rules. Who makes them? You can't live here; you can't live there. You can live here if you're white; you can't if you're not.

A new customer walked in and sat at the corner stool. Ray went over to serve him.

Maybe, he'd go over to Madison and check that apartment house, Armando told himself. It'd be the last straw, he thought, if they're willing to rent to a Japanese but not a Mexican.

"So Frankie," he could hear Ray saying to the new customer, "got the part?"

"Aw, just a damn walk-in part," Frankie said, who seemed a little drunk. He was about forty, semi-bald, wearing an open-collared shirt. "Some asshole robbed me of the part I wanted."

"A'ways that way, huh?" Ray said.

"One of these days, they're gonna find out I'm a helluva actor and give me one of those parts I deserve," Frankie said.

"Yeah, sure," Ray said.

"My tab still good?" Frankie asked.

"A'most up to the limit."

"C'mon. My usual straight."

"Right."

Armando noticed that after serving Frankie, Ray went over to the cash register, took out a bill and made an entry.

Ray came back over to Armando.

"Actors and would-be actors," Ray whispered. "Lotta 'em went to City College's acting school. Few made it; most still dreaming."

"Hey, Ray," Frankie called. "Whattahell you talkin' to him for? C'mon over. Lemme tell you 'bout the part I'm gonna go in for tomorrow."

Ray ignored Frankie.

"Hey, Ray! Why waste your time talking to that Mexican?"

Armando clenched his teeth, trying not to hear what he was hearing.

"See what I gotta go through?" Ray said sofly to Armando. "I should've kept going to college."

"Hey, Ray!" Frankie called again.

"Aw, Christ..." Ray muttered.

Armando said nothing.

"Hey, Ray!"

"C'mon, Frankie. I'm talkin' to Armando."

"Armando..." Frankie repeated. "I'm Frankie. Frankie Livingston."

"Yeah. Right, Frankie."

"You gonna keep talkin' to that Mex or you're gonna come here and talk to your own kind."

"Shit like that still going on?" Ray asked Armando.

"Not as bad as it used, to be" Armando said.

"C'mon, Ray," Frankie went on. "I need 'nother one."

"You had 'nough, Frankie," Ray said.

"Enough!" Frankie protested.

Ray ignored him.

"Actors..." Ray whispered to Armando. "Just do a walk-in scene and you're an actor...."

"Hey, Ray! C'mon!"

"I'm cutting you off, Frankie. I'm lowering your limit until you're cleared."

'After all these years!'

"No more, Frankie."

Frankie staggered up. "This damn fucking joint!" He slammed his empty glass hard on the counter, and headed for the back door. "After all these years, I get treated worse than a Mex."

Armando took a deep breath. He glanced over at the back door and watched Frankie staggering out.

"Makes you wonder how guys like him manage to live so long," Ray said.

CHAPTER 4:

Lowney Handy

After leaving Christine Barrington's home, George drove his old Ford out of exclusive Remington Park and headed north toward his office on Sunset Boulevard. Up ahead, on the hillside, the gigantic HOLLWOOD sign was conspicuous as ever.

He still had not gotten over the tall, reddish-blonde girl speaking Nihongo. Without a trace of accent, too. If he had shut his eyes and listened to her, he'd really have thought she was a Nihonjin.

The first time he had ever heard a haole speaking Nihongo was in Fort Savage, Minnesota, when he was training to be an interpreter. The instructor, a haole officer, was pretty good. But he had an accent. You knew he learned his Nihongo by studying it. With Christine Barrington it was a natural Nihonjin voice.

And, that Japanese garden! Imagine a Japanese garden in the heart of Remington Park! With a real Japanese bridge and koi fish in the pond.

He slowed as he approached Santa Monica and stopped when the street light turned yellow, then red. That's the difference between high-class, educated haoles and low-class uneducated ones, he told himself. The high-class haoles were interested in the culture of Japan while the low-class kept hating Japan for the Pearl Harbor attack over ten years ago. And some of the damn low-class bastards blame him for the attack.

After what he had gone through in the war!

Aw, stop complaining, he said to himself. He came out okay. Not even a scratch. Guam, Iwo Jima, Okinawa. Not like what had happened to two of his interpreter buddies in Guam. One was killed by an American who took him for a Japanese soldier; the other by Japanese fanatic who would not surrender.

The light changed to green.

He pressed the accelerator and continued on.

A block up were several young GIs getting off a bus and looking around. Apparently, hoping to see actors and actresses standing at the street corner. Now that the Korean War was over they would be in a peace-time tour of duty in the States or overseas.

The GIs reminded George of a great book that came out in 1951. "From Here To Eternity." It was a best seller. The novel's setting was Hawaii, written by James Jones, a soldier stationed in Hawaii before and during the war. George was about to graduate from Cal State that year. When he read the book he was so captivated by it he decided he would write a novel that also takes place in Hawaii. If a haole from a small town in Southern Illinois can do it, why can't he? He was born and raised in Hawaii and knew the people better than Jones.

In the publicities and promotions of the book, George had read that a lady called Lowney Handy had helped Jones write his novel. Lowney, who had no children, and her husband, Harry, who was the superintendent of an oil company in Robinson, Illinois, had heard of a young ex-GI from Robinson who was trying to become a novelist. An aspiring writer, Lowney, who had nothing published, was willing to devote her time to Jones' novel. She and Harry provided Jones a room in their home where

Jones could write every day without interruption.   Lowney, thereafter, became Jones' mentor and drove him to keep writing.

That month in 1951, rather than writing about Hawaii, George had decided to write about his own combat experiences in the Pacific.   How he had landed with the American forces in Guam and how he had saved several Japanese families from jumping down the cliffs.   Then he wrote about the invasion of Okinawa, the island of his father and mother, where he had tried to get Okinawan civilians out of caves and save them from being blown up by Americans who were tossing grenades and dynamites into the caves.

For him, the most poignant and amazing experience in the Okinawan invasion had taken place during the battle of Shuri Castle, the ancient capital of Okinawa.   The battle had gone on for days.   Thousands of Japanese soldiers, as well as hundreds of conscripted Okinawan laborers, were confined in miles of tunnels under the castle.   The Americans kept bombarding the castle continuously for days, hoping to annihilate the Japanese soldiers.

When the Americans finally attacked the castle, they discovered that the bombardments did not destroy all of the tunnels and that Japanese soldiers were so well protected in the tunnels that they were still able to withstand the attacking Americans.

It was only when the American battleships in the bay fired their big guns at the castle that many of the Japanese soldiers were killed and the tunnels destroyed.   When the Americans were finally able to attack the tunnels, they discovered that most of the Japanese soldiers had evacuated the tunnels and had escaped down to the southern tip of the island to continue the fighting.

It was then, when George and his fellow interpreters were interrogating the Okinawan laborer POWs, that George made a startling discovery. One of POWs was Seiyei Tsukayama, his father's brother who had lived with them in Maui before returning home to Okinawa. Uncle Seiyei was in rags, unshaven and starving. George would not have recognized him if not for his name and a closer examination. Uncle Seiyei, of course, did not recognize George. His nephew in the American Army! The last time Uncle Seiyei had seen George was ten years ago when George was just a young boy.

George took his POW uncle aside, away from the rest of the POWs, and told him who he was. Uncle Seiyei was shocked. He called George by his Japanese name. "Hiroshi! You are really Hiroshi!?" When uncle kept bowing low to him, George reached over, took his hand, and hugged him. No words needed to be said. They both cried.

George gave Uncle Seiyei his pack of cigarettes, his box of C rations, and assured Uncle that he would visit him at the POW camp as soon as things were more stable.

After detailing the rest of the Okinawan battles that went on from April 1, 1945 to June, 1945, George ended his story by visiting Uncle Seiyei at the Ishikawa POW camp, and trying to locate his other relatives in central Okinawa where the battles were not as fierce as they were in the southern tip of the island.

When he finally finished his novel two years later in 1953, George wrote Lowney Handy and told her about his great American war novel, BATTLING YOUR OWN PEOPLE. Will she help him have it published? Lowney Handy wrote back immediately and said to send her the first chapter of the novel. Which he excitedly mailed in a 9 x 10 brown envelope that same day. First class!

He just knew that Lowney Handy would love his novel. That she would have Charles Scribner's Sons of New York, who published "From Here To Eternity," publish his novel, too. No more confrontations with taxpayers after that. No more suits and ties. No more 9 to 5 hours. He could go back to Maui, become a barefoot boy once again, and continue writing at his pleasure.

Three days later, he received a 9 x 10 brown envelope from Lowney Handy, his savior. He could see himself autographing his book everywhere in the country, in bookstores, in schools, in libraries. He could see his envious Baldwin High School classmates on Maui congratulating and heralding him for his great accomplishment. And he could see his former girlfriend, Alice Watanabe, who would not marry him because he was a low-class Okinawan now wishing she had married him.

Very ceremoniously, very delicately, George opened the envelope and took out the first chapter of his great American classic.

Across the first page, in a bold unmistakable inscription was S-H-I-T! Puzzled, George looked at the envelope.

It was addressed to him! Besides, how many George Tsukayamas are there in Los Angeles?

When he turned to the second page, there were more S-H-I-Ts. And scribbled at the edge were Lowney Handy's frank evaluations of BATTLING YOUR OWN PEOPLE, "This is not only a piece of shit. It stinks like it!"

In the following page, she went on relentlessly: "Whodahell ever told you you're a writer? Even my beginning students here at the colony can write circles around you. Get off your high horse and either dip your head in horse manure or come up for a breath of fresh air and read the great books written by real writers."

She did not let up in the other pages either. "Your title is the only redeeming value of this manuscript. The rest of your writings don't deserve such an intriguing title.

"Writing is an art," she went on. "No different from a painter painting a scene. Every detail is planned and put together from the beginning to the end.

"You're so-called novel is not a novel. It is a bad example of an essay written by a sixth grader," she continued, now picking on several sentences and paragraphs. "You personally saw combat in Guam, Iwo Jima and Okinawa. Good. Very brave. But I don't feel your bravery, your sacrifice, your fears. Granted this is only the first chapter, but you must capture the reader from the first page, or the reader will dump your novel in the cess pool where it now belongs.

"I am a teacher," she continued. "I'm not a publisher nor an agent. Jones had to learn to write some of the scenes, and was willing to write and rewrite them to make you feel you're part of the scene. This is the essence of good writing. The writer becomes the character. And it is the character who moves the scene; not the writer. I don't expect you to know this. You're at a stage where you think you can write because you have a great story to tell, not realizing that the reader does not feel the way you do. The reader asks you to entertain him, make him laugh; make him cry; make him afraid what's coming up next. But, for God's sake! Don't you dare bore the hell outa him. There's enough boredom in the world."

She concluded her tirade: "Writing is spiritual. Let your spirit guide you; not your ego nor your ambition. Forget self; forget who you are. Just remember that when you have the faith of a grain of a mustard seed, you will grow and learn what it takes to become a writer."

LOWNEY HANDY.

George did not fully realize how painful Lowney Handy's condemnation was. Tears were streaming down his face. A part of him had just died. After two years of hard, dedicated work! To be told not only that his story was not a story but it was a badly written child's essay. A piece of shit. And smelled like it.

He was about to rip apart Lowney Handy's envelope. To hell with her! He knew he had a good, interesting story. And no Lowney Handys in the world are going to tell him otherwise.

He laid the envelope on his dining table desk, wiped his eyes, and laid his head down on his arm. If there was any consolation from Lowney Handy's comments, if that's what it can be called and not a condemnation, it was the trouble she took to read the chapter he had sent her. He was sure that if she had read the rest of his story she would take back her shitty words and praise his writing.

Nearing Sunset now, the devastating letter still fresh in his mind, he remembered wanting to go down to Santa Monica Beach and start swimming back to Maui.

CHAPTER 5:

The Concentration Camp

Shigeru "Shig" Ito, George Tsukayama's age, was also a vet of the Second World War. Unlike George who served in the Pacific, Shig had served with the segregated all-Nisei Japanese unit in Europe, the 442nd Regimental Combat Team.

That day when he was wounded in his back, he was afraid the young Hakujin field doctor was going to say he would be paralyzed for the rest of his life. The medic, a fellow Nisei shot him a dose of morphine to ease the pain, and told him the doctor would do everything possible to keep him from being paralyzed.

The patient on the next cot, a Hakujin who became a friend a few hours ago, consoled, "You're gonna be okay, Shig. You're gonna be okay."

That was ten years ago and Shig was grateful that the doctor had prevented paralysis. The doctor, however, warned him that there would be a big scar and the pain would be unbearable at times.

The doctor was right. There was a big, jagged scar just above his waist, and the pain was unbearable at times. Especially on days when the air was wet, muggy and humid, and he was forced to use a cane.

Today was one of those days, a drizzling, windy Southern California day…

He was now busy folding a customer's clothing in his

laundromat, Ace's Cleaners, on Santa Monica, three doors away from Vermont. He did not particularly enjoy running a laundry business. But It was better than gardening like some of his Nisei vet friends were doing. Besides, running the laundromat did not bother his back as much as pushing a lawnmower.

Shig was attending night classes at LACC, preparing to go on to a state college after his sophomore year. His major would be agriculture. Something he knew about. He had grown up in Gardena, Los Angeles County, where Japanese truck farmers had done most of the farming. His father was quite successful leasing land from the Hakujins and planting celery, tomatoes and strawberries.

Ace Cleaners was rather small, six washing machines, three dryers, and a section for dry-cleaning customers whose clothes he sent out to a dry cleaner on Normandie two blocks away. At the back, next to the cash register, were the counter for folding just-washed laundry, a desk, a table, chairs for guests, and a bathroom. The entrance was on Santa Monica. A back door opened to the big parking lot of Ralphs Supermarket where most of his customer shopped.

Shig's wife, Susan, a Nisei registered nurse, sometimes came in the late afternoons to help during the busy hours. She would bring their three-year old daughter, Alicia, from the nursery and Alicia would enjoying spending the rest of the day with Daddy.

Shig's enjoyment was to shoot the bull with customers who had been coming to the shop for many years. Two of them were George Tsukayama and Amando Fuentes who lived in the same apartment close by on Madison. They would occasionally go to Ray's Bar across Vermont for a few drinks. If business was slow, Shig would close up shop and join them.

All three were veterans, he and George in the Second World War, Amando in the recent Korean War. As veterans who had gone through deadly battles, they tried to laugh off some their experiences and not mention in detail their buddies dying and wounded alongside them.

"The damn war," Shig would say shaking his head, "all those killings."

"Ain't that the shits," Amando would always agree, "we're out there about to be killed while the leaders back home are telling us what great heroes we are."

"That's the way the ball bounces," George always concluded. "The poor takes a beating in a war; the rich stay home and get richer."

"Hey, whattahell you guys complaining about," Shig said. "Your families weren't behind barbed wire fence like mine were."

"That really was the shits," Amando said. "Locking up your families and asking you to volunteer in the Army."

"I don't know if I would have volunteered if they had locked us up," George said grimly.

"You guys in Hawaii were lucky," Shig said. "That damn Roosevelt knew if they locked up all the Japanese in Hawaii, who would do the work in the sugar cane and the pineapple fields?"

"They could have imported Mexicans," Amando said, laughing.

"The Pacific Ocean is not the Rio Grande," George said

"There's always the damn gringos who sent the Japanese into those camps," Amando said.

"Yeah. Sure." George said. "Gringos who don't know the difference between sugar cane and pineapples."

Shig, listening silently would shake his head. Gringos, he thought. Like General DeWitt, commander of the Armed Forces in the West Coast and the then Attorney General of California, Earl Warren. Those two, more than anyone else, were responsible for fanning the war hysteria and leading the people to believe that all Japanese in the West Coast were potential spies and saboteurs. "The only good Jap is a dead Jap," DeWitt declared. "They should all be put away."

And the people of California, Oregon and Washington believed DeWitt and Warren.

Yeah, he now thought, continuing to fold the dried laundry for his next customer, getting angrier thinking of the concentration camp he and his family and all the Japanese in the West Coast, were placed in shortly after Pearl Harbor.

It was odd that the government waited until harvest time in the spring of 1942 that it ordered the evacuation. Farmers like Shig's father and other Japanese growers were ready to harvest their crops that month. Suddenly, they were ordered to abandon their crops and report to the evacuation centers. They were given less than a week to do so. All they could take with them were their personal belongings. Nothing else.

That's when the Hakujin vultures descended. The generous ones offered ten cents on the dollar for whatever personal belongings the Japanese families owned, furniture, pianos, cars, trucks... The ruthless vultures did not offer anything for the crops about to be harvested. They waited for everyone to leave, then harvested the crops for themselves.

Shig, his father and mother and an older sister, left with only the clothes on their backs. They were allowed to take just one suitcase per person to the evacuation center, which, for them, was

Santa Anita Race Track in Arcadia.

Their living quarters were horse stables that reeked horse manure, horse urine, and old hay.   There were about 10,000 Japanese confined in the race track.

They survived the race track for several months, then were shipped to various so-called relocation camps throughout the western states, ten in all, that housed a total of 120,000 Japanese. Shig and his family were loaded on a train and shipped to Heart Mountain, Wyoming, an isolated desert in the middle of nowhere and settled there with 10,000 other evacuee prisoners for an unknown duration.

They all existed in crude, makeshift army barracks behind razor sharp barbed wire fences, Hakujin army guards with rifles watching them from high towers.   They were told that the guards were there to protect them from outside agitators.   If so, why were machine guns and rifles pointed inwardly toward the evacuees?

Shig, 17 at that time, was still going to high school. Schools were established in the camp and he was able to finish his junior year.   Then, during his senior year that spring of 1943, a few weeks before he would be graduating, Japanese-American men who so far had been classified as undesirables, were suddenly asked by President Roosevelt to show their loyalty to the United States by volunteering in the Army.

In the concentration camps, many were against Roosevelt. How dare he lock them up, then ask them to volunteer in the Army!   The agitation turned to bitter turmoil between those against volunteering and those for volunteering.

Vincent Hasegawa, a former teacher at LA High, believed in showing the Hakujins that he was as Americans as they were.   He painted sketches of young Japanese boys saluting the American flag and pledging allegiance to it. He wrote letters to the camp newspaper declaring that it was a great opportunity for Japanese-Americans to show their loyalty to the country of their birth.

No sooner did the article come out than Vincent Hasegawa was caught in the bathroom by several camp agitators and beaten up. While in the camp hospital nursing his bruises and a patched eye, Vincent Hasegawa became even more vocal. He challenged each of his assailants to settle the fight like men. No one accepted his challenge.

After months of confinement in the camp, Shig couldn't wait to get out. The Army was the answer. Like other fathers who had sons of military age, his father, he was sure, would forbid him to volunteer. Surprisingly, though his father was a strong Japanese nationalist, he was not as bitter as other fathers in the concentration camp. Philosophically, he said Shikata ga nai. It can't be helped.

He told Shig that right or wrong, America was his country. It was only proper that he was willing to fight for it.

With his father's blessing, Shig, although wary of the camp agitators, volunteered.

After passing a rather short physical exam, he was sent to Camp Shelby, in Jackson, Mississippi, for basic training. He had never been in the South before. He quickly learned that although the Japanese were treated unjustly because of their race, the Negroes in Mississippi were treated almost criminally by the Hakujins. They were banned from white restaurants, banned from white toilets, banned from drinking water from the same fountain as the Hakujins. And there were signs at the edge of towns, "Don't let the sun set on you Nigger!

Once, when he and his buddies boarded a bus, they stepped to the back where the seats were empty. The white bus driver stopped the bus. He told Shig and his buddies they could not sit there. The whites sat up front; the blacks in the back. Shig and his buddies looked at each other. They were neither white nor black.

He began hating Hakujins as never before. When the war started, he was called a damn slant-eyed Jap and sometimes stoned or forbidden to enter ice cream shops and restaurants. He had to endure several fights, not with just one Hakujin, but gangs of them and was beaten up.

All the hatred and intolerance by the damn Hakujin were nothing compared to what the Negroes in Mississippi were going through. And many of the Negroes were drafted into the Army and placed in segregated troops.

Most of the Nisei in Camp Shelby were from Hawaii. There was a cultural difference between the mainlanders and the Hawaiians. The mainlanders were not easygoing and friendly as the Hawaiians. The mainlanders, because of their upbringings with Hakujins, spoke proper English and pronounced their words like Hakujins.

Shig's first confrontation with a Hawaiian was during close order drill. The Hawaiian, a corporal, would mispronounce the commands and Shig would be confused. "One, too, tree, fo'," the corporal kept commanding. After several more unclear commands the corporal said, "Righ' flank righ'! Left flank left! One, too, tree, for..." Shig marched into the soldier to his left, then to the soldier to the right.

"Whatsdamatter, you!" the corporal scolded Shig. "You no understand English? Righ' flank, you step to da righ't. Left flank, you step to the left."

"Yes, sir!" Shig responded.

"What! You wise guy!" The corporal said. "No 'sir' me. Me not one officer."

As basic training went on, the mainlanders began understanding the Hawaiians and their culture. And when the Hawaiians discovered that mainlanders had volunteered from concentration camps, they began to respect the mainlanders.

CHAPTER 6:

The Laundromat

Christine loaded the trunk of her Chrysler with a couple bags of dirty linens, towels, Levis, shirts and blouses. She drove out of her driveway and headed up Amber Street toward Hollywood in the gloomy midmorning smog. Up until a month ago, Cecilia, her cleaning girl, did the laundry at Christine's home. Cecilia, however, left for her home in Mexico and did not know when she would return, if she ever would. Then, too, the washing machine which needed to be repaired was not working anymore.

Christine had found Young's Chinese laundromat on Vine near Santa Monica, and had been taking her laundry there for the past month.

When she arrived at Young's this morning, struggling with the bags of laundry, she discovered to her dismay that Mr. Young had closed his shop. A sign on the door said: "Move Chinatown."

Rubbing her eyes, sniffling from the smog, she drove slowly down Santa Monica, looking both sides of the street, hoping to see signs of a laundromat. She stopped at a dry cleaner, inquired if they did laundry and when she got a firm no, got back into her Chrysler and continued down Santa Monica.

Shortly, as she approached Vermont, the street light turned yellow, then, red, then green. Noticing Armando standing behind his pickup, she made an abrupt left, and drove into Ray's

Parking lot.

Surprised, Armando rushed over to her Chrysler.

"Hey, Christine," he said, "today's Tuesday. No class."

"I'm looking for a laundromat, Armando," she said. "I can't find any around here."

"Laundromat?" Armando said. "You came to the right man."

"I did?"

"Friend of mine runs one. Across Vermont. Three doors down from the corner."

"I should've have come directly to you instead of roaming all over Santa Monica Boulevard."

"Where's your laundry?"

"In the trunk."

He stepped to the rear of the Chrysler. "Open it."

She unlocked the trunk.

Armando reached down into the trunk and took out the bags of laundry.

"Leave your car right there," he said, "nobody's driving nowhere."

"Nobody's going anywhere," she corrected.

"Right, Miss Barrington. 'Anywhere.'"

"What about your flowers?" she asked, nodding toward the flowers in the back of Armando's pickup. "And your parked cars?"

"They're gonna be okay," he said, stepping over to the sidewalk with the bags of laundry, his left leg dragging slightly, "I'll take you over to Shig's."

"Shig's?"

"My friend,'" he said.

As they crossed Vermont, he asked, "How're you doing in

your painting class?"

"Oh, pretty good, I guess. Like how you are doing in your English class?"

"Y'know, I wish I could speak like you," he said. "Not only proper English; pronouncin' the words...'prop-er-ly,'" he added, rounding his lips, and chuckling.

"Oh, Armando, you're doing fine."

She kept walking alongside him, the steps of his left leg making odd scrapping sounds.

They finally approached Ace's Cleaners.

Armando pushed the door open, and stepped in with the two bags, Christine following.

"Oh," he said, "Sorry. Ladies first." He bowed and stepped aside to let her in.

"Thank you," she responded, bowing back, going along.

"Hey, Shig," Armando called out. "Look who I got here. A new customer."

A Japanese man who was busy folding a batch of just-dried laundry, looked up, quite surprised.

"She ain't just 'nother customer," said Armando, "she's smart, talented and got lotsa class."

"Aw, Armando," Christine said, flushing.

The man stopped folding.

"This is Shig," Armando introduced, stepping up to the folding counter with Christine. Then, catching himself, said, "Oh, I'm sorry. I'm s'pposed to introduce the lady first. –This here is Christine, Shig. Christine Barrington."

Christine extended her hand. "Hello. How do you do?"

"Hi," Shig greeted, shaking her hand, looking at her curiously.

"See, what'd I tell you?" Armando said. "She's got class."

"Just like you, huh?" Shig said.

"Well, yeah, in a way," Armando laughed. He placed the bags of laundry into one of the baskets.

"Nihongo dekimasu ka?" Christine asked Shig.

Shig looked at her.

"Nisei han desu ne?"

Recovered, Shig responded, "Hai, Nisei desu."

"Hey, Shig," Armando interrupted, "I never knew you could speak that language."

"Why not?" Christine said. "He's one of us?"

Shig, still astounded, chuckled.

"Wow!" Armando said to her, "What else can you speak?"

"A little Spanish, too," she said.

"Me, I'm Mexican, but I can't speak no Spanish. I know, I know. 'Any Spanish,'"

"Not a word?" Christine tested.

"Aw, a few," said Armando. "Bad street talk."

"Cholo talk," Shig interrupted, and chuckled.

"Words you don't say before a lady," Armando said.

"Or a gentleman," Shig said, raising his head.

"You?" Armando said, dismissing Shig with a wave of his hand.

"Cabron..." Shig said.

"Hey, watch your language," Armando said.

Familiar with a few Spanish street words, Christine said, "Si, no mas."

Shig and Armando looked at her.

"Por favor," Christine went on, "keep speaking so I can learn more Spanish street words."

"Naw," Armando said, "you don't wanna learn them words."

"Those words," she corrected.

"Yeah. Those words. –Well, I better get back to the parking lot," Armando said, stepping over to the door. "See you back at the lot, Christine."

"Si, Armando. Gracias."

"Por nada," Armando said to her. "Hey, Shig," he said opening the door. "Maybe, you, me and George we can have a few at Ray's when you've closed up."

"Good idea," Shig said.

After Armando shut the door behind him, Christine asked, "How long have you known him?"

"Armando?" Shig said. "Been my customer for almost three years."

"He doesn't say much about himself, does he?"

"Naw. 'At's not his style," Shig said. "All of his life, he's being taking the good with the bad."

He continued folding.

She watched him for a moment.

"You grew up here in Los Angeles?" she finally asked, hoping to start a conversation.

"Yeah," he said. Like Armando, he seemed the silent type.

"Didn't you speak Nihongo to your parents?

"A little," he said. "Where'd you learn Japanese?"

"I was born in Japan."

He stopped folding. "You were born in Japan! No wonder you speak Japanese like a real Japanese."

"Domo arigato gozaimasu."

"Us Niseis, we gradually forgot Japanese," he said. "You know, 'you're in America, speak English!'"

"That's what I heard."

"The war," he said. "It had lots to do with it."

"That's what my friend Carole told me."

"She's Nisei?"

"Born and raised right here in Los Angeles. Until she was placed in one of those camps."

When Christen told him that Carol Ikeda was at Heart Mountain, Shig, surprised, asked if Carole's Japanese name was 'Yoshiko.'

"Yes," said Christine. "Carole Yoshiko Ikeda."

"Holy…!" he said. "We were classmates."

"Oh, my goodness," she said.

"We all knew each other," he said. "Just a small high school in camp."

"I'll have to call Carole and tell her I met you."

"What a small world," he said.

"Carole and I are best friends," she said. "From our SC days."

"She went to USC?"

"Got her masters from there."

"Masters! Wow. Congratulate her for me."

"I sure will. She'll be so surprised, if not shocked, that I met you."

"Carole Yoshiko Ikeda…" he muttered.

"When Carole and her family came back to Los Angeles after the war, they were treated awfully," she said. "Nobody would rent them a house or an apartment. They had to stay with old Mexican neighbors who welcomed them back."

"Yeah," Shig said. "I heard things were still bad back here. To the Hakujin, a Japanese was still a Jap."

"There was a shortage of gardeners back then," she said. "My dad put in the *LA Times*. '*Gardener wanted. Preferably Japanese.*'"

"Preferably Japanese?! Back then?!"

"Guess who came knocking at our door next day?" she said. "Carole's father."

"You're kidding."

"He was shocked when Dad spoke Japanese to him."

Shig laughed. "I would've been shocked, too."

CHAPTER 7:

A Coffee Break

George had not taken his mid-morning coffee break yet. He decided to stop at Norm's on Sunset, the gang's hangout, before heading back to the office.

Stepping into Norm's with his briefcase, he looked around the crowded restaurant, and saw no one he recognized. Some of the guys would either come in later or had already taken their break and had gone back to the office.

He stepped past the noisy, occupied tables, sat at one of the counter stools, and placed his briefcase carefully on the floor beside him.

"Hi, George," Sally, the slim, friendly Latina waitress in crisp white uniform greeted. "The usual?"

"Right."

"Coming up," Sally said, stepping back, placing a slice of bread into the toaster at the inner counter. She then placed a cup before George and poured coffee into it.

"Hey, George," she whispered, "okay I ask you a tax question?"

"Sure," he said, sipping.

"How much of our tips are we supposed to report?"

"All of it."

"Every penny?"

"All income is taxable," he said. "Unless exempt by law."

"And if we don't report all of it?"

"You go to jail."

They looked at each other until George chuckled.

Sally leaned closer over the counter, looked to her left; her right.   "Now give it to me straight," she said, confidentially. "How are they gonna check how much tips we make each day?"

He leaned over to her and whispered, "It's between you and God."

She looked at him.

He chuckled again.

"Really, how much are we supposed to report?"

"Sally," he said, "I'm an IRS agent. I can't tell you to cheat the government."

"Who's cheating?"

He held his head sideways, grinning.

"What you're saying," she whispered again, "I report what I think is reasonable. Right?"

"You're saying it," he said, still grinning.

They looked at each other and smiled meaningfully.

"Gotcha, George," she said, turned, retrieved the toast, placed it on a small dish with a small block of butter, and served him. "More coffee?"

"Yeah. Thanks."

Pouring, she said, "I'm glad I can talk to you. Your IRS buddies, I don't dare ask them anything."

"Why not?"

"They're …so straightlaced. They'd probably report me if I asked them the same question, I just asked you."

He said nothing.

She went over to serve a customer who just sat on the counter corner.

Sipping more coffee, he thought, she's right. How're you gonna know how much tips a waitress makes in a day. Ten bucks? Twenty? And why pick on waitresses when there's millions of dollars either not reported or hidden by clever lawyers and accountants who took advantage of loopholes in the tax laws. Depreciation, oil depletion, overseas accounts, capital gains and losses and many other ways to "legitimately" reduce their clients' income.

Oh, whattahell are you worried about? Let the politicians come up with ways to close the loopholes or create new ones for their voters.

He thought of Christine's tax return, and wondered why he was so concerned about her charitable deductions. All he needed to do was to verify the fair market value of those clothing deductions and make sure that the City of Hope received them for resale at the prices claimed. That way, the downtown office would have no reason to question his decision.

He took a long sip, trying to forget about taxes. After another sip, his mind floated to the new novel he had just started.

It had been two years since Lowney Handy condemned his first novel.

Three days after he had received that "Shit" letter back in 1953, he had received another letter from her. He had hesitated to open it. So he was not a writer according to her. So he didn't have what it takes to become a writer. Well, he wasn't going to take anymore crap from her. Someday, he'll prove to her and to the rest of the world that he is a writer.

He had taken a deep breath and finally opened the envelope. To hell with what she has to say.

It was a long three-page letter full of typos she didn't bother to correct. She rewrote on the edge or over some of the words she wanted to emphasize. As he scanned the letter, he was surprised that she had not said, "SHIT" at all. It was a much gentler and kinder letter than the first one. Actually, the rough and tough woman apologized for the things she had said before.

When he read the letter once more, he was comforted, relieved and hopeful. Lowney Handy said she had helped several students in the colony have their works published. But only after years of learning their craft. Writing, she said, is no different from other endeavors. A doctor goes to medical school to become a doctor; a lawyer goes to law school to become a lawyer; and, a writer must learn to write before he becomes a writer.

"I'll help you," she wrote, "but only if you do what I tell you to do. Like everything else, success is measured by how much you're willing to put into it. I'm willing to be your teacher only because you had been willing to finish your so-called novel and because your attempt must have taught you a little about writing.

"The first thing I want you to do is to burn everything you have written so far," she said. "I want you to have a fresh start on a new novel. But, even before you start, I want you to copy the works of great masters: William Faulkner, John Steinbeck, Raymond Chandler and James Jones.

George took a deep breath.

What is she saying, "Burn everything you have written so far?" The novel that had taken him two years to finish. No way was he going to burn it! And about copying the great masters? Plagiarize them?

Then, he reread his novel. It certainly wasn't as bad as Lowney Handy said it was. Actually, there were some great moments in it. Especially the scenes when he went searching for his mother's sisters and brothers in devastated Okinawa. And the scene when he saved the lives of a whole family who were about to blow themselves up with hand grenades. Lowney Handy had not read those scenes because they were not in the first chapter he had sent her.

Two weeks later, he received another letter from Lowney. Her perception startled him. "You have not burned your novel, have you?" she said. "And you have not started copying like I had told you, have you? Rewriting that novel of yours will not free you from your first attempt at writing. And being afraid of copying the great legends indicates you don't have the confidence to become a great writer. I'm a busy teacher. I have several writers here in the colony who someday will be great writers. Only because they have been listening to me.

"I don't have time for losers," she went on. "If you don't do as I say, you're a loser."

"Ready for more coffee?" Sally said, startling him.

"Huh? --Oh, no," he said. "No thanks."

"You're not still thinking about what we talked about, are you?"

He shook his head.

How ridiculous that she would think his mind was on tips.

He glanced at his wristwatch. He still had a few more minutes before heading for the office.

Sally took the pot to the other customers.

He took a sip and again thought of Lowney's letter. Well, he'd copy those writers, starting with James Jones and see where they'd get him.

Starting that week, he began copying his favorite novel, *From*

Here To Eternity.   Lowney had said it would enhance his concentration and, "You'll forget that time and space exist. You will be transported into the world of the novel and forget self; forget who you are; forget that there is anything else in the world except the world you are copying."

He began appreciating From Here To Eternity even more than before, the story line, the characters, the locales, the twists and turns of the story.

He had to admit Lowney was right. He would tell her that someday, he would want to come to the colony and finish his novel.

Lowney, as before, wrote right back. She was glad he was beginning to learn what writing is all about. Keep copying, she said, and better things will come to you.

In another letter, she said, "Be honest and devoted to your characters, utterly. Remember, you are not you anymore; you are the characters and the characters are you. If the characters want to take a crap, let them; if the characters want to fart; let them. And for goodness' sake! Don't be a moralist. Your responsibility is to the characters. Honestly and truthfully.

He read Lowney's letter over and over until he was getting to know what she was saying. How foolish he had been, he told himself, that he had wasted two years writing his novel when he didn't know the basics of writing.

What better subject for his novel, he told himself, than writing about people he knew and using them for his characters. He should write about a time and period that is familiar to the readers. And start with the premise that the novel may be fictitious, but possible and real.

The time and period of his story would be the first week after the Pearl Harbor attack. The place would be Maui, Hawaii, his island. The plot would be the welcoming invasion of Japanese troops on Maui, and the effect it would have on the Japanese on the island. The characters would be a takeoff from the Okinawans on Kapuna, Maui, where he was born and raised.

He sent Lowney the first chapter, not afraid what she thought about it. After all, he was now her serious student.

Lowney wrote right back. She was glad that he was starting a new novel. She marked the novel severely, with some encouraging notes. He was beginning to project himself into the characters, she said. He was letting the characters move and tell the story; not he the author.

In the second chapter he sent her, she again criticized it. This time more severely than the previous. She said he was not progressing as fast as he should. Then, astonishingly, she said, "You have not burned that first novel, have you? Burn it now! If you don't, don't bother to send me anymore chapters. That bunch of bullshit you wrote is still hindering you. You must get away from all that."

Now howdahell did she know he had not destroyed his novel, he thought. She once said she and he can contact each other through the air waves. He, of course, didn't believe her. But now... After displaying her mental power several times, he was afraid she was capable of reading his mind.

That evening, he gathered his 500-page manuscript, carried them to the apartment's waste barrel and, with deep, choking breaths, reluctantly but resolutely, dumped every page into the barrel.

Miraculously, he was overwhelmed by a freedom he had not experienced since writing the manuscript. As Lowney had expressed, "You will feel a catharsis taking over, a cleansing of your soul, an unburdening of a ton of bricks on your shoulders."

He rewrote the third chapter and sent it to Lowney. When she returned the chapter, again with markings and corrections but not severely, she, for the first time, said his writing has improved and he is on his way to become the writer he wants to be.

CHAPTER 8:

The Texan

Half-an-hour after the tall, attractive Hakujin lady left his laundromat, Shig was still marveling at how well she spoke Japanese. She spoke it far better than he a Japanese.

Well, she had an advantage. She grew up in Japan and had no hangups. Nobody told her, "Be an American. Stop speaking Japanese!"

That's the way it had been with Shig and his fellow Japanese-American Niseis. Until they could barely understand and speak Japanese.

The No. 2 dryer came to a stop.

He went over with a cart, transferred the dried laundry into the cart, and came back to the counter to fold them. The routine was killing him. It was a good thing that he was attending night classes at LACC and looking forward to graduation so he could go on to a four-year college and pursue his goal of becoming an agricultural teacher or a state farm inspector. He'd of course have to end his laundromat business, and move to Pomona or up to San Luis Obispo to get his degree in agriculture.

It'd be nice to be associated with farmers again, he thought. And to be out in the open fields and speak the farmers' language, crops, fertilizers, planting, harvesting and marketing. It'd bring back his boyhood days working in the fields with his dad.

The soil. Yes, the feel of warm, vibrant soil in his hand.

Something he had not realized how much he had missed until the basic training days in Mississippi. The California soil was much richer, much finer and fertile, but the Mississippi soil gave him the same feeling of warmth and security as soil did everywhere. Except, of course, the dirt, the mud and the soil of the battlefields in Italy and Germany which were always tainted with fresh human blood.

Those damn bloody days, he remembered, going on with the folding. Kill or be killed. The shelling, the machine guns, the rifle shots and the painful screaming of the wounded, all came flashing back.

The worst day had been in the early winter of '44. It was freezing cold, windy and dark in the dense forest. The 442nd had just liberated the French towns of Bruyeres and Biffontaine at a high cost. Even before their outfit had a well-deserved rest, the General had ordered them to go up into the Vosges mountain and rescue a bunch of Texans surrounded by Germans. Others from the Texans' own division had attempted to break through the German lines, but were pushed back. When they tried the second time and failed, the General turned to the 442nd. The Nisei outfit, all veterans of many other battles, had by now a reputation as being the best fighting outfit in the European front.

Shig's company, already battered from the battles of Bruyeres and Biffontaine, was ordered to spearhead the rescue. When they reached the Vosges forest, they discovered that the Germans were extremely well-fortified with artilleries, machine guns, mortars and Nazi veterans. They were determined to repel any American attempting to reach the trapped Texans.

While climbing up through the dense, dark, treacherous forest, Shig's company could barely see each other, let alone a few feet ahead of them. They climbed up the steep hills and mountain cliffs holding each other's hand so they wouldn't be isolated in the darkness.

The alert Germans opened fire on the 442nd killing many of them. Those surviving dove into ravines and holes or hid behind the big trees. Shig could hear the screaming and moaning of the wounded, and wondered when he'd be next.

As some of his company finally broke through the German lines, most of them wounded, the Texans, those who were still able to stand, greeted them with grateful, opened arms. Many of the Texans were wounded and needed immediate medical care.

Shig came across this one Texan, wounded pretty badly and bleeding in his stomach area, barely able to stand. Shig knew that the man would be a gonner if he didn't get him back to the medics right away. With the battle still raging all around them, Shig held the guy up with one arm, had the guy cling on to him, and they both started backing away from all the treacherous grenades, artilleries and mortars.

When the heavy shells exploded around them, they dropped to the ground and began crawling-crouching their way to the American line. Although the guy was in pretty bad shape, he was able to carry his own weight and tried to make it easier for Shig to help him.

Out of nowhere, one of the damn artillery shells landed into the trees above them. Shig and the Texan hugged the wet, muddy ground, praying they would be spared.

Sharp shrapnel hit the branches and ricocheted everywhere.

Suddenly, Shig felt a flashing hot metal striking his back. It seemed just a superficial wound. When he reached behind and looked at his hand, he was shocked. It was covered with blood.

It was then that he discovered he could hardly move his body, the initial numbness growing into excruciating pain.

The Texan glanced over at Shig's blood-soaked hand. "You're hit!" he said.

Shig nodded painfully.

"Go ahead," said the Texan. "I'll be all right."

"We're both gonna make it or we're both not gonna," Shig said, still hugging the ground, more shrapnels ricocheting around them.

The Texan, weak as he was, attempted to get up on his knee.

"Get down!" Shig cried out, pulling the Texan down beside him.

The Texan rose again.

"Medics!" the Texan cried out. "Medics!"

Shig again pulled the Texan down.

"C'mon," Shig said, struggling, "let's gettahell outta here!" And they both began crawling-dragging-crouching on their hands and knees toward safer grounds, both supporting each other, both suppressing their painful moans and curses.

They finally reached a relatively safe area.

One of the medics from Shig's outfit hurried over, and shot him a dose of morphine. He tended to the wounded Texan who had lost much too much blood and was weakening.

What followed were vague and unclear to Shig. He was lying on a cot and did not know how he got there. He could feel a big roll of bandages around his midsection and his back.

In the same crowded medical tent next to him was the Texan. Most of the other cots were occupied by fellow wounded Niseis.

Shig asked the Nisei medic about the Texan, "How's he doing?"

"Not too good," said the medic.

"Not too good!" Shig protested. "After what we just went through?!"

"If we don't get him to the hospital right away," said the medic, shaking his head, "I don't know…"

Shig tried to rise from the cot, but fell back down.

"Hey, Buddy," Shig called the Texan, "you can't give up. Not after what we went through back there."

The Texan, weak and weary, turned his head toward Shig. He smiled a tight waning smile. "Yeah," he said, "that was one helluva trip back there.

" —Hey," the Texan went on, "whatcha your name?"

"Ito," Shig said. "Shig Ito."

"Benton," said the Texan, reaching over touching Shig's hand, "Eric Benton."

Shig squeezed Eric's hand.

As moments of private thoughts went by between him and Eric, Shig gazed across the aisle and noticed that it was occupied by someone covered with a GI blanket. The man was silent and did not seem interested in anything going on around him.

"What's wrong with him?" Shig asked the medic.

"He don't want anyone to know he's a POW," the medic said

"He's a Kraut?!"

The medic nodded silently.

Eric, having heard the conversation, said angrily, "He's taking over a cot meant for one of us?"

The medic nodded.

"Sonofabitch…" Eric cursed.

Shig looked over the POW. The Kraut was still silent, his eyes focused on the triangular tent top.

"Bastard..." Shig said.   "They tried to kill us; now we're saving 'em."

"Fuckin' Krauts..." Eric cursed again.   "Starving us a whole week, showing no mercy for our wounded, and now..."

"Speaks English?" Shig asked.

"Yeah," the medic replied, "not too bad."

"What'd he say?" Eric questioned.

"He wanted to know why Japanese were fighting Germans when Japan and Germany were allies."

"Bastard!"   Eric tried to get up.   "I'd like to get my hands around his neck."

"Hey, c'mon, man," the medic said, "we don't want you losing any more blood."

Eric lay back down. "Yes, sir."

After a moment, Eric, struggling to stay awake, said to Shig, "If you're ever my way in Texas, be sure to look me up." He tried to dig into his pocket for his wallet.

The medic took out the wallet from Eric's pants pocket, pulled out an address card and handed it to Shig. The medic then placed the wallet back in Eric's pants pocket.

Shig accepted the card from the medic. "Austin, eh? Austin, Texas."

"Yeah," said Eric.   "Nice place. Friendly people. You'd like my family. Where're you from?"

"California."

"Your address?"

Shig had to think it over. His address? What's his address? Certainly not Gardena, California, anymore.

"Hey, medic," Shig called his fellow Nisei. "Do me a favor. Write this down."

"Sure," said the medic, taking out a pad and a pencil.

"Shig Ito. Block No. 30, Barrack 19, Unit E, Heart Mountain Relocation Center, Heart Mountain, Wyoming. Got that?"

"I was at Heart Mountain, too," said the medic."

"You, too?" Shig said.

The medic handed the note to Eric.

Eric struggled to read it. "...Heart Mountain Relocation Center... Nice place?"

Shig and the medic exchanged brief glances.

"Don' forget, Shig," Eric said, "If I don' make it, you go on over and call on my folks, y'hear? Tell 'em how we met."

"Yeah, sure," Shig said. "But you better make it. Don't make me feel I got banged up for nothing."

"Yes, sir," Eric said. "I want the folks back home to know what you guys from Heart Mountain did for us Texans."

Shig again exchanged short glances with the medic and, grinning, said nothing.

Not as severely wounded as Eric, Shig was sent to a field hospital. Eric, on the other hand, was sent to a medical hospital in Southern France.

Shig had kept in touch with Eric, writing to him at the hospital and having Eric send his short replies to his former outfit's address. Then after a few weeks, when Eric stopped answering his letters, he checked with the medical hospital in Southern France. He was told that Eric Benton did not make it through a major operation.

Shig thought of writing Eric's father and mother. What would he say to grieving parents of a soldier who almost survived from battle wounds, and did not make it? Besides, he really did not know Eric? Had Eric lived, they most likely would have been best of friends for the rest of their lives. But, now, how could he extend that friendship to his father and mother when they don't know how close he and Eric had become during those few moments they were about to die together?

Shig wrote his sister in Heart Mountain and told her about how he met Eric Benton. He told her that he really intended to visit Eric in Texas when he returned to the States. Now…

He went through the short letters Eric had written him before his major operation. Eric seemed upbeat. Then came the news from one of the volunteers at the hospital.

While recuperating from his wound, walking and exercising as much as he could, Shig could still feel the hot flashing pain from the shrapnel that penetrated his back. Wanting to erase that horrible moment, he kept reminding himself that a total stranger had become a close friend and they had planned to reunite when the war was over.

He tore the letters. It was another phase of many phases in his life. He then took out Eric's address in Austin, Texas, and tore it, too.

The tumbler in the No. 3 dryer came to a gradual stop.

Shig went over, dug out the laundry and placed them in the cart. He finished folding the laundry from the previous dryer, then began folding the laundry from the No. 3 dryer.

CHAPTER 9:

IRS Office

George left a tip, picked up his briefcase, and was about to leave when Sally thanked him for his advice.

"What advice?" he said.

"You know," Sally said, "reporting a reasonable amount of tips."

"Sally," he said, grinning, "I said no such thing."

Sally looked at him, straight-faced, then smiled. "Oh, sure, George."

He paid the cashier, and was about to step out of Norm's, when Sally, picking up her tip, said, "I"ll be sure to report this," and waved the quarter.

"All of it," he said, smiling at her.

Outside, he crossed Cahuenga, and kept on walking down Sunset. Passing the downstairs' IRS Collection Office, he noticed several delinquent taxpayers waiting for their turn to speak to a collection officer who would be making arrangements for late tax payments, interest and penalties.

There were times when there would be famous actors, athletes, and movie producers among them, but not today.

Coming to the next building, he pushed open the old squeaking door, and climbed up the narrow stairway to the second floor.

As expected, the large, opened, upstairs office was almost

empty, most of the agents out on audits. At the corner overlooking Sunset were the two mid-twenties haole secretaries, Helen for group one and Julie for group two. In the two cubicle offices also overlooking Sunset, were the supervisors, Bill Granger and Warren Michaels, both haoles in mid-thirties.

George stepped up to his desk which was alongside the desk of his friend, Greg Irving.

Greg had just stepped out of the bathroom in the back and came over to his desk. A graduate of UCLA a couple of years ago, Greg, quite dashing in a dark suit and a neatly placed matching tie, was now in his second year of night law school at USC. Greg had gone to LA State College, which made him a fellow alumnus, then had transferred to UCLA for his BS.

Sitting, Greg said softly, "Your case that was transferred to me, I just came from there."

"That professor from Occidental?"

"Yeah. Him. That know-it-all economics professor."

"So. What happened?"

"After I got through with him, he thought you were a better agent than me," Greg said, chuckling.

He looked at Greg curiously.

"I threw out more contribution and entertainment deductions."

"In addition to mine?"

"You shouldn't have allowed any of them," said Greg. "He didn't have receipts or cancelled checks to prove them."

"Bastard," George said. "Calling Bill and asking him to transfer the case to another agent. He must've thought a white agent would be better than an Asian agent."

"What made you allow that much of his promotion

expenses?" Greg asked.

"Don't tell me you knocked them out, too."

"I told him he doesn't have to agree with my findings," Greg said. "He could protest and have an informal hearing with my supervisor or request an appellate hearing downtown."

"He's gonna?"

"I doubt it. He knows if he squawked, even more of his deductions gonna be thrown out."

George chuckled. "You made me look good."

"And I made myself an asshole."

"Better you than me," George said.

The phone on Helen's desk rang. A second or two, then, "George. Line one."

George stepped over to the phone on a stand against the wall.

It was Christine Barrington.

"Oh, hi, Miss Barrington... --Oh, yes. Christine."

"My CPA, Tom Hoffkins, just called," she said. "He wanted to know how you were coming along with my tax return."

"There's really no issues with your tax return, Christine."

"Really?"

"Don't lose any sleep over it. If there's any problem, I'm sure Tom can handle it. Tell him I'll finish the audit as soon as I can."

"Oh, thank you."

"Anything else you want to know about your return?"

"Not really. I was just wondering. Remember my friend, Carole?"

"Your classmate at SC?"

"Well, she's more than just a classmate. She's coming home for the weekend. I'm having her over for dinner. Would you like to join us?"

Oh, oh. He let a moment of silence go by.

"Would you?"

He tried to think of a reasonable excuse.

"You'll enjoy her company, George. She's been to Japan since the war and has some great stories."

Oh, Christ. He'd be through writing for the day. He could go down to Little Tokyo, meet some Hawaiian friends, and have a few.

No reasonable excuse popped up.

"Would six on Saturday be okay?" she went on.

Oh, whattahell.

"Is that too early?"

"Oh, no," he responded. "Six will be fine."

"Oh, that's wonderful," she said. "I'll prepare dishes your mother used to serve you."

"Great," he said, trying to sound enthused.

"I'm sure Carole will be happy to meet you."

He recalled the last blind date which had turned out disastrous.

"*Omachishite imasu*," she said. I'll be waiting.

"Hai. Domo."

No sooner did he hang up, then Helen said, "Oh, how sweet."

"I'm working on her case," he informed.

"Oh, sure," said Helen. "On a Saturday night."

When he returned to his desk, Greg said, "I didn't know you speak Chinese."

"Chinese?"

"Hai. Domo," Greg said.

"Schmuck," George returned.

"Hey," Greg said, "you speak Hebrew."

"And a little English, too," he said.

After reviewing the tax return on his desk, Greg said, confidentially, "How're you doing with that lady in Illinois?"

"Lowney? We're beginning to understand each other better," he said.

"No more 'shits'?"

"Not as bad as before," he said.

"One thing you gotta say about her," Greg went on. "She's honest. No bullshit."

"That's for sure," he said.

"Don't forget," Greg said. "I get the first autographed copy of your book."

"Hell, yeah," he said, "you're the only one knows I'm interested in writing."

Going through his next audit, the figures vague and meaningless, he wondered what would Lowney say about his new novel taking place during an unforgettable time and place in Hawaii.

From Here To Eternity was written from the Haole point of view before and during the war. His novel was from the viewpoint of the local people that only someone who was born and raised in Hawaii could write. It was a tragedy turned into a tragic-comical situation of misguided loyalty and misplaced values.

He glanced over at Greg, who was busy analyzing the tax return of his next audit.

He wondered what Greg would say about him writing a story involving a Japanese man in Hawaii wanting Japan to win the war.

CHAPTER 10:

The Brawl

Class was over at the college and Armando decided to have a drink or two before heading back to his apartment.

He stepped into Ray's through the back entrance. All the stools in the semi-dark bar were occupied by after-work men and women. At the far corner stool was Frankie, the semi-bald, would-be actor who was already feeling no pain and was the loudest among the loud crowd. He was getting some attention from admirers who also were would-be actors.

As expected, there was no waitress. Armando ordered a Bud from Ray and took it to one of the open booths in the center. After that encounter with Frankie over a year ago when he first came to Ray's, he and Frankie had somehow made peace. He still had not forgiven Frankie for calling him a "Mex" and a "Wetback," but was civil to him.

As the crowd thinned out, Shig and George stepped into the bar through the front entrance on Santa Monica. They noticed Armando and immediately headed his way. George still had his suit on, apparently not having gone home after work. Shig, as usual, was in his casual T-shirt and Levis. George stepped over to the bar, ordered a couple of Buds from Ray, and brought them to the booth.

"Been here long?" George asked.

Armando lifted his half-full bottle. "My first."

"Not crowded," said Shig, looking around.

"It was." Except for Frankie and couple of guys at the corner, the bar stools were empty now.

"That loud-mouth jerk's here again," said George, nodding toward Frankie.

"So what else is new?" Armando said. "As long as nobody's listening to him, he'll be all right!"

Three of them sipped from their bottles, each to his own thought. Finally, Shig said to Armando, "That girl you brought over yesterday, where'd you meet her?"

"Right here," Armando said.

"She parks her car here?"

"What's wrong with that?"

Shig turned to George. "You should've seen him walking in with that lady. A Chicano with a tall, blonde, classy woman."

Frankie in the corner called Ray. "How 'bout 'nother shot?"

"Right, Frankie," said Ray, taking a opened bottle over and pouring into Frankie's glass.

"I see your Jap customers are back," Frankie whispered to Ray, but could be heard all the way to their booth.

"Hey, c'mon, Frankie," Ray said. "They're friends."

"You sure know how to pick 'em," Frankie said, nodding to the two other customers near his stool, chuckling.

One of them, as drunk as Frankie, said, "I 'member no Japs sat in the same bar as us."

"Yeah," said the other, also drunk, "No Japs or Chinaman allowed."

Armando glanced over at Shig and George, hoping they'd ignore Frankie.

"Assholes," George said, loud enough so Frankie could hear

him.

"What'd you call us!" Frankie screamed across the bar, jumping up from his stool.

"Hey, c'mon, Frankie," Ray tried to calm him.

"You heard what he just called us!"

"'At's for what you called him."

Armando could see that George and Shig were about to jump up from their seats. "They're drunk," he said, "take it easy."

"Just once more!" George threatened. "Just once more…"

"Sonofabitch!" Shig fumed, controlling himself.

"Hey, Mando The Man!" Frankie called him. "What's your friends so fired about?"

"I think you've had enough, Frankie," Ray said.

"'Nough?" Frankie protested. "It's those two who's causin' you trouble."

"Yeah, yeah, Frankie," Ray said. "One more and 'at's it."

"Ray!" Frankie protested. "I don' get you. Whattahell you're siding with 'em for? I'm your best customer. Don' I always pay my bills?"

"You're okay for now."

"You damn right, I'm okay. What 'bout them two over there?

"They're cash customers."

"Those Japs?"

Armando could see George taking off his wristwatch, loosen his tie, and about to take off his coat.

"Hey, George…" he said. "He's drunk."

"Bastard! Just once more," George said. "Just once more."

"Hey, you two!" Frankie called out. "You ain't mad at me for callin' you Japs, are you?"

Before Armando could stop him, George was up on his feet,

stripping off his coat and tie, and dashing over to Frankie's corner stool.

Armando was now up. So was Shig.

George grabbed Frankie's collar and was shaking him.

"You fucking white trash!" George screamed into Frankie's face.

Ray reached over across the bar and tried to untangle George's grip. "Hey, George," he said, "take it easy. He don't know what he's saying."

"I ain't drunk," Frankie said, trying to push George away. "I can take care of myself."

Armando and Shig were now beside the two other drinkers, waiting to see if they'd try to help Frankie.

"Get him, Frankie!" the drinker beside him said. "Show 'em we don't take no shit from Japs."

"Yeah, Frankie," his other friend said, "Japs and Chinamen ain't s'uposed to be in here."

"C'mon!" George screamed, letting go of Frankie and stepping toward the back door, "C'mon out!"

"I get out there I'm gonna beat the shit outa you, you fucking Jap!" Frankie said, stepping toward the door."

"Yeah," Ray said, "take your troubles out there in the parking lot."

When the two other customers followed Frankie, Armando and Shig followed them out.

It was almost dark, the sunlight faded over the tall brick buildings.

George waited for Frankie to come out into the parking lot.

"Get 'em, Frankie!" his first friend encouraged. "Show 'em you ain't 'fraid of him."

"Yeah, Frankie," the other said. "Beat the shit outa him. Damn Jap-Chinaman!"

As Frankie took a fighting stance, both fists up and threatening, George kept away, letting Frankie advance toward him. Frankie was a couple of inches taller than him and about 25 pounds heavier.

"Get 'em, Frankie," his first friend called him. "Show 'em, Frankie!"

Armando stepped up to him. "You better shut up!" he threatened.

"What?" the man said. "You're gonna do something 'bout it?"

Armando did not hesitate. He threw a left hook that landed flush on the man's chin. The man went down and stayed down.

Shig was waiting for the other man to help Frankie. "You want the same thing," he threatened, ready to swing at the man.

The man quickly backed away. "I ain't involved in this," he pleaded.

Armando watched George maneuvering away from the advancing Frankie. Ray had come out of the bar and stood watching, not saying a word, just watching.

When Frankie swung a wild powerful right, George backed away. Just as Frankie was about to swing another right, George stepped forward, clutched Frankie's arm, and jerking Frankie toward him, twisted his body, and gave Frankie an over-the-shoulder throw that sent Frankie flying onto the hard pavement.

Frankie landed on his back and the side of his face with a heavy thudding sound, his breath blowing out like a deflated balloon.

George advanced and, grabbing Frankie's collar, lifted him

up to his knees and was about to punch him when Ray rushed forward.

"Hey, George," Ray said, untangling George's grip around Frankie's collar, "you don' wanna kill the guy."

George twisted his hold on Frankie's collar, and choking him, screamed into his face "You damn sonofabitch!"

Ray kept trying to have George let go of Frankie. "C'mon. He's had 'nough."

George screamed. "You ever call me a Jap again, I'm gonna flip you into the traffic! Get that!"

Frankie, his face ashen, his throat gagging, held his hands up helplessly, pleadingly, his knees barely holding him up.

Armando stepped over. "Let him go," he said.

The man Armando had cold-cocked was now on his feet, staggering, wiping blood from his mouth. "You, too," Armando said, "you had 'nough?"

The man kept nodding.

Frankie touched his face where it had scrapped on the gravel and looked at his blood-smeared hand.

Ray reached for the bartender's towel on his shoulder, and offered it to Frankie who wiped his face. "You okay, Frankie?".

Quite sober now, Frankie nodded, looking at the droplets of blood on the towel.

"What hit me?" he stammered.

"Must've been something from up there," Ray said, looking up at the sky, grinning.

Frankie looked up at the sky, shaking the cobwebs in his head.

Armando, looking on, fought to keep from laughing.

"Hey, c'mon, you guys!" Ray said to everyone, "Get back in the bar. First drink's on the house."

"Hell, yeah," Frankie said, "I need a drink."

His friend, who had gone down from Armando's blow, repeated "Hell, yeah. I need a drink, too."

As George and Shig followed Armando back into the bar, Frankie and his two friends followed them in.

Ray poured shots for Frankie and his friends at the stools, then brought over three Buds to Armando's booth.

"Hey, George," Ray said, awed, "you're a black-belt?"

"Outa practice now."

"Outa practice," Ray said, quietly, "I'd like to be outa practice, the way you threw him."

"He's not hurt, is he?" George asked.

"Naw," said Ray. "A little shook up 'at's all."

"You got a black belt?" Armando asked George.

George shrugged, put his wristwatch back on, stuck his necktie into his coat pocket, and laid the coat on the back of the seat. "That was some left hook," he said to Armando. "The guy didn't know what hit him."

"Glad he din't get up," Armando said.

Over at the corner stools, Frankie and his first friend were still nursing their wounds when Ray offered them fresh towels."

"What was all that about?" Armando could hear Frankie asking Ray. "Whattahell was he so upset about?"

Armando looked over toward the stools, shaking his head.

Ray was also shaking his head, grinning.

"Hell, I've got nothing 'gainst him," Frankie said. "What's he got 'gainst me?"

"Frankie," Ray said, "would you call a colored man a 'nigger' to his face?"

There was a moment of silence as Armando, Shig and George

listened to Ray telling Frankie about the sacrifices Japanese-American soldiers made during the Second World War.

George, still a little winded, was sipping his beer silently. Shig was doing the same. Armando was glancing back and forth between the stools and his two Japanese friends.

He could now hear Frankie saying to Ray, "Get 'em a round. On me."

Ray hesitated. "You don' have to, Frankie."

"I wanna."

In a moment, Ray came to Armando's table with three Buds.

"On Frankie," Ray said.

All three turned their heads toward Frankie, who was looking down at his glass.

"Thank him," Armando said.

"Right," Ray said.

"Yeah, thank him," Shig said.

"Thank him for me, too," George said.

They lifted their bottles, nodded toward Frankie, and sipped.

CHAPTER 11:

Damn Buddhahead

Walking back to his apartment, George thought the brawl out in the parking lot was not really fair. He was sober and Frankie was drunk. When Frankie started swinging wild drunken blows all he had to do was wait for an opening. He ducked the blows and took advange of Frankie's unbalanced charge by pulling Frankie's arm forward and executing his favorite judo throw. If he had really wanted to hurt Frankie, he could have clutched Frankie's arm, bent it behind his back, and forced Frankie to fall forward with a broken arm.

George wondered what his venerable judo Sensei *teacher* would have said, he getting involved in a street fight with a drunkard. No doubt, Sensei would have chastised him for using his judo skills in a senseless bar brawl.

He had taken up judo while attending Japanese intermediate language school and had developed his skills further in high school. Taller and heavier than the average Nisei, he attained his brown belt at 14 and his black belt at 16. After Pearl Harbor, all the Japanese language schools were shut down and judo tournaments were discontinued. He was able to develop his skills further while training for combat in the Army.

Aw, Christ, he thought, whydahell was he thinking of judo when he should be concentrating on his novel.

Opening his apartment door, he took off his coat and tie and hung them in the small closet alongside the narrow bathroom. He kicked off his shoes and put on his pajamas.

His first-floor apartment, like the rest of the apartments in the old, faded, three-story brick building, did not have a bedroom. It was a combination living room/bedroom that adjoined a tiny kitchen. The dining table against the wall was his desk and it was there that he did his writing on a new portable typewriter.

Back in '47, when he arrived in Los Angeles, he had heard about haole landlords discriminating against Japanese, but did not think it would apply to an ex-GI college student. He was already accepted at LA State and wanted to live in the Hollywood area where it seemed nice, safe and glamorous.

He was staying temporarily at a downtown motel and was paying far more than he could afford. All he wanted was a room or an apartment near the campus. Having encountered a couple of blatant Jap-hating landlords, he went through the college newspaper and came across an ad "Apartment for Rent. Open to all."

Taking a deep breath he had knocked at the manager's door. A elderly man and a white-haired woman answered. Both haoles. Oh, boy, George thought, here we go again.

Surprisingly, the couple said there was an opening and took him to a first-floor apartment. It wasn't luxurious, not even roomy, but it would do. All he needed was a space where he could do his studies, cook his meals and take his showers.

He immediately made a deposit. That was 8 years ago, and he was still in the same apartment. The rent then was $38 a month. Today, $48. Later, he discovered that the old brick building was owned by a Nisei who had hired the haole couple to manage it. The couple, originally from Ohio, had a son married to a Japanese war bride.

Sitting at the hard, straight-backed chair, he reached over for Lowney's last letter and read it for the umpteenth time. Her criticisms were as severe as always, but alongside them now were some encouraging words. "You're getting there," she said. "You're showing signs of projecting yourself into the character so that it is not you the writer who feels, sees or hears, but it is the character who does."

Rereading the last sentence, Christ, he thought, it's like hypnotizing yourself and letting another mind take over.

He had long passed the line of no-return with Lowney. He believed in her. Totally. "Utterly," as she put it. She was honest. No holds barred. Brutally frank at times, nevertheless, sincere and caring. From what he gathered in the magazines and newspapers about her, she really was a highly educated, sophisticated lady. The kind of a high-class haole lady he never met or knew. And her husband, he learned, was a Harvard grad and was the superintendent of a big oil refinery in Southern Illinois.

Words, she said in the letter before him, were just a way to convey thoughts, some beautiful and joyful, some ugly and painful. The word "Jap," to him, couldn't be uglier and more painful. Whenever he heard it, his insides churned and growled and exploded, wanting to hurt and even kill whoever used it against him.

Of course, it went back to the war days. The ridiculed, bespectacled, buck-tooth Jap in wartime propaganda cartoons, newspapers, and magazines.

The day after Pearl Habor, rumors were rampant that all the Japanese in Hawaii would be placed in concentration camps.

One of the camps would be on the uninhabited and barren island of Kahoolawe off the coast of Maui.

Sixteen at that time, George thought that was a bunch of bullshit. How could the military ship thousands of Japanese to Kahoolawe. Except for sheep and goats, nothing existed there. There was scarcely any water, let alone food, on the island. What would the Japanese prisoners eat? Wild grass? Kiawe beans? Sheep and goat manure?

More importantly, who would be working in the sugar cane and pineapple fields if the Japanese workers were jailed? The economy of all Hawaii would be at a standstill. Would the rich haoles be willing to work in the fields?

George had gone to school the day after the attack. He was glad when the students were told to go home. There would be no classes, indefinitely.

He would have played hookey anyway. With everything going on after Pearl Harbor who could concentrate on studies?

He had gotten off the bus In Wailuku rather than returning home.

Barefoot, he walked down Market Street and hung around the corner of Vineyard and Market, knowing that his friend Yosh would eventually show up. The few people gathered on the sidewalks seemed in a daze whispering frightenedly to each other.

Most of the mom-and-pop stores and shops on Market Street were closed.

There was hardly any traffic in the usually bustling town. A prominent department store, the Nippon Center, had its sign removed and was now called the Victory Store. The jewelry store near Vineyard called Tokyo Jewelry was now New York Jewelry.

Shaking his head, George could not help but chuckle to himself. If the Japanese troops landed, they'd probably put up the original signs and become Japanese shops again.

In about ten more minutes, Yosh showed up. Three years older than George they had been roommates at Maunaloa Pineapple Camp on the island of Molokai last summer. Yosh and George's brother, Jiro, had been close friends at Baldwin before Jiro went on to University of Hawaii. Yosh actually went to Molokai to gamble with the young high school kids.

"Hey, howzit," Yosh greeted in his George Raft style, speaking through the side of his mouth. As usual, Yosh was dressed in his peg-legged gabardine trousers, aloha shirt, shiny shoes, a gold-plated watch shining on his wrist.

"Hey, howzit," George imitated Yosh.

"See how Market Street changed overnight?" Yosh said, looking up and down the street.

"Yeah," George said, grinning. "No more Japanee flags."

"Bunch of two-faced bastards," Yosh said.

"Tomorrow, Japanee flags 'gain, huh?" George said.

"Whodahell knows?"

"You no t'ink da Buddhaheads gonna land?"

"Could be."

"Christ," George said, "We gotta go back Japanee school."

"Just you young kids."

"Damn Buddahead teachers," George said. "I used to get my head slapped every day."

"The Japanee school teachers dey gonna be more mean."

"Yeah? You think so?"

"Dey gonna t'ink dey samurais."

"You kiddin'," George said.

"Aw, no worry," Yosh said.   "Damn Buddhaheads. Whattahell dey wanna take over Hawaii for? All we got here is a bunch of bobura pumpkin heads."

"Maybe the Japanee soldiers dey wanna try lay da hula-hula kanaka wahines," George said.

"Dey bettah watch out. Dem kanaka wahines, dey tough. Force 'em into bed dey chop off your balls."

George laughed.

"Yesterday," George said, "right after the attack, t'is guy, Montoku, from across the Kapuna river, he comes running over and tells my old man Japanee soldiers landed at Waikiki Beach."

"What!"

"He heard it over the Japanee short-wave radio."

"'At's da best one yet. ...Landed at Waikiki Beach."

"He's a kibei. One of those guys born on Maui, sent to Okinawa, then came back."

"Them kibeis," Yosh said, "they're all like dat. Lost in Japan for not being one of 'em; lost here in Hawaii for not being one of us."

"Da guy, Mantoku," George said, "his neighbor reported him for listening to a short–wave radio."

"Japanee neighbor?"

"Porlegee."

"Just like a Porlegee."

"When the police raided Matoku's house," George went on, "dey thought Japanee soldiers a'ready landed."

"On Maui!"

"Mantoku had on his old Japanee army uniform."

"No shit,' Yosh said, shaking his head. "He dat pupule, eh?"

"My old man gonna go over to the police station and tell 'em

Mantoku he not all there. Y'know. He crazy."

"Your old man, he bettah watch out. Dey gonna lock him up, too."

"Dey lock him up for dat," George said, "dey gotta lock up all the Buddaheads on Maui."

"Not me," Yosh said, "I gonna go down da armory and volunteer in the Army."

"When?"

"Right now," Yosh said. "Get in early and control the crap games."

"I wish I was a'ready eighteen," George said. "I volunteer with you."

Two-and-a-half years later, George did volunteer in the Army. He was sent to an interpreter's school in Minnesota and had to relearn the Japanese language.

Just before he was sent to the Pacific front, he and several of his interpreter buddies were ordered to go to different Army camps to show the haole GIs what a real Jap looks like. It was a direct order from the commanding general.

While fighting in the Pacific he was always aware that he could be shot by a Japanese or an American. There were times during the Okinawan battles that he was fired upon by both sides. He was not hit, but one of his interpreter buddies was killed by an American.

Once, near a cave overlooking the sea, he tried to save a young Okinawan girl of about twelve from jumping down the cliff. The young girl, whose entire family had already jumped stared at him, distrusting, her eyes blazing fearfully and hatefully. She took another step to the edge.

"Don't!" George pleaded, holding his hand out to her,

begging her.

"I'm not going to hurt you."

The girl inched closer to the edge.

"Don't do it!"

The frightened girl was apparently told by the Japanese soldiers that Okinawan women captured by Americans would be raped, mutilated and hanged.

She hesitated a second.

"C'mon!" he said, reaching. "Give me your hand."

The girl looked down the cliff, at him, back down the cliff.

"I'm an Okinawan like you," he now said. "My father and mother, they're from Ginoza Village."

The girl stared, undecided.

While she stood there, he began singing an old Okinawan song that he remembered from his boyhood days.

Tinsagu Nu Hana Ya. Singing it, he could recall his mother telling him that flowers are beautiful, but they are not nearly as beautiful as the lessons your mother taught you.

The young girl glanced down the cliff where her entire family lay dead. She looked over at him, her feet dragging away from the edge of the cliff.

As he reached farther out for her hand, she finally offered it to him.

She rushed into his arms, crying, saying in a mixture of Japanese and Okinawan, "Why, why? Why didn't you come sooner?"

He guided the young girl away from the cliff and took her to the rest of his squad where they offered her food and water.

The sergeant who witnessed the crises came over and shook his hand. "Too bad you couldn't save her family," he said. "You think we could have her talk to the others?"

Having won the young girl's confidence, George led her to a cave and told her to speak to the people in there. The girl stood at the mouth of the cave and called out, "Oi! Oi! Please come out! The Americans will not harm you!"

After a suspenseful moment, an old lady, holding the hand of a child of about three, came out of the cave, still distrusting. The girl George had saved rushed up to the old lady and child, and brought them safely into the open. Moments later, other women emerged from the cave with their children.

If there were any glory in the war, George now thought, saving that young girl and the others was the glorious of them all. In writing about it, there was no need to dramatize it. It was all there."

CHAPTER 12:

The Medal

Mom Diaz had called Armando early last night. She reminded him it's been over a month since his last visit. His excuse was a lame one. He was busy with his school work and his parking job, and was not able to get away. Then when she said she'd prepare his favorite Mexican dishes if he'd come for dinner tomorrow night, his studies and parking lot job went out the window.

"Really?" he had said. "Chili relleno and menudo?"

"And brown rice, chicken enchiladas and tortillas."

Although a Mexican, he was not familiar with home-cooked Mexican dishes. Ever since visiting Mom and Pop Diaz after his release from the VA hospital, he could never have enough of Mom's delicious, mouth-watering dishes. They were so much better than the tacos and burritos he used to have at the orphanage and at Mexican street stands.

Now, driving to East Los Angeles on First Street, he recalled his first visit to the Diazes. It haunted him. He had promised Rudy, his Army buddy, that he would call on Rudy and his family when they returned home from the war.

Rudy had not made it back. Armando was confined in a hospital ship crossing the Pacific, and was later stuck in an Army hospital in San Francisco. The Army doctors had to perform further operations on his amputated left leg, and the plastic surgeons had to work on the deep shrapnel scar on his face.

In the beginning, he did not really enjoy visiting Rudy's parents. The conversations were always strained and three of them made conscious efforts not to talk about the war.

He told them only that Rudy, a sergeant and he a corporal, were in charge of a squad on a hillside waiting for an attack by the North Koreans. The squad was made up of young and inexperienced but dedicated soldiers exposed to combat for the first time.

He had spared Mom and Pop the gruesome details of what really happened that day.

He did not tell them that the squad was greatly outnumbered. And that when the North Koreans made their suicidal charge up the hill that day, screaming, yelling, blowing bugles, cursing in whatever English they knew, he, Rudy and the rest of the squad waited patiently in their trench, their fingers ready to press the triggers of their machine guns and rifles to start the counterattack.

When the unsuspecting North Koreans were almost upon them, Rudy suddenly opened fire with his machine gun, followed by Armando with his machine gun and the others with their rifles. The first wave of the North Koreans were easily gunned down and the other waves quickly retreated.

No one in the squad was killed or wounded. They knew the North Koreans were regrouping. The next attack would be even more suicidal and even more violent than the first one.

They waited breathlessly, their ears fearfully attuned to every sound and movement down the hill and around them.

Rudy and Armando studied the others in the squad. They were okay, holding their ground.

Suddenly, more screaming, more bugles, more yelling in broken English.

The squad immediately opened fire. The attack came from all directions, right angles, left angles, firing blindly, going down, getting up, charging recklessly as though hopped up. When the machine guns fired at them from the left and right and the remaining squad picked them off, the North Koreans had no choice but to retreat and regroup.

Rudy, Armando and the rest of the squad waited again. Nervously. Anxiously. Knowing that the fanatic North Koreans would not stop. Crazy bastards! Dying was a sacrifice they seem to enjoy.

The squad knew they'd eventually be wiped out if their reinforcements did not reach them in time. Wheredahell were they!

The third attack finally started. It was even more fanatical and determined than the first two, this time lobbing grenades at random, not really knowing where the machine gun and rifle firings were coming from.

One of the aimless grenades landed between Armando and Rudy. Before Armando could react, Rudy reached for it and, in the same motion, heaved the grenade back at the attackers.

Armando was relieved when he noticed the reinforcements jumping into the trench and joining the fight.

The North Koreans did not let up. Without regrouping, they kept charging up the hillside.

Suddenly, another grenade landed beside Rudy.

This time he had no time to throw it back. He dove on it. When the grenade exploded, his body took the full impact, shrapnel zig-zagging and crisscrossing everywhere.

In that split second, Armando saw Rudy's body on the ground, couple of the soldiers besides him wounded.

He dashed over. "Rudy!" he cried out.

Rudy lay there, blood gushing from his mouth and his forehead, his jacket ripped at his stomach, his insides exposed.

"Rudy!" he cried out again, holding Rudy's head on his lap, trying to comfort him.

"Corporal!" one of the squad members yelled. "They're getting closer! A whole bunch of 'em!"

They were about to be overrun. He laid Rudy's head as comfortably as he could on the mud, and darted back to his machine gun.

Tears running down his face, he screamed and yelled at the fanatical gooks, wanting to kill, annihilate every one of them sonsofbitches, hating them as he'd never hated anyone so much.

"C'mon!" he yelled, firing his machine gun. "C'mon, keep coming! Keep charging, you fucking gooks!"

Not letting up, he kept squeezing the trigger, swinging the machine gun left to right, right to left, exposing himself, rallying the rest of the squad to keep firing.

Suddenly, something struck his leg and rolled on the ground. A grenade! Reaching for it, he was about to heave it at the now retreating gooks when a flashing explosion shook the ground around him. He did not feel the pain at first. Then, it came. Gradually. Then awfully. He could feel warm blood flowing down his left leg. And quickly felt an additional pain. This one in his face. He rubbed his right cheek, brought his hand before his eyes, blood all over his hand.

"Sonsofbitches!" he cried out. "Them fucking sonsofbitches!"

He began feeling weak and delirious. He kept firing his

machine gun, then collapsed on the mud still cursing the North Koreans.

How could he now tell Rudy's mom and dad what really happened that awful day?

They had lost their son. What more could be said?

Those who saw Rudy sacrificing his life for them reported the heroic act to the company commander, who, in turn, wrote a detailed report and sent it to battalion headquarters. The report reached the high command of the American Forces in Korea, then eventually went on to the President of the United States.

Rudy's mom and pop were invited to the White House to receive the highest medal in the United States Armed Forces from the President. Posthumously.

The medal was now displayed in a showcase at the Diaz home. Beside it was a photo of Rudy in full uniform. Whenever Armando approached the showcase, his eyes would moisten and his throat would tighten as the scene of Rudy diving on the grenade flashed before him.

Mom, of course, was proud to receive the medal from the President of the United States. But it was a small consolation. A medal for her son's life!

Approaching the Diaz home, Armando slowed down a block away, preparing as always to steady himself and check his emotions. Rudy was gone. Nothing would ever bring him back. And he hoped and prayed Rudy's mom and pop would soon get over the death of their son, their only child. A child who dreamed of going on to college and becoming a school teacher. And, along the way, becoming a boxing champion.

He was now across the street from the Evergreen Cemetery in East Los Angeles. The old and historical cemetery was home for the very rich and very famous of Los Angeles. The new plots were now for the humble, the sacrificing and the working class of the city. Also for the recipient of the country's highest military award.

He stepped up the steep front steps of the Diaz home, the yard bordered by large hibiscus and ginger flowers. He had climbed up those steps a million times. A million painful times. Yet, still felt like a lost man approaching a strange home. A family home he had never known growing up in an orphanage.

He and Rudy were supposed to have climbed up the steps together and be greeted triumphantly by Mom and Pop. Where was the glorious return of a couple of brave soldiers from the battlefields into the folds of a warm and loving home?

Before he could knock on the door, Mom was already there opening it.

"Armando!" she cried out, wrapping her arms around him, holding on to him as she would have Rudy. As always, she was dressed attractively in a starched cotton dress, her dark, silky hair combed back into a bun.

"What's been keeping you from coming home?" she said.

He returned her hug and kissed her cheek, unable to truly express his hesitation in "coming home," as she put it. Despite his injuries he had made it back; Rudy had not. Why did he keep feeling pangs of guilt gripping him whenever he returned "home?"

Quite a few with whom he had served in Korea did not make it back. He felt for their families. But not nearly as much as he felt for Mom and Pop Diaz. They still expected their son to step into the front door.

Pop Diaz stepped up to him. A truck driver, he was a little

bigger and heavier than Rudy. Otherwise, he was an image of Rudy.

"How're you doing , Son?" Pop greeted. "Ever'ting okay?"

"Fine, Pop," Armando returned. "Fine."

Pop held on to Armando's hand. "You're looking good."

"Come," Mom said, from over at the table where the aroma of delicious home-cooked Mexican dishes filled the warm living room.

The dishes, as expected, were great, the conversation very subtly steering away from the war.

Armando caught his own reflection in the framed photo and suddenly felt there must be something he could do for Rudy, his mom and his dad.

CHAPTER 13:

Revelation

Christine was in her upstairs studio finishing the landscape painting of her Japanese garden when Carole called.

She looked at the clock above her head. Four o'clock. She had expected the call so they could catch up with the latest news. And to prepare her to meet George.

"--Of course, I'm disappointed," she said when Carole revealed she could not be in LA over the weekend.

"And he's a professor at San Diego State?" she said after Carole tried to explain why she wasn't coming up. "Hanson Goodland...? And he speaks Nihongo...? How long have you been seeing him...? And you never mentioned it all this time...?

"Oh, by the way," she interrupted, "I met an old friend of yours. From the Heart Mountain days. Shigeru Ito... Yes, Shig Ito. You'll have to meet him on your next trip up... I sure will. He'll be glad you remember him.

"—Carole, I better start preparing dinner. ...George, of course, will be disappointed you won't be able to make it...

"Yes. Please. Do. Don't leave out any details.

"Sayonara..."

Still in her casual painting outfit of T-shirt and Levis, she went downstairs into her bedroom closet and changed into a white blouse and blue skirt. She applied a light touch of lipstick, powdered her face lightly, studied herself in her big mirror and, satisfied that she looked all right, went into the kitchen where all the ingredients for her special dinner were ready to be cooked: sliced chicken, onions, shitake mushrooms, bamboo shoots and long rice. The regular rice in the automatic rice cooker was already done, ready to be served.

She brought the electric frying pan into the dining room, placed it in the middle of long table, then brought out all the ingredients and the pot of rice.

She placed two plates across from the frying pan with chopsticks beside them. Not knowing whether George drank beer, whiskey or sake, she left his empty glass beside the plates with napkins, and did not bring out the drinks.

The door bell rang.

George, a man of appointments, must have waited until precisely 6:00 pm before ringing the bell.

He stood at the doorway in a sports coat, dress shirt, no tie, creased trousers and shiny shoes, his hair combed properly in place.

"Hi," he said, smiling warmly, offering her a bouquet of colorful red roses. "Sorry if I'm a little late."

"*Ira'shai*," she welcomed, thanking him for the beautiful flowers. "Late?" she said, a half laughter, restraining from remarking that an IRS agent is never late for an appointment?

She caught him studying her outfit, which was quite different from the day of the audit.

"Dozo," she invited. "Please. Come in," and held the door open.

She led him into the spacious dining room where the frying pan was now sizzling hot. As she placed the flowers in a vase, George looked around expectantly, then a little puzzled.

"Oh," she said, "Carole won't be here. She forgot she had a previous engagement." Then added, "There goes our Nihongo session."

"That gets me off the hook," he said. "My Nihongo wouldn't be up to par with hers. Or with yours."

"You speak it very well," she said.

"Yeah, sure," he said self-deprecatingly. "Static, bookish and classroom Nihongo."

"Come," she invited, indicating a chair across the table. "We'll have dinner while it's being cooked. Okay?"

"Sure," he said. "Chicken hekka."

"Chicken hekka?"

"Hawaiian style."

"Ever cooked it?'" she inquired.

"It's very simple," he said, standing from the chair, "let me do it."

Fascinated, she watched George placing the chicken in the pan, let it brown for several seconds, set it to one side, then placed the other ingredients in, the onions, bamboo shoots, shitake and the long rice. He cooked them for several minutes, the chicken on the side now even more brown. He poured a touch of shoyu sauce and brown sugar into the vegetables and chicken, careful not to overdo them. He continued stirring the sizzling ingredients expertly, the tantalizing aroma mouth-watering.

She discovered that George enjoyed a glass of beer before dinner, which she was glad to get him. Not really a drinking person, she poured herself a small glass of wine.

The chicken hekka was at last done.

George, playing the host and not the guest, ceremoniously filled the plates, then filled the bowls with rice.

Using her chopsticks, she reached into her plate, placed hekka into her bowl and, lifting the bowl, began eating. Slowly at first, tasting every morsel, then hungrily, amazed how tasty the hekka was.

"Goodness, George," she said, "who would have thought you could cook. A wonderful cook at that."

"For an IRS agent, huh?" he said, grinning.

He now filled his own plate and began devouring his hekka.

She glanced over her bowl of rice and thought how different he was from the IRS agent she met a few days ago.

Trying not to stare, her thoughts floated back to her young days in Kobe and wondered if her boyfriend, Shoichi Murata, have turned out as gentle and fine as George. She and Shoichi had corresponded steadily up until Pearl Harbor, vowing they would meet each other again soon. Either in Japan or in America.

"You're millions of miles away," she now heard George saying.

"Oh, I'm sorry," she said, catching herself. "Ever had taste, sound or smell bring back memories?"

"My hekka brought back memories?"

She nodded, stirring the food in her plate. "Fond memories of Japan," she said.

"Your childhood boyfriend?"

She felt her face suddenly flushing. Was it that obvious? "Him, too," she said finally.

"He must've been a nice boy," he said.

"Yes, he was."

"Why don't you contact the bureau in Kobe," he said. "Find out what happened to him."

"The bureau?"

"Or, whatever they call it over there in Kobe. They'd have records of every family in the city."

"I wrote to him in care of the census office," she said. "The letter was returned unopened."

"Ever thought of going back? You know, find out what's happened to the Murata family?"

"Not after what happened to Mom and Dad,"

He stopped eating, took a sip of beer and laid his glass down.

"Another one?" she asked.

"One glass during dinner is all I can handle. Noticed you didn't finish your wine."

She shook her head.

"I forgot. Daughter of missionary parents."

"Oh, that's not the reason," she said. "My face turns lobster red and I get intoxicated too easily. You seem able to control yourself very well," she added. "One glass and that's it."

"Not when I'm with my drinking friends."

"Oh?"

"Thought I was a 'holier than thou' IRS agent, huh?"

"Well, you're the first IRS agent I've ever met."

"You know," he said, "I shouldn't have accepted your dinner invitation. Not when I'm auditing your tax return."

"You think I'm bribing you?"

"The appearance of being too friendly with a taxpayer who is being audited could be misinterpreted," he said.

"George Tsukayama!" she said, her voice rising, "my inviting you to dinner, if you recall—"

"Yeah, yeah, I know," he quickly said, "you wanted me to meet your friend."

"Exactly. Nothing more, nothing less."

He looked down at the table.

"The idea! As far as my tax return is concerned, I could have had my accountant handle everything without ever meeting you."

"Yeah, I know," he apologized.

"On the other hand," she said, "I'm glad I met you. Even though you're an IRS agent."

They looked at each other. They laughed.

She took a tiny sip of her wine. "From what I've seen of Maui," she now said, "the people seemed warm, friendly and happy."

"I'm not?"

"Well..."

"I may not be warm and friendly, but I'm happy."

"I'm glad you think so."

"I'll be a lot happier," he said, "if you'd offer me another glass of beer."

"Of course," she said, stepping into the kitchen, opening the refrigerator, taking out a bottle of beer, and pouring into a fresh glass.

She was back in a second.

"Mahalo," he said, accepting."

"Mahalo?"

"Thank you in Hawaiian," he said. *"Mahalo nui loa.* Thank you very much.

Do itashimashite," she returned.

He lifted the glass. *"Kampai."*

She glanced over at him again. Other than being an IRS agent she knew nothing about him. Absolutely nothing. Oh, he was Nisei, served in the U.S. Army and came to California to attend college. He surely must have other interests than taxes. Maybe, he has a girlfriend, is engaged, or was married and has children to support. And here she was trying to match him with Carole.

He was at least interested in her paintings, she went on speculating, sipping her wine delicately, hoping her cheeks won't turn lobster red, wondering what was he thinking right now, drinking silently, his eyes down on the table.

He seemed one of those stoic Nihonjins, hardly relaxed, always working, always sacrificing for a better tomorrow. What in the world made him become a IRS agent? Did he enjoy harassing and intimidating taxpayers? Does he feel important carrying a U.S. Treasury Department badge?

And him born and raised in paradise.

Oh, why am I so concerned about him? Trying to match him with Carole. She's too cheerful and too pleasant for him. What would they talk about? Tax laws? People whose tax returns he'd examined? How he'd intimidate cheating taxpayers?

"How many tax returns do you examine in a day?" she asked, trying to fill the gap in their conversation. "A dozen?"

"Huh?" he said, not in the same train of thoughts.

"Tax returns," she went on. "Do you examine several of them each day?"

"Several?"

"Aren't you expected to examine a number of them each day?"

He shook his head. "We're expected to do the best we can. There's no mandatory quota."

Another moment of silence.

"Do you golf?" she now asked.

"Golf?" He shook his head. "And I don't go fishing either."

"You don't golf; you don't go fishing. What do you do in your spare time? --You do have spare time, don't you?"

He laughed that pleasant, enigmatic laughter of his again.

"I wish I could paint like you," he said.

"I really wanted to become a writer," she said.

"Oh?"

"But painting became my first love."

"Ever had anything published?" he asked.

"In a national magazine once," she said. "The rest in our local church magazine."

"Anything I can read?"

"You really want to?"

"Yeah. Sure. I'd like to."

"My latest article came out some time ago," she said, stepping over into the living room, and bringing back a magazine that was published while she was still attending church services.

"So," he said, accepting the magazine, "you're a published writer."

"If that's what you want to call me."

He turned to her article, and began reading it, sipping his drink.

She started clearing the dining table, taking the frying pan back into the kitchen first, then the dirty dishes. Placing the plates into the dishwasher, she glanced over at George who was absorbed in the article.

It was a subject he was already familiar with. Shoichi Murata.

It was entitled, "Searching For A Friend."

It told about meeting young Shoichi Murata at the Christine Church in Kobe. She had learned to speak Nihongo from Shoichi and Shoichi learned to speak English from her. They both attended church services together and were able to understand the sermons in both Nihongo and in English One day, she said to her mother, "Someday, I'm going to marry Shoichi."

"Yes, Dear," her mother seemed amused.

"You think Dad would perform the wedding ceremony?" she went on.

"I don't see why not?" Mom said, stepping away.

Following Mom into the living, she went on, "I hope his father and mother won't object Shoichi marrying me."

"The Muratas? Object?"

"I'm not Japanese."

"Well," Mom said, sitting on the couch, pulling out a magazine from the nightstand, "I'm sure they'd prefer Shoichi marrying one of his own people."

"How about you, Mom?"

"Me?"

"And Dad?"

Mom look at her and smiled warmly.

And so, while still only eleven years old, they embraced their promising world with wonderful expectations.

But December 7, 1941, was not what they had expected. The catastrophic event changed the entire world, not the least theirs.

After putting all the dishes in the dishwasher, she took out the freshly baked apple pie from the oven, placed it on the cutting board and, slicing it into generous pieces, put two of them on the plates.

She glanced over at George who had turned to the last page of the article. She stepped into the dining room, studying George, hoping he had enjoyed the article.

"Hey," he said, putting the magazine down, "this is a pretty good piece of writing."

"You liked it?"

"Well written," he said, "and very interesting."

"Thank you," she said. "Glad you think so."

"A nice, young, human-interest story."

"Being in Hawaii on Pearl Harbor day," she said, "you'd really understand how it affected everyone."

"Yeah," he said. "How can we ever forget that day."

"I knew nothing about politics," she said. "All I knew was that many of our servicemen were killed that day. And Japanese pilots were shot down." He said nothing.

"Americans hated the Japanese," she said. "I could not hate them. In a way, they were my people."

He nodded. "And there was Shoichi."

She nodded back.

"Never heard from him after that?"

She shook her head, her eyes misty. "I could only hope and pray that he and his family were fine."

She suddenly remembered the plates of pies in her hand.

She placed his plate beside the magazine. "My Mom's recipe," she said. "My favorite."

"You just baked it?"

She nodded.

"I didn't think anyone baked pies anymore."

Not hesitating, he brought a forkful up into his mouth, then another.

"Well?" she questioned, studying him, then taking bites from her own plate.

"Very good," he said. "Better than the bakeries," and continued devouring the rest of the pie.

After a moment, she said, "Honestly, what do you do on your own time?"

He looked away.

"I've practically told you all about myself and my mom and dad."

A moment of silence.

"George?"

He finally looked up at her. "I live in a dream world."

"A dream world? You?"

He nodded.

"You're getting treatment for it?"

"Yeah," he chuckled, "in a way."

"Psychiatric treatment?"

"Well, not exactly," he said. "You've established yourself as a painter. Me, I'm trying to become a writer."

"A writer?!"

When she probed further, he told her all about Lowney Handy. And explained that he had been corresponding with Lowney Handy for the past two years.

"Oh, George! That's great!"

He shook his head. "Not until I have something published like you."

"It was just a magazine article."

"But you're a published writer."

"Well, yes. I suppose so. But you, you're going to be a published novelist."

He looked at her across the table, his head held sideway, then quickly took a sip of beer.

"What's your novel about?" she went on probing.

He remained silent.

"I know," she said, "I know. You're not supposed to talk about it."

His silence was annoying. But she remembered that in one of the creative writing classes she took at SC, the professor emphasized not to talk about what you're writing about until you're finished with the material. "Talking about it before then," he had said, "would dissipate your story."

"How long will it take to finish it?"

He shrugged. "Depends."

Oh, Christine, she scolded herself, so many questions when he really doesn't want to talk about it. What a revelation! A stoic Nisei IRS agent writing a novel. And corresponding with a famous teacher.

"I'm waiting for Lowney to invite me to the colony," he said.

She reached across the table and squeezed his hand. "To have so much faith in your writing. In yourself."

He squeezed back, then quickly let go.

"I've eaten all of your food," he said, getting up, "had your delicious pie, drank your beer and had an interesting conversation. It's time for me to go."

She rose also.

"I'm sorry Carole couldn't make it," she said. "Maybe next time."

"Yeah. Sure," he said, stepping toward the living room door. "I'm not sorry she couldn't make it," he added, chuckling. "Now, don't tell her I said that."

"It was nice of you to have come," she said, "and get to know the real you."

"I wish all the taxpayers would say that," he said.

"Not until they really get to know you," she said.

She held the door open and followed him out to his car.

"Well, "she said, "good luck on your novel."

"Thanks," he returned. "I hope to see one of your paintings in an art gallery someday."

"*Domo,*" she bowed gratefully. And standing there close to him, she instinctively hugged him. "I'm so glad to have met you, Tsukayama-san."

He resisted a moment, then returned the hug.

CHAPTER 14:

Li'l Tokyo

Instead of driving up to Santa Monica Boulevard and heading home, George headed south to Wilshire.

In a way, Christine was sure odd, he thought. After all these years, she still thinks about that boy in Kobe. A boy she last saw when they were both what? Eleven years old? A sort of Japanese loyalty. Why not? She was, after all, a Japanese at heart.

He passed Conklin and Jupitar Streets, turned left on Wilshire, and drove toward downturn LA.

In a way, he himself, was a Japanese, at heart, too, he told himself. An Okinawan Japanese who grew up disliking Japanese customs. All that bowing and superficial politeness.

Aw, he probably felt that way because he's constantly reminded by the Naichis non-Okinawan Japanese that Okinawans were second-class Japanese. That their customs, language, traditions and behavior were closer to Chinese and Kanaka Hawaians than Japanese.

And what's wrong with that? He grew up with Chinese and Kanaka kids and always felt close to them. Like Okinawans, they, especially the Kanakas, were happy people, always singing, dancing and laughing.

Christine, in a way, was like a Kanaka, he thought. Totally non-prejudiced toward other races. It must be her religious upbringings. Everyone is God's children. If she had been older when telling her mother she'd like to marry Shoichi someday, would her mother had approved?   Her daughter marrying a Japanese!

In a few more minutes, he was on First Street in downtown LA, heading toward Little Tokyo.

It was his usual routine on Saturday nights.   He'd work on his novel all afternoon, wash up, then drive down to Little Tokyo for a Japanese dinner.   If he ran into his Japanese-Hawaiian friends, he'd go to Civic Bar with them and have a few.   If still early, he'd join them at one of the nomiyas Japanese bars where the waitresses were former war brides who usually were divorcees or on-the-run wives.

He parked on First, walked over to the basement poolhall on the corner of First and San Pedro, and went downstairs.   He looked for his friends, Tad and Mits.   Not finding them he came back up the stairs and headed for Civic Bar across the street.

Stan, the owner, in aloha shirt and khaki trousers, looked toward the door as he entered the long, dimly-lit bar.

"Whaddyasay, George," Stan greeted, turning away from a lone haole customer occupaying one of the bar stools.

"Hi, Stan," George returned, and sat at the bar.   Stan, a forty-year-old Hawaii Nisei, was one of the oldtimers in J-Town.   He had left the islands long before the war as a merchant seaman and never returned.   He still spoke with a heavy pidgin accent, however.

An unofficial mayor of J-Town, Stan not only knew everyone, but everything that went on there.   He knew where the floating craps games were, where a new haole girl worked, who and where the bookies were, and who to look up if you want someone beaten up.   He even knew the mama-sans who had connections with abortionists.

"Looks like your friends not here yet," Stan said.

"It's still early," George said, glancing over at the other customer.

"The usual?" Stan asked.

"Yeah," he said, taking out a bill from his wallet.

Stan reached into the refrigerator, came up with a bottle of Bud, and placed it before him.

"I don' wanna talk shop--," Stan said confidentially, "but lemme ask you something." He glanced over at the other customer. "I know gamblin' winnin's, dey taxable. What 'bout losses, dey deduct'able?"

"Only up to the winnings," George said.

"In other words, "Stan went on, "no gamblin' loses on your tax return?"

He shook his head. "Only If you're in the gambling business."

"But 'at's not legal in California, right?"

He shook his head.

"So dey got you comin' and goin'."

He nodded.

"Damn tax laws," Stan said. "Can't beat 'em-- Hey, I got not'ing against tax laws," he quickly added.

George laughed.

"See da guy over there?" Stan tossed his head toward the other customer.

George glanced over.

"Came all da way from Alabama. Lookin' for his wife."

"Ex-GI?"

"Yeah."

The ex-GI seemed lost and abandoned.

"Kinda remind me of Takako and her husband," Stan said. "Y'know Takako the waitress at Ichiban Nomiya."

"Oh, yeah. Her husband came from Kansas looking for her."

"No way, she gonna go back, she told him. Not'ing but cornfields, cornfields, cornfields."

"And wheatfields, wheatfields, wheatfields," George joined, laughing.

He looked over at the ex-GI again. Poor guy must have thought he was doing his wife a great favor bringing her to America.

George finished his beer, got off the stool and left his change on the bar. "See you, Stan."

"Yeah, okay, George. I'll tell Tad and Mits you was here."

He stepped out into the cool night air and headed for Atomic Nomiya a few doors away from Civic Bar.

"*Ira'shai!*" Mama-san welcomed as he stepped into the small stifling bar. "'Ello, Georgie-san."

"Hi, Mama-san," he returned.

Mama-san, the middle-aged owner of the bar, was in a colorful tight kimono, her makeup quite heavy. She indicated an empty booth against the wall. "Come. Sit here."

There were several noisy customers at the bar stools and a few others in the semi-dark booths, none of whom he recognized.

"Mariko-san, she busy righ' now," Mama-san said. "She come join you bery soon. Okay?"

"Okay," George said, sitting alone.

His friends, Tad and Mits, were not there. They must have gone to another nomiya.

"Wan' bee-ru? Sake?" Mama-san inquired.

"Beer," he said.

"Hai, bee-ru." She walked off behind the bar where Mariko, the young, pretty, dainty waitress in a tight sweater was talking to a Japanese national in Nihongo. "Mariko-san," he could hear Mama-san saying, "your friend, da tax man, go ovah talk to 'im."

"Hai," Mariko said, excusing herself and coming over to George's booth with a bottle of beer and a glass.

"Hi, Mariko," George greeted. "Busy, huh?"

"Oh, Georgie-san, nevah too busy for you." Unlike the other waitresses her English was quite good.

She accepted the ten-dollar bill he had placed on the table. "Bring back change," she said, stepping over to the cash register, ringing it and coming back with change.

Taking the first sip, looking over the glass, he said, "Mariko, your home, Alabama?"

"Ah-la-ba-ma? No. I-ri-no-i."

"Not Alabama?"

"Why you keep sayin' Ah-la-ba-ma?"

"Just asking, is all," he said.

"T'is Ah-la-ba-ma gal you rookin' for," she said, "she owe tax money?"

"Oh, no," he quickly cut her off, "nothing like that."

"Me," Mariko said, "I no owe no tax money. Ever't'ing paid up."

"Yeah, I know," he said, wondering if everyone who knew he was an IRS agent thought he was looking for delinquent taxpayers. Christ, after putting in his eight hours, he couldn't care less if a taxpayer owed the U.S. Government a million bucks. Unless it was a part of his audit.

Mariko, he thought, would be a great character for his novel. A girl having arrived from Japan just before Pearl Harbor, now a bar girl in Wailuku, Maui. He wanted to capture her accent and her loyalty to Japan.

"This place in Illinois," he said, "you didn't like it there?"

"Oh, yes."

"So what are you doing here?"

"Had to get 'way. Y'know…"

He waited for her to go on.

"Husband, Hal, he bery goo' husband."

"And you left him?"

She nodded. "Somet'ing missing."

He took a sip, listening intently.

"Baby boy, t'ree years old, he die."

"Oh."

"Must get 'way. A'ways t'inking 'bout baby, Michael Kiyoshi. I blame Hal; I blame myself."

"What happened?"

"Fall off tractor. Cotton field."

George winced.

Mariko's hand was up to her mouth.

He waited.

"Rike night-tu mare," she went on. "Hadda get 'way."

He nodded. Sympathetically. Her story would have a place in his novel.

A Japanese mother recovering from a son's tragic death.

"Your husband, he ever been here?"

"Two times," she said, holding up her fingers. "I wanna go back. But, him and me, we still cry when t'inkin' of Michael Kiyoshi."

He said nothing.

"Hal, him, number one best husband," she volunteered.

"Treat me rike I am queen. I try to be good wife, but..." She pressed her hand over her mouth again.

A real different angle, he told himself. A war bride who loves her haole husband and can't see him suffering.

"He owns his own farm?" he asked.

She nodded. "Many acres. Once belon' to grand-u-faddah, then fa-ddah, now him. Cotton, corn, wheat."

"He doesn't mind you working here?"

"He no wan' me workin', but I tell him I must keep busy. It is goo' for me. I am with Nihonjin friends. Remember young, happy days in Japan."

Wow, he thought. A nice nostalgic angle.

He took another sip.

"Ever been back to Japan?" he asked.

She shook her head.

"No family? Brothers? Sisters?"

"Oh, yes."

"Don't you miss them?"

"Very much."

"And you've never been back?"

"Mama and Papa dey don' want me back. Ever since I marry 'Merican."

He finished his beer.

He ordered another one.

CHAPTER 15:

Takarazuka

Christine watched George's car pulling out of the driveway. Well, well, well. An IRS agent becoming a novelist. She had felt that his heart really wasn't in his tax work. He seemed too kind, too warm, and too personable to be an IRS agent. During his first visit, he'd been more eager to get over his examination than to look for violations and errors. It was just a job.

She shouldn't have asked what his novel was about, she chastised herself. After all, she, too, would have been annoyed if he had asked what her next painting would be.

Was he writing about his horrible experience fighting against Okinawans who could have been his own relatives? she asked herself. Or, maybe, about growing up on Maui, a second-generation Japanese boy not understanding the culture of his parents.

Whatever, she was glad to discover another side of George Tsukayama. Maybe, she, too, could become a novelist. She had already written several stories. They could have been novels.

Oh, Christine, you've not attained your full potential as a painter and here you are thinking of becoming a novelist.

She wished she and George had spoken more Nihongo. She guessed after what he and other Niseis went through during the war, they'd rather forget they're Japanese and be treated as Americans. They had been called awful names during the war and didn't want to be reminded of those days.

But, what was so wrong with speaking Nihongo? It was a beautiful language, reflecting the deep and refined culture of Japan. Besides, that war had ended ten years ago. The Korean war was just over and the soldiers were returning home calling the Koreans awful names. When was all this name-calling end?

She went upstairs to her studio with a cup of coffee and stood looking at her paintings on the four walls. Also, at rough sketches of Shoichi and Carole she had done long ago and wanted to do an oil painting of them. It was too bad that Carole couldn't make it for dinner tonight. On the other hand, she was glad that Carole had met someone she seemed interested in.

Sipping her coffee, she opened her drawer and brought out her old photo album. The first pages were of Mom, Dad and her in Kobe. Mom and Dad had been lucky, she thought. They had met each other in church during their college days. They were meant for each other. Their lives were fulfilled, until…

She took another sip and went through more photos. Kobe, 1937. The last year she was there. Dear God. That long ago!

The photos of Shoichi popped up.

Takarazuka. The Hollywood of Japan. Where she and her classmates had gone to see a musical. Oh, how exciting that had been. Her first Japanese musical. She could still sing parts of it. "When the clouds came drifting by, and you and I were there watching them sailing by…"

She glanced over at the neglected sketch at the far wall. Has it been that long ago when she sketched it? How old was she then? Ten? Eleven?

She and Shoichi had escaped from the rest of the class and went for a walk across the long wooden bridge which spanned across the Takarazuka River.

Dressed in her school uniform of blue skirt and white blouse, she had sat at the edge of the bridge and looked down toward the dainty homes along the river. Shoichi, in his uniform of brown trousers and white shirt, had sat beside her, a couple of kids struck by the peace and serenity of the colorful scene and the sound of trickling water below them.

"Oh, how I wish I could paint that beautiful scene," she said to Shoichi in Nihongo.

"Do a sketch," he suggested.

"That's a good idea," she said. "I can do a painting of it later."

She brought out her pad and pencil and quickly sketched the river, the banks and the houses along the river.

Then she inserted a young boy and girl on the edge of the bridge looking down at the scene below them.

"Who are those two people?" Shoichi wanted to know.

"Who else could they be?"

After a passing silence, he said, "Honto. You are leaving for America at the end of the month?"

"I have to."

"You're never ever coming back?"

"Of course I am," she said. "When I'm a little older and I can travel by myself."

They sat there silently as she kept sketching.

"Will you forget me when you go to America?"

"Forget you? Silly boy."

"I wish you were not going away."

"I have to. I can't live here alone."

"You could stay with us."

She looked at him. "I thought about that."

"And?"

"Mom and Dad. They'd be lonely without me."

"Hai," he said, "*so desu neh.*"

"You could come to America and live with us," she said.

"I thought about that."

"And?"

"My okasan and otosan, they would miss me."

She was finishing the sketch, which was not as beautiful as she'd hoped it to be, but gave her a basis for a painting.

"You and me," he went on, "we're different, but…"

"Different?"

"You have reddish hair," he said, touching her hair, "and I have black hair. Your have blue eyes and I have brown eyes."

"But deep inside we're the same," she said.

"Hai," he agreed. "*So desu, neh?*"

After another moment, he said, "You don't mind people staring at us? You know. You an American, me a Nihonjin."

"They're just wondering why I'm not with another American and why you're not with another Nihonjin."

"Christine-san and Shoichi," he said, his hand on her shoulder. "We look different to others, but we're not really different, are we?"

"*Kokoro wa Nihonjin desu,*" she said. Our hearts are Nihonjin.

"Hai, so desu," he said, rising. "C'mon, we better go to the theatre before the show starts."

"Hai." She placed her sketch into her handbag and got up.

They went back across the bridge and joined the lines of people waiting patiently to get into the theatre.

Her coffee cup was now empty. As she stood up, her eyes caught the sketch against the wall. She stepped over and studied it. It was a rough sketch by a child. It needed more definition. She could refine it before doing an oil painting of it. Yes, that would be her next project, an oil painting of her and Shoichi enjoying the beautiful view from the Takarazuka bridge.

CHAPTER 16:

Texas

Shig transferred the wet laundry from washer No. 3 to dryer No. 1, and watched the hot tumbler spinning and protesting in squeaking, nerve-racking rotations. Bored and hypnotized by the endless spinning, he wished he was already a full-time student at either Cal Poly San Luis Obispo or Cal Poly Pomona.

His mind rotated back to when he and Susan had first started the laundromat five years ago. Then rotated further back to when he first met Susan.

He was hospitalized in a couple of VA hospitals on the East Coast, then was transferred to a Midwest hospital near Chicago. His wounded back had gotten a little better, and fortunately his rehabilitation period was not as long as other Vets who had been wounded more severely.

Among the many nurses at the hospital was Susan Hashimoto, a tall, attractive Nisei from Glendale, California, not too far away from his hometown, Gardena. Susan and her family were sent to Manzanar Relocation Camp in the Sierra Mountains right after Pearl Harbor.

A couple of years before the war ended, Susan was allowed to leave Manzanar camp and attend a nursing school in Cleveland from where she graduated right after the war. She chose to work at the Veterans Hospital near Chicago, knowing there would be wounded Nisei veterans hospitalized there.

Susan invited Shig to her home in North Chicago on his first pass from the hospital. Her father and mother were glad to meet someone who had lived close to them in Southern California.

Before long, Susan became more attentive to Shig at the hospital and they were soon dating.

He was a wounded Vet without a job or any particular skills. Should they get married now or later when he learned a trade? "Now," meant he would work part time and attend college. "Later," meant they would hold off marriage until he was out of college. They chose "now."

Shig found a job at Curtiss Candy Company of Baby Ruth fame near the wharf as a warehouse clerk and started night school at a junior college under the GI Bill while Susan continued working at the Veterans Hospital.

He and Susan lived in a cramped apartment on the Southside and hardly saw each other, let alone eat together. After several months, he threw in the towel. Worst of all was the bitter, cold, Chicago winters which affected his arthritic back.

They decided to get out of Chicago.

But where? To California, where they heard Japanese were still not welcome? Where they heard those who returned after the camp days were barely surviving?

When Shig mentioned Texas, Susan was shocked.

"Texas! Of all places, why Texas?

It was then that Shig told her about Eric Benton. Although he had lost Eric's address, if Texans were as friendly as Eric had been, they would have no trouble settling there. Besides, it was much warmer than Chicago.

They packed all their belongings in the back of their old Ford Pickup, mapped out the direction to Austin, and were on their way in a few days. It was freezing cold in Chicago and the farther south they went the less cold it got.

Driving through small towns in Northeastern Texas, they discovered, at least perceived, that they were in the deep South. Shig's memories of the basic training days in Mississippi reminded him how puzzled he and his Nisei buddies were about white toilets and black toilets; about riding in the front of the busses or the back; about signs designating whites only restaurants.

Shig was sure the big cities like Austin would be different. The University of Texas was there and the people would surely be more liberal, more understanding and tolerant. With Shig's disability checks and Susan's nursing salary, they could live comfortably.

That first night in Austin, they drove into a motel with a "Vacancy" sign and was told no rooms were available. No rooms were available in other motels, too, until they came into a segregated part of the city. The room was unpainted and the bathroom needed plumbing work. But, it at least was a roof over their heads.

Next day, while Susan went looking for an apartment near the UT campus, Shig went to register as a new student. The registrar, a heavyset, light-haired girl pronounced Shig's name as "She-get-roo Eye-to."

When he informed the unsmiling, curt girl that he'd be attending school on the GI Bill of Rights, she was confused. "You were in our Army?" she questioned."

Oh, boy.

"If you're from California," she went on, "why aren't you goin' back there?"

"I heard that University of Texas is a great school," he said, hoping that would appease the girl.

"Yes, it is," said the girl. "But you're Jap'anese, aren't you?"

"Yeah."

"We have many ex-GIs here," she tried to explain. "Some of 'em were wounded fighting the Jap'anese during the war. Will you be comfortable bein' among 'em?"

"Look," he said, annoyed, "I fought in the Army too."

"'Gainst your own country?"

"Against the Germans!" he tried to control himself.

A blond, crew-cut male registrar in the next window stepped over. "What's wrong here, Agnes?"

"I'm trying to explain to 'im that he might be more com'fortable attending a college in California," she said.

The young man studied Shig. "You're from California?"

"Born and raised there."

"So why d'ya wanna attend UT?"

"I heard it's a nice friendly school," he said, glancing over at the girl.

"Yes," said the young man, "UT is known for its friendliness. Aren't the schools in California just as friendly?"

"Look," he said, "are you turning down my application?"

"Oh, no. Not'ing like that. You're most certainly welcome here. We just wanna make sure this is the right school for you."

"I'd like to speak to your supervisor," Shig said.

"We're not rejecting your application, Sir."

"Then you're accepting me?"

The young man turned to the young girl. "Stamp it 'Accepted,'" he told her.

The girl now asked, "Have you found living quarters near the campus?"

"Not yet," he said. "My wife's looking for one right now."

"She might be able to find one out on the outskirts," she said.

Later that night, back at the motel, Susan revealed that she couldn't find an apartment near the campus. They were either filled, will be filled or were just for Americans."

The apartment they finally found was a good forty-five minutes ride from the campus. It would do for now. Until they could relocate much closer.

With their savings, it would be better to buy a home, Shig thought. Preferably near campus and not having to deal with a landlord. After graduation, they could sell the house and turn over a profit.

Susan's nursing job at a clinic in a disadvantaged neighborhood paid about half of what she was earning at the VA hospital in Chicago, but she felt she was at least contributing to the poor and helping them as best as she could.

School had not yet started and Shig spent most of his time walking around the huge campus and orienting himself to the different departments. Some of the department heads, ex-GIs like himself, were quite friendly. One of them had landed in the Normandy invasion and had heard about the Japanese-American soldiers fighting in France and Germany.

Shig and Susan could not get used to the loud, raucous next-door neighbors. Their vibrating music penetrated the walls and their constant bickering and fighting were as though they were all living in the same apartment.

Shig went through all the ads in the Austin Sentinel, searching for an inexpensive house. Having experienced rejections in California before the war, he was aware that he'd be confronted with rejections here, too. But not as vocally and hatefully. All subtleties were thrown out the window. They were told the houses were not for foreigners; that they should return to wherever they came from; that they, the sellers, would be condemned if they sold their homes to undesirables.

Are these the friendly Texans Eric Benton had told him about?

Shig and Susan decided to go to another state. Maybe, Arizona, New Mexico or Nevada. Where it was not as warm as Texas; certainly much friendlier than the damned Texans.

Shig, in the meantime, had received a letter from his sister, Tamiko, who had relocated back to Southern California. She said things were still bad, but were gradually easing. Some of the Hakujins were actually welcoming the Japanese back to California, she said. They're beginning to admit that the evacuation had been wrong.

Encouraged, Shig and Susan decided to head back home. But not before Shig had the satisfaction of writing a letter to the editor of the Austin Sentinel. Trying not to sound bitter or hateful, he wrote a draft, then another, then a final one.

"Dear Editor:

I fought with the 442nd Regimental Combat Team made up of Japanese-Americans in Europe. We were the recipient of many citations, including a Medal of Honor, and the Presidential Citation that cited our courage and dedication to our country.

The highest casualty we encountered in the war was at the Vosges Mountains in northeast France near the German border. When we had beaten the Germans in Bruyers and Biffontaine nearby, we had expected to be pulled back and have a much-deserved rest.

Our General, however, ordered us to rescue a battalion of American soldiers surrounded by the Germans. Other Americans had attempted to free the trapped battalion, but were driven back. Because of our combat record, the General ordered us to rescue them.

The American Battalion was the First Battalion of the 141st Regiment from Texas. They had been surrounded by the Germans for days and were desperately in need of food, water and medical attention.

I don't know whether our battle saving the Texans was ever told in your newspapers. It was the toughest battle we ever had. And, Sir, we did encounter some tough battles throughout Italy, France and Germany.

After we fought the Germans with fixed bayonets, grenades, rifles and artillery, we finally overran, killed or captured them, and rescued the Texans. Our casualty was over 800. The Texans we rescued were about 200.

During the battle, I came across one of the Texans who needed immediate medical care. He was wounded pretty badly. Being much smaller than him, I helped him crawl to safety trying to escape the slaughter that was going all around us. We managed to get away from the onslaught and was approaching our medics when a shell exploded in the trees above us. The Texan was not hit. I was.

Recovering in our medical tent together, I learned that the Texan was Eric Benton from Austin. He invited me to visit him when the war was over. He said everyone in his battalion would be forever grateful to us for rescuing them. He assured me that all Texans would remember the 442th Regimental Combat Team. He especially wanted me to come to Austin and meet his father and mother.

Eric and I wrote to each other after we were separated. Very sadly, Eric did not make it from an operation in a field hospital.

In fond memory of Eric Benton, a brave soldier, I am writing this to you hoping there would be many other warm, friendly Eric Bentons in Texas.

Unfortunately, I have not met any of them. All I have met so far are confrontations and hatred. There were instances when my wife and I were *refused service in your restaurants. When motels wouldn't accept us. Most humiliating was when we tried to purchase a home and was told the home was not meant for foreigners.*

Where are the friendly Texans that Eric Benton told me about?

Sincerely,

Shig Ito

The editor of Austin Sentinel published Shig's letter a couple of days before he and Susan were ready to move back to Southern California. The column was entitled:

IS THIS WHAT WE'RE ABOUT?

Shig had not revealed his address. His phone had already been disconnected. He and Susan wanted to leave as soon as possible and never ever hear of Austin, Texas, again.

The editor came out with another editorial the following day, wanting to invite Shig for an interview. The editor apparently had done some research on the 1st Battalion of the 141st Regiment and was shocked that nothing had been told about the 442nd Regimental Combat Team rescuing the lost battalion.

The editor said he had been deluged with phone calls from all over Texas wanting to meet Shig Ito. They could not say enough about the courage, bravery and sacrifice that the Japanese-American soldiers went through in rescuing the Texas Lost Battalion.

Some expressed willingness to help Shig buy a home in their hometown. Some invited Shig to be a guest at their home as long as he wanted. A former officer in the 1st Battalion of the 141st Regiment wanted Shig to come and speak to the National Guard in his hometown and tell them about the rescue. Another suggested that the Governor of Texas declare all members of the

442nd Regimental Combat Team be honorary Texans.

On the morning Shig and Susan were about to leave, there was a middle-aged Hakujin couple at the doorsteps of their apartment. The couple had found Shig's address from the UT registrar's office. They were Eric Benton's father and mother.

After introducing themselves, Mrs. Benton, unable to suppress herself wrapped her arms around Shig and cried. Mr. Benton hugged Susan, unable to say a word.

Eric had written them about how Shig had saved his life and about the letters they had exchanged. Mrs. Benton had looked forward to meeting Shig all these years. Shig had become a son she had never met.

The Bentons, high school teachers and alumni of UT, wanted Shig and Susan to come and live with them. Shig could attend UT and Susan could find a nursing job at the university.

Shig would have gladly accepted the invitation. It was too late. His mind was already set in Southern California. He was, however, grateful that he was not leaving Texas with the bitterness and hatred he had felt since arriving there.

There were, after all, many Eric Bentons in Texas.

Shig transferred another batch of wet laundry into a dryer.

It was the dryer he had worked on and it did not squeak nor protest against the new heavy load.

CHAPTER 17:

Mom

Christine was surprised when she parked at Hal's and Armando approached her with a medium-sized, framed photo of a young man in Army uniform.

"This here was my buddy," he said. "Rudy Diaz."

"Was?"

He nodded solemnly. "Never made it back."

She looked up at him. He avoided her eyes.

"Look," he finally said, "you wanted to paint me."

"Yes."

"Here's somebody you really wanna paint," he said, handing her the photo.

The young man, a Latino in dress Army uniform and cap, was about Armando's age, handsome, stoic, a determined expression.

'What makes you think I want to do a painting of him?"

"Because…"

She waited for him to go on.

"He was like a brother I never had."

She kept waiting.

'We never met until our Army days," he finally said. "Then. from basic training to the end, we were always together."

He stopped again.

"Look," he said, "you think you wanna do a painting of him?"

"I want to do a painting of you," she said.

"Me, I'm nobody."

"And he was?"

"Him," he said, "he's a real somebody. He was awarded the Army's highest medal."

"The Medal of Honor?"

He nodded.

Haltingly, painfully, he related what happened. "...And suddenly, just like that, he was gone. Wasn't for him I wouldn't be here talking to you."

So that's why he did not want to talk about his war experience, she told herself. He blamed himself for his friend's death. He lost his leg and incurred that the terrible scar, but had survived.

"So..." he said. "Wanna do it?"

"I've never done a painting from a photo."

"What's the difference?"

"Well, for one thing, "she said, "when I'm painting someone, I can see that person before me, alive, breathing, speaking. I get to know a little about him. I get to feel a part of him. You know, an extension of myself."

"So. You don' wanna?"

"I did not say that."

"Look," he said, flustered, "what if I took you to meet his mom and dad? Y'know. Get to know them."

"He was from LA?"

"Hometown boy. Grew up in East LA."

"Seems he was an extraordinary man," she said. "I'd like to know more about him. Hear him talking to me, watching him looking at me. You understand what I'm saying?"

"Yeah. I think I get you. You gonna have time after your last class today?"

"It's the only class I have."

"Wanna go over and meet Rudy's mom and dad?"

"Yes. I would be glad to."

It was mid-morning when she returned to the parking lot, and Armando was waiting anxiously. He seemed relieved that she had not changed her mind. He apparently had given Ray an excuse to leave for an hour or two.

"Give Mom this," he said, handing over a bouquet of roses before getting into his pickup.

"I'll be glad to pay for them," she said.

"No way," he said. "They're from me to you."

"And from me to Mom?"

"You got it."

As they drove down to First Street and on to East LA, Christine thought that meeting strangers was one thing; meeting them for the sake of getting acquainted with a dead son was another. Would Rudy's parents have to relive that horrible day when they first learned about their son? Perhaps she should not have accepted Armando's challenge. That's the way he had put it in his clever manipulating way, a challenge.

They finally came to a home across the street from Evergreen Cemetery. Armando led the way up the concrete front steps of the yard, then to the front door.

He knocked.

Shortly, a middle-aged lady opened the door. She was in a simple dress, her hair combed neatly, a big smile on her pleasant, radiant face.

"Armando!" She greeted him with a warm hug. Noticing Christine, she quickly said, "Your friend?"

He nodded. "Mom, this is Christine. This is Mrs. Diaz,

Christine."

"Hello," Christine said, and offered the flowers.

"Oh," Mom said, "roses. My favorite. Come in," she invited. "Please. Come in." She led them into the small but warm family room and as they sat on sofa, she asked, "So you want to do a painting of Rudy?"

"Like I said, Mom, she's a good painter," Armando said. "A real good one."

"I'd like to know more about your son, Mrs. Diaz," Christine began.

"Please," said Mom. "Don't feel you're a stranger in our home. I'm either 'Maria' or just plain 'Mom,' like he calls me." She patted Armando's arm affectionately.

"Is Pop on the road today?" Armando asked.

"He drove up to Fresno," said Mom. "He won't be back until late tonight."

"Mom," Christine addressed, "I hope I'm not bringing back painful memories."

"Armando warned me," Mom said. "I think I can talk about Rudy without getting too upset."

Christine took a deep breath. She looked once more at the photo that Armando had handed her, and asked, "What kind of boy was he? Serious? Happy? Studious?"

"Oh, he always made good grades. He wanted to be a schoolteacher. Y'know, work with young kids. Help them make something out of themselves."

"He was also tough," Armando interrupted. "A champion fighter in the Army. Nobody could beat him."

"He wanted to go professional, but his dad wanted him to stay in school," Mom said. "Go to college."

"He was always talking about finishing junior college. then go on to UCLA," Armando said.

"Tony said he'd keep supporting him as long as he went to school," said Mom.

"What was his best subject?" Christine asked. "Math? Science? English? History?"

"Not only American history, Mexican history, too. He spoke Spanish--proper Spanish he learned from his grandpa and grandma, my mother and father."

Mom reached over to the coffee table and, bringing up a photo album, turned the pages. "We used to send Rudy to his grandparents in Guadalajara, Mexico, every summer vacation," she said. "Here's a picture of him with Grandpa and Grandma," she indicated a photo of a young boy in short pants and T-shirt holding the hands of an elderly couple.

"So cute," Christine said.

"Here's another one," Mom turned the page. "A year older."

She turned to another page. "He was becoming a teenager in this one.'

"And a young man," Christine added.

"He was just learning to take responsibilities," Mom said. "He used to say he would take care of Grandma and Grandpa when they got old."

Mom buried her mouth in her hands.

Armando broke the silence. "My Spanish, he used to say, was like a typical gringo."

"Oh, Armando," Mom said, "how could you speak Spanish when you didn't grow up a Mexican?"

"There was a dozen of us at the orphanage, but they were all like me-- English and cholo Spanish."

"We always taught Rudy to be proud of being a Mexican," Mom said. "His ancestors in Mexico, they were heroes in the revolution."

"Eisenhower was his American hero," Armando said. "A great general before he became president. Rudy knew all about the Normandy Invasion and how Ike spent months and months preparing for the landing."

"Wars, wars," said Mom. "We never learn. Young boys dying before becoming men."

"Yeah," Armando said, "dying before knowing what life's all about."

"And just that to show for it," Mom said, leaning over to the showcase and indicating the Medal of Honor in it. "Me and his father, we're proud of what he did. But who won the war? Us? The Communists?"

"Nobody wins in a war," Armand said.

Christine could say nothing.

Mom closed her tear-filled eyes.

Armando moved over and put his arm around her.

A long moment of silence went by."

"Many times," Mom now said, "I sit here looking at Rudy's photo and the medal. So many promises in his life. So many things he looked forward to. And, then…"

Armando looked over at Christine and exchanged painful looks.

At that moment, Christine felt she knew how much love Rudy's mother had given him. And how he had become the man he was.

CHAPTER 18:

The Letter

Christine had enlarged Rudy's photo at an art shop on Sunset Boulevard, and placed it on a stand in her studio. The 6 by 12-inch photo was now life-size. It made Rudy alive, breathing, talking, his brown eyes much clearer, his jaws more powerful, the corners of his mouth breaking into a warm smile.

Yes. That's what she needed to make Rudy a living model. Someone like Armando or George posing for her in their Army uniform. Or even Shoichi in his Japanese Army uniform.

Her eyes darted over to the letter on her desk. She quickly returned to Rudy's photo. She'd read the letter again later when she was not preoccupied with the sketch.

Rudy looked so young, she thought, her mind still lingering on the letter before she could shake it off. He seemed much younger than when he died at twenty. His expression, however revealed a fearless, matured man ready to overcome all obstacles. He was a pillar of strength. A soldier unafraid to tackle the demands of his time.

She listened to her mind's ears and could hear Armando describing Sergeant Rudy Diaz, a warrior, a hero. She could hear Armando telling her how Rudy had hurled a grenade back at the enemy, then had stared at another one before diving on it.

Yes, that was the legacy of Sergeant Rudy Diaz, she said herself.

On the easel before her was a stretch of white paper. She would draw a rough sketch of the photo on it, analyze it, become an extended part of it and feel Rudy was alive.

She started the sketch with a dark pencil – the outline of his face, his deep features, the light shadows under his cap. She then went on to the delicate lines around his face. Next, she added the details, his hair, his eyes, his throat, then went on to sketch the Sergeant's stripes with several ribbons which he had received before his death.

Stepping back, she looked at the sketch and, before she could study and analyze it, felt a deep groan in her throat. She shut her eyes and shook her head. Where was Rudy? The Rudy she had come to know, alive, vibrant and full of life. What was before was only the skeletal form of him.

Painfully, she unpinned the sketch from the easel, then as she crumpled it into a ball and was about to drop it into the waste basket, her eyes darted over to the letter on her desk.

The letter again. It preoccupied her thoughts, making everything else meaningless.

She was having a cup of coffee downstairs yesterday morning when the phone had rung.

It was not a salesperson nor a solicitor nor anyone she knew. It was the Reverend from the Wilshire Methodist Church. She had not gone to church for years and had made it known to her friends she was no longer interested in church work.

The Reverend, whom she had not met, said there was an old letter addressed to her. Would she come and get it.

A letter addressed to her at the church?

She wondered if the new Reverend was enticing her to renew her membership. Most of the members knew why she had given up her faith. Apparently, not the new Reverend who knew nothing about Mom and Dad.

Curious, she drove over. It had been a lifetime since she had last stepped into the church. The front steps were the same as she remembered, the interior somewhat repainted, the pews brighter, the elevated front splendid as ever.

The new Reverend was waiting for her with an envelope as she stepped into the huge, ornate building and walked up front. He was about forty, tall, dark haired, a warm friendly smile greeting her. "I'm Reverent Bill Atkins," he shook her hand friendlily. "I'm the new pastor here. I'm afraid we've never met."

"I'm afraid not," she said, careful not to be committal, but friendly enough.

The Reverend handed her a dog-eared letter. "I guess this has made its rounds," he said. "One of our members who knows you gave me your phone number."

Puzzled, she accepted the letter. It was from Hokkaido, Japan, the northernmost island. Who did she know there?

The Reverend watched her for a second, then indicating the pew said, "Why don't you sit here. If there is anything I can do for you, I'll be in my office." He then disappeared into the doorway up front.

She stood there staring at the envelope.

Suddenly startled, it can't be! she told herself. It just can't be! Yet, it must be. Who else would write to her from Japan? She studied the handwriting. The crossing of the "T's" and the doting of the "I's." It's been nearly fifteen years!

Taking a deep breath and sitting at in the pew she began opening the envelope.

A sweet smell of Japanese powder floated out.

It was from him! Shoichi!

Ohmygod!

She wiped her eyes. Still unable to focus on the letter, she took another deep breath, calming herself.

Dear Christine-san, the letter began.

I pray that this letter finds you happy and well. It has been a long time since we last wrote to each other, neh? Many things have happened since. To me, and I am sure, to you, too.

When I think of you and me in Kobe during our young happy days, they seem yume no yo datta. They are dreams. How quickly the years went by.

She could no longer contain herself. She lowered the letter and, pursing her lips together, sobbed.

She brought the letter back up.

When I became eighteen and had graduated from high school, I was drafted into the Army. I requested to be in the medical corps and not be required to carry a weapon. I, of course, did not tell them about my Christian upbringings.

I was assigned to the medical corps and sent to Okinawa just before the invasion there by American troops in 1945. Most of the island was destroyed and many were killed, soldiers as well as civilians. I was tendering to one of our wounded soldiers when I was captured and became a POW. Very fortunately, one of my American guards was a Christian. When he discovered I, too, was a Christian, he treated me very well.

At that moment, Christine-san, I thought of you and was very glad that you taught me English. That American soldier, Andrew Kimball, and I became friends. We were both on God's side and we still write to each other today.

When the war ended, I returned to Kobe and discovered that most of the city was destroyed. Our home in the Kobe Hills was no longer there. My sister survived the bombings, but not my father and mother.

Christine had to stop once again. She pressed her hand against her mouth and fought back another burst of sobs.

People were in rags and had hardly anything to eat. There were many young children adopted by American soldiers. They lived in Army camps and were fed by the soldiers.

After searching for a job for many months, I finally found one at the American Red Cross in Kobe. Again, I was grateful to you for teaching me English. I became an interpreter for the workers at the Red Cross building. They were the janitors, the houseboys, and the kitchen help. The big advantage working there was that we always had much food. Some were leftovers and others were surplus. But we were happy to be treated so kindly.

It was about this time that I met an Army chaplain who conducted services for American soldiers. He invited Japanese Christians to attend his services. too. He was a Captain from California, your home state.

I began attending English classes at the Red Cross. To learn not only to speak better but also to improve my writing. The director wanted me to become good in English so I could communicate much better with the American soldiers assigned there.

The Captain encouraged me to become a minister. He said Japan needed time to heal and to rebuild the country. He recommended me to the church officials in America which made it possible for me to attend a seminary school in Osaka.

I received a degree in Christian Ministry and was sent to Sendai in northern Japan to help revive our church there. Not too long afterward, I met Aiko. She and her family were members of our church. We were soon married. We now have two children, a boy, 5, and a girl, 3.

Two years ago, I was transferred farther north to Hokkaido. Aiko and I and the children love it here very much. It is very cold during the winter, which makes us appreciate the beautiful Falls and Springs even more.

I don't know if this letter will ever reach you. I hope and pray it will. Aiko suggested that I write you when I told her about our young love. She said she would like to meet you, your father and your mother someday.

Lo and behold! I learned that our ministry wants to send me and my family to America next year to attend graduate Christian Seminary School in California. I had lost all of your letters and did not know how to reach you. Aiko, again in her wisdom, suggested that I address a letter to a Christian Church in California and pray that it would find you.

We hope our prayers will be answered and that one day soon we can all get together. We also hope that your children are being brought up as good Christians as your father and mother had brought you up.

May God Bless you, Christine-san.

Shoichi Murata

Christian could no longer fight herself. She could hear her sobs bouncing off the walls.

Reverend Atkins hurried over.

"Are you all right?" he asked, deeply concerned. "Did the letter bring bad news?"

At last, containing herself, she said, "Good news. News that can't be any better."

"Thank heaven," the Reverend said. "For a moment... Is it from a friend in Japan? Someone we might know?"

Christine shook her. "I don't believe so. But he and his family are devout members."

"If they should ever come to California, please bring them here," the Reverend went on.

Christine nodded. "I'll remember to do that."

Returning home, she ran up the stairway to her studio, and

began answering Shoichi's letter. She told him that she was not married and that her father and mother were happily together in the spiritual world. Now that she has Shoichi's address, she told him, she would like very much to come to Japan and visit him and his family. On the other hand, she said, when he and his family came to California, please remember that you are all welcome to stay at her home.

Please extend my love to your wife and your children.

Christine.

She folded the letter into an envelope, stamped it with extra stamps, hurried downstairs, and placed it in the mail box for the postman.

She now took her eyes off Shoichi's letter and took a deep refreshing breath. Then lowering her head she said something she had not said for a long time. "Yes. Lord, You work in mysterious ways."

She returned to the new blank sheet of paper on the easel.

Feeling somewhat released from Shoichi's heart-warming letter and feeling assured that her letter would find him and his family well, she could now devout herself to Rudy's sketch.

It took a couple of hours, then another hour to add the finishing touches.

Stepping back, she studied the sketch, added more finishing touches, then satisfied, finally decided to the oil painting.

It took hours, days, and several nights of complete dedication to finish it. She felt it was quite good. But how good to another pair of eyes? Ultimately, it would be Rudy's mom and dad who would have to be satisfied. Would they approve?

The phone rang. It rang again. And again.

She finally answered it. "Hello."

"Hello, Christine. This is George Tsukayama."

"Oh, hi, George."

'I've finally finished the audit of your 1954 tax return."

"You have?"

"I went over to the City of Hope and went through the list of all the donations you made there. They all checked out fine. I also called Tom Hoffkins about the Buick. He deducted what it was worth at that time."

"I always knew I could depend on Tom," she said. "He's as honest and careful as the day is long."

"And so are you," George said.

"Thank you, George. Now that you've finished your audit, does that mean I won't see my favorite IRS man anymore?"

He laughed that good-natured laughter of his.

"I tell you what," he said. "Since you had me over for dinner, let me take you out. How's that?"

"That would be wonderful, George. Domo."

"How about tonight? It's about time I took a break."

"From your writing?"

"Yeah. Get away from it. Refresh my mind."

"I'm all for that."

"I'll come by... --How about six?"

"Six will be just fine," she said. "–Oh, is this a suit and dress affair, or just a casual outing?"

"Casual," he said. "Very casual."

"Sounds fun," she said. "I'll be waiting."

CHAPTER 19:

Stars and Stripes

George, in old Levis, faded aloha shirt and a pair of much-worn tennis shoes, was on Santa Monica heading for Remington Park. He was still flabbergasted that Shig and Armando knew Christine.

No way were they speaking of the same Christine, he thought, when he had dropped by the Laundromat.

"Hey, George," Armando said, "you're just in time to go to Ray's with us."

"Not tonight" he said.

"Not even for just a couple," Shig said, folding a new batch of dried laundry.

"Gotta go out to dinner."

"Boy, oh, boy," Armando quipped. "The man's got a big dinner date."

"So where're you taking her?" Shig wanted to know.

"Beverly Hills Hotel," he said, raising his head, proudly.

"They serve Japanese food there?" Armando questioned.

"She's not Japanese," he said.

"Hakujin?" Shig questioned.

"C'mon," George said impatiently, taking out a bill from his wallet, "where's my laundry?"

"You're taking out a Hakujin woman so you don't wanna associate with us anymore, huh?" Shig said.

"She's Hakujin, but she's one of us," he said.

Shig looked at him, over at Armando, back to him.

"She was born in Japan," he said.

"Hey," Shig said, handing over the bundle of laundry, "I just met a Hakujin woman who was born there."

"Christine?" Armando interrupted. "'At's who you talking about?"

George looked at Armando and Shig. No way were they talking about the same Christine.

They not only knew her; she was a friend of theirs.

Not wanting to reveal he was auditing her tax return, he explained that he met her through a mutual friend.

This was the first time he was taking out a haole girl. He had not even known a haole girl he could ask out. At LA State, whenever a Japanese guy was seen walking around campus with a haole girl, some haole guy would invariably comment, "Look at that bitch with a Jap!"

It was all right for a white guy to be walking around campus with a Japanese girl, but not a Japanese guy with a white girl.

He wondered if Christine was aware of the white man's attitude toward mixed dating. On the other hand, he told himself, she thought of herself as being more Japanese than a Caucasian.

At Christine's door, he could hear her playing the piano in the living room. A Tchaikovsky classical. He took a deep, anxious breath and knocked, expecting to wait a few minutes.

The piano music stopped abruptly.

In a couple of seconds, Christine was at the door.

'Hi!" she greeted, smiling that warm, radiant smile of hers, her bluish-greenish eyes radiant as ever.

"Hi," he returned, taking in her blondish hair combed back into a bun, her white blouse partially hidden under her casual sweater. "Waited long?" Isn't that what she expected him to say?

"All afternoon," she said. Then laughing, she added, "I didn't know what to wear."

"You look great."

She, too, was in Levis and tennis shoes, her matching pullover casually over her shoulders. Her makeup was hardly noticeable, her perfume just a slight touch, almost as though she had not intended to have any on.

"I guess we're both ready to go for a workout," she said, looking down at his tennis shoes.

"Japanese custom," he said.

"Workout after dinner?"

"To dress casually, yet maintain an air of dignity."

"My dignity is to show you I have no dignity," she said.

He joined her in laughter.

"Oh, before I forget," she said, as he opened the car door for her, "I'd like to show you something when we come back."

He looked at her.

"I hope you'll like it."

"Now, you're acting like a true Japanese."

"I am Japanese," she said.

He closed the car door, went around to his side, and got in. They were downtown in about twenty minutes, going through the seedy skid row section when Christine observed, "With all the resources in this country we still have people without shelter."

"Hey," he said, "it's not your fault."

"In a way, it is. We contribute to the Salvation Army, the

Missions and the Red Cross, but we're not reaching these people who really need help."

"Don't you know," George said, almost hitting a pedestrian staggering across Main Street, "even in the best of times, they'll always be people hanging around skid row. It's a way of life for them."

"It doesn't have to be," she said. "Many of them should be placed in psychiatric hospitals where they can get proper medical care."

Can't argue against that, he thought.

On several occasions, he had put on old patched Levis, wrinkled t-shirt, frayed shoes and had stepped into one of the skid-row bars, feeling he belonged there. It made him appreciate what the people there were going through. And, who knows, one day he'd be able to write about them.

Striking up conversations at the bar stools by reverting to the simple life he had lived on Maui, he was able to talk with some of the drunkards and drug addicts. Most of them blamed their wives, their parents and the military for their predicament. Above all, they blamed the whole fucking country that didn't give a shit about them.

He was glad when he finally saw First Street coming up.

Yeah, he thought, parking at the corner of First and Los Angeles Streets, there'd be skid rows in any city. And Los Angeles was the most attractive because of its mild weather and the generosity of the Salvation Army, Red Cross and the Missions.

He was about to help Christine out of the car when she got out before he could.

They walked up the steep narrow stairway of Kawamoto

Restaurant. The restaurant was partially filled, most of the patrons Nihonjins, a few haoles. The familiar sweet aroma of fried tempura, sukiyaki and teriyaki fish floated in every corner of the room. Just beyond the stairway, to the right, was a woman playing nostalgic Japanese numbers on a piano. At the piano bar was a couple of Japanese nationals in dark suits, reminiscing, singing along with her.

A kimono-clad, middle-aged waitress finally greeted them. *"Ira'-shai!"*

She spoke Nihongo to George, then English to Christine.

When Christine responded in Nihongo, the waitress was dumbstruck. She studied the tall and attractive Hakujin woman. *"Okyaku sama no Nihongo wa totemmo subarashi desu."* Your Japanese is *excellent.*

"Domo arigato gozaimasu," Christine responded.

The waitress led them to a lacquered table near the piano bar where they sat across from each other. She handed them colorful menus, asking Christine, *"Nihongo yomemasu ka?" Do you read Japanese.*

"Hai, sukoshi yomemasu," Christine answered.

"E-eh," George intervened, "Kono hito wa Nihongo yoku yomemasu."

She reads Japanese very well.

"Ah, so," the waitress said.

The waitress turned to George and asked, "You Nisei?"

"Hai." George replied. "Hawaii Nisei."

"Ah so, Hawaii Nisei," the waitress said. "Bery nice place, Hawaii."

She took their drink order and disappeared.

"Have you been here before?" Christine asked George,

studying the paintings on the walls.

"Coupla times," he said. Nodding toward the piano bar, he added. "Same girl at the piano."

"Same waitress, too?"

He shook his head. "Never saw her before."

"Do you remember the song she's playing?" Christine asked, now humming along with the pianist. "After The War Is Over."

"Oh, yeah," he said. "We all sang it wishing the war would end soon."

After humming a little longer, Christine looked back at the paintings. "They show the old days of Li'l Tokyo."

"History of the Japanese pioneers who settled in LA."

"It's amazing how they survived the racial intolerance during the old days."

"And it's my generation who complains the most."

The waitress shuffled over with Kirin beer for George and hot tea for Christine, and placed them daintily on the table.

"Tonight," said the waitress, "we have-o bery special teriyaki salmon. *Bery good.*" She placed chopsticks and napkins before them.

"The salmon, it's fresh?" he inquired.

"Hai. Bery fresh."

"Care for the salmon?" he asked Christine.

"If you don't mind, I prefer shrimp tempura and sashimi."

"Hai," the waitress noted. Okusama wa shrimp tempura to sashimi desu, neh?"

"I'll have the salmon," he ordered.

Stepping away, the waitress, bowing, expressed, *"Domo arigato gozaimashita."*

"Did she say, 'okusama'?" Christine asked.

"She was just being polite," he said.

"By addressing me as your wife?"

"Aw, she didn't mean to insult you."

"Oh, it wasn't insulting," she said. "I just thought it was funny she would take it for granted we're husband and wife."

"Want an apology?"

"Oh, George."

At the piano bar, the two businessmen rose from their barstools and went to their table.

The piano player finished her last number, rose, and disappeared through a side door.

"Those songs she was playing," Christine said, "they brought back fond memories of Kobe. Especially the pre-war songs. Those two," she said, referring to the two businessmen at the opposite table, "they must be homesick."

"Yeah, singing all those old songs," he said.

Shortly, as they were enjoying their drinks, the waitress approached their table with hot platters of shrimp tempura and teriyaki salmon. She apologized for being late, even though she was early.

"Oh, *sumimasen*," the waitress said to Christine, "*Okusama wa ohashi tsukae masu, neh?*"

"Yes, of course, she uses chop sticks," he intervened. "And by the way," he added, "she's not my okusan."

"*Okusama dewa nai?*"

"E-eh," Christine said. "*Tomodachi desu.*" We're just friends.

"Ah, so" the waitress said. "You look bery happy together."

"Domo arigato gozaimasu."

"*Do itashi mashite,*" the waitress bowed deeply.

"Well," Christine said, as the waitress stepped away, "that's cleared."

The teriyaki salmon, as promised, was excellent, the miso soup as expected, sumptuous. He quickly noticed that Christine brought the edge of the soup bowl very daintily up to her lips and sipped the soup very delicately like a true Japanese lady.

Not trained properly in using chopsticks, George very consciously tried to hold his chopsticks as Christine did, but found it cumbersome. He reverted to his childhood Hawaiian ways and felt comfortable shoving the salmon into his mouth.

"I thought the girl would return and play more nostaligic songs," Christine said.

"Why don't you take over?" he said.

"That wouldn't be proper," she said. "The girl makes her living playing here."

"She's on a break," he said. "She won't mind."

The waitress, standing attentively nearby, said to Christine, "You play piano?"

"Well..." Christine hesitated.

"She's very good," he said.

"Ah so," said the waitress. "Come, come," she waved her hand toward the piano, "play, play."

"Go on," he said.

Christine, hesitating, looked at the waitress, back at George.

"Come on," he encouraged, rising, stepping over to the piano with his glass of beer.

Christine rose. "Well, if it's all right."

She stepped over to the piano, adjusted the stool to her long legs, stretched her fingers a few times, then began playing an old Japanese song, *"Shina No Yoru."* China Night.

The waitress, George immediately noticed, seemed uncomfortable. It was a song taking place during the Japanese occupation of China and was no longer acceptable, if not forbidden. And it certainly was not sung in public.

George looked over at the other patrons in the restaurant for their reaction. The Niseis, he noted, did not seem to give a damn what the song was about. It was a beautiful song of the old days. The two Japanese businessmen seemed concerned, then broke into warm smiles.

They walked over to the piano bar with their drinks, sat, and began singing.

They applauded loudly when the song ended and raised their glasses to Christine.

"Bery good!" they said. "Bery good!"

George told them she grew up in Kobe.

"Ah, so. Kobe gal," one of the businessmen said. "No wonder she know bery famous Japanese song."

"How about this?" Christine said, following up with a lively, fast-paced Japanese army martial music, and humming it.

The two businessmen looked around the restaurant expecting reaction from the other patrons. When there was none, they began humming along with Christine, softly at first, then began singing it loudly.

George remembered the military march from boyhood days and began humming along. So what if it was a Japanese military song? The war was over ten years ago. Who cared what it once represented?

He raised his glass to the two businessmen and hummed louder.

Having a Japanese playing the march in public would have

been in bad taste, if not insulting, but Christine was a haole. Who was going to hold it against her?

Christine switched to a classical number, running her fingers expertly up and down the keyboard to the delight of everyone in the restaurant.

In a few minutes, several other patrons surrounded the piano bar and listened to other classical music, applauding enthusiastically, requesting more and more.

Christine, now upbeat, started playing and singing the latest popular songs.

George was surprised that she was playing all the numbers without a music sheet. As the patrons kept applauding and requesting more numbers, he tried to act as though none of it surprised him. He raised his beer glass proudly and sipped after each number. After all, Christine was his *Okusan*.

The two businessmen ordered drinks for everyone.

Christine, as expected, declined but thanked them and everyone else for their enthusiasm.

The crowd was disappointed as Christine and George returned to their table.

When George asked the waitress for their bill, the waitress revealed that it was already settled by the two businessmen.

Driving home, still worked up by the songs at Kawamoto, he and Christine continued singing *"Shina No Yoru."*

"Oh, what a wonderful evening," Christine said, moving over closer to him, holding his arm. "Can't remember when I had a better time."

"Turned out great," he agreed, placing his free hand around her shoulder. "Boy, the people in the restaurant, were they surprised. An American playing all those Japanese songs. And singing them!"

"It brought back so many wonderful memories," she said, snuggling closer. "Kobe, Takarazuka, Osaka, Kyoto... I wish I were there right now."

"With your Shoichi?"

"Yes," she said. "With my Shoichi. And with you, too."

He gave her shoulder a warm squeeze and he could feel her hand wrapping tighter around his arm.

Driving into Christine's wide driveway, he wished they could have taken a long drive down to Venice or Santa Monica beach and enjoyed the ocean view up and down the coastline. It would have been like being back home on Maui, parking at the beach with a date after a movie or a dance.

Yeah, he thought, his arm still around Christine, those young high school days.

"Don't forget," Christine now said, moving toward her side of the door, "I have something to show you."

"Oh, yeah," he said, having completely forgotten.

"C'mon," she said, stepping to the front porch, "it's upstairs."

She held his hand and led him upstairs into her studio.

When she turned on the light, there before him in the middle of the studio was a huge painting. Maybe 36" by 48".

It was a Mexican soldier with sergeant's stripes.

When Christine finally told him who the soldier was, George could almost see the soldier's blazing eyes, hear him commanding his men against the enemy, encouraging his men to drive the enemy back.

He looked over at the photo in Christine's hand. Then looked at the portrait. Except for its size, he could hardly distinguish one from the other.

"It's terrific!" he said, for lack of a better description.

Greatly relieved, Christine let out a deep sigh, her eyes glistening. "You think so?" she said. "You really think so?"

"I've gone through lots of painting in my audits," he said. "This is as good, if not better, than most of them."

"Oh, thank you," she put her arms around him. "Thank you. I was afraid you wouldn't think it was any good."

He held her in his arms and felt the warmth of her body pressing against him.

"So much talent," he said. "A first-class painter, a classical pianist, and to top it all, a wonderful singer."

"Oh, George," she kissed his cheek, holding on to him, and kissed his cheek again.

He hesitated a moment, then held her firmly. He found himself moving his lips from her cheek to her soft, warm, delicate lips, deliriously wondering if all this was actually happening. Him, a barefoot Maui boy actually kissing this beautiful, classy, haole girl.

CHAPTER 20:

The First Kiss

After a warm goodnight kiss at the front door, Christine, still a little delirious, stood there watching George driving away. Goodness! What an evening it turned out to be.

While George was studying her painting upstairs in the studio, she had held a long breath. When he said it was better than most paintings he had seen in his audits, the relief was so overpowering she could not help letting her impulse get the best of her.

Was she too aggressive, too forward, hugging and kissing him? She was so happy, so overwhelmed, she couldn't restrain herself. Did he think she was a typical white girl kissing every man she could?

No. Of course not. He knows better. And besides, didn't he kiss her back? Yes, a long, warm, passionate kiss which surprised her. She had never been kissed by a Nihonjin before. She and Shoichi. as close as they were, never kissed. But then they were just eleven years old. And, perhaps, at that time, she believed Japanese men and women never kissed.

When George mentioned that he was waiting to be invited to the writers colony in Illinois, she inquired whether he'd be returning to Southern California when he finished his novel. Southern California, he had said, was his home away from his real home on Maui.

That meant he would have to relocate himself. Why couldn't he stay at the upstairs garage apartment?

He couldn't afford to live in Remington Park, he had said. And what would the neighbors think? Him, a Japanese, living in Remington Park?

She should have expected that. Although a Nisei, who had proven his Americanism, he was still wary about what so-called haoles considered him. A Japanese spy who had bombed Pearl Harbor.

She had gone through the same thing with Carole. If you don't feel like an American, she had told her, how can you expect other Americans to accept you as a fellow American?

She knew it was not that simple. There still was a strong anti-Japanese feeling in California. Primarily because of the war. The Japanese, however, were now being slowly accepted into the fold, assimilating, moving into neighborhoods that were once forbidden.

George shouldn't feel isolated from other Americans, she had told herself. He, himself, must feel he is a true American.

It was, of course, easy for her to feel that way She had never experienced racial prejudice. Except, of course, a little of it growing up in Kobe. But it was because she looked so much different from the other kids. A blue-eyed, little blonde girl playing with dark-eyed, dark-haired Japanese children.

"George," she had said, when she told him the upstairs garage apartment could be his writing sanctuary, "it could be your writing sanctuary."

"I can't afford it," he had said.

"Oh, George," she had returned, "I'm sure I can get along quite well without collecting rent from you."

And they had laughed.

Now, alone in her studio studying Rudy Diaz's portrait, she thought of doing final touches to the cap, the ribbons and the stripes. Then, studying the painting more intensely and hearing George's wonderful, encouraging voice, she warned herself not to overdo it. She had gone through the same phase with other portraits and had ruined them.

What a relief it had been to at last show the portrait to someone! Not to just anyone. To George who, though not an expert, had judged many paintings throughout his IRS audits. He had seemed mesmerized by it, studying the details, his eyes riveted to Rudy's eyes.

It really was more than a look-alike portrait, she told herself. It was a replica of the photo, honoring a man who had made the supreme sacrifice. It suddenly occurred to her! Why didn't she think about it? The ribbons and the medal! They were missing.

But the photo was taken long before he was awarded them. Still, she could have painted them.

Then, again, maybe it was a good thing she did not. She could still hear Mom Diaz, "My son's life for a medal."

No, don't overdo it, she told herself. Leave it alone. It's done. Finished.

As she kept appraising the painting, she could painfully remember staring at a bare, blank canvas on the easel. Nervously, anxiously, when she made the first stroke, she could feel a great burden lifting off her shoulders. It was a beginning of many strokes, thousands, millions, some broad, some infinite, all nevertheless, contributing to the end result. Ten hours a day, every day, sometimes at nights, obsessed, never satisfied, doing some parts over and over to the finest detail.

When she thought it was at last done, she had sat on the floor a long moment, eyeing the portrait from down that angle, not sure, doubtful, wondering how it would look to a pair of different eyes.

Not wanting to reveal the progress of the portrait to Armando, she had stopped going to her art class at LACC. One day soon, she would have to show it to him. Now that it had received a favorable appraisal from George, she was sure Armando would be impressed by it.

She would eventually have to show it to Mom and Pop Diaz, too. That would be something, a 24-inch by 36-inch portrait of their son in their home.

While painting it, she had envisioned the portrait displayed at a public venue, a place where many could see it. Not only as her work, but more importantly as a portrait of a Mexican-American hero. Rudy's parents had gone all the way to the White House to receive the medal from the President. How many knew about it? Or read about it? Especially the Mexican-Americans in East LA.

The idea had gradually come to her. Moreso as she was approaching the end. Why can't the portrait be placed at the high school Rudy had attended? Or at the boxing gym he had trained. Or at the East LA College where he had attended before joining the Army.

She knew it would take political muscle to have the portrait placed in a public domain. A move that has to be introduced by a county supervisor or a city councilman. And they, the politicians, would have to be enticed by political ambitions.

As she had thought about it, feeling a strong need to finish the portrait as soon as possible, she had suddenly realized that Uncle

Jess Balkin, once Dad's architectural partner, contributed quite a bit to politicians.   Uncle Jess could surely approach the supervisor or councilman who represented East LA.

She would call Uncle Jess, who was not a true uncle, but was considered one ever since she could remember.   He came to family gatherings with his children and attended church services with the Barringtons.   He had even attended her graduation ceremony at USC.   When Dad and Mom died in that awful accident, Uncle Jess called almost every day from his office.

He knew of her ambition to become a painter and had always come upstairs to her studio to see her latest works whenever visiting Remington Park.

He would most likely come over to study the painting and suggest where Rudy's portrait could be placed.   An artist in his own right, and a social activist, he was always interested in the welfare of the underprivileged, the minority, the prejudiced.   He would surely be interested in a Mexican-American hero and see to it that the recipient of the highest medal in the United States Army be given proper recognition.

Next day, she called Uncle Jess in his downtown office.   Busy as ever, Uncle Jess did not hesitate to take her call.   After the usual warm greetings, she told him why she was calling.   Uncle Jess was intensely interested.   Give him a couple of days, no, a day, he said, and he would make some calls to the right people and get the ball rolling.   In the meantime, he would like very much to see the painting before she showed it around.

CHAPTER 21:

The Portrait

George dashed out of his apartment right after reading the letter.

His life had changed dramatically ever since the dinner at Kawamoto. And tonight, a couple of weeks later, it would change even more.

Lowney had at last invited him to come to the colony to finish his novel. It was a step closer to having his first novel published.

When Christine opened the door to let him in, he reached for her and, not saying a word, held her and kept kissing her.

"Wow, George," she uttered. Ever since that Kawamoto night, they always stood inside the doorway, exchanging warm kisses.

"Guess what?" he said, finally letting go.

And he told her about Lowney's letter.

"Oh, George!" She reached over, holding him. "At last."

"Of all times," he said. "Just when we're getting to know each other."

"How long are you going to be gone?"

"It's up to her. I'll have to do whatever she wants."

"Still…" She pulled out of the embrace and sat on the sofa nearby.

He followed her.

Look," he said, "we're both gonna be busy. You with your paintings; me with my writing."

"And be half a continent away."

"Things will work out."

She went into his arm. "I hope so. George. Oh, I hope so."

"We'll stay in touch."

Nodding, she pulled away from his arm. "I almost forgot. I met with Uncle Jess and the supervisor and the city councilman for East LA today. They're both interested in setting up a memorial for Rudy Diaz."

"Hey, that's great. What about your portrait?"

"I suggested it be placed at a recreation park or a school library," she said. "I should have known Uncle Jess would have bigger ideas. He wants it displayed in City Hall."

"City Hall!"

"And he also wants a street in Los Angeles named the Rudy Diaz Highway."

"Wow! A street name after Rudy!"

"I'd like to tell Armando," she said. "But I'm afraid he'll run over to Mom and Pop and announce it before I'm absolutely sure it's going to happen."

"Don't worry. Politicians, they're really not leaders. They'll do what the people want."

"That's what Uncle Jess said. They wouldn't dare object to the memorial. Many Mexicans fought in the war. How many of them have really been recognized for their heroisms?"

"It's the same with us Niseis," he said. "Out of all the heroes who were wounded or died in Europe and the Pacific, just one received the Medal of Honor. All the others, and there's been a lot of them, got the second highest medal, the Distinguished Service Cross. You know why? Politics. And the reluctance of Niseis to glorify one of their own."

"I read that there was a Nisei awarded the Medal of Honor in the Korean War."

"Hiroshi Miyamura. He was in the European Front as a replacement in the 442nd. Then was called back into active duty in the Korean War.

"He was a one-man army in the trench that day," he added. "The men under him were all white kids. When they retreated back to headquarters, they told the high command what he did and how he had saved their lives."

"Thank heaven he was recognized for it."

After a moment, she asked, "When do you plan to leave?"

"In couple of days."

"That soon?"

"Hey," he said, "other than you coming into my life, this is the next best thing happening to me."

"I'm happy for you. But it seems so unfair…"

"Yeah, I know," he said. "But one day we'll look back and be glad we had all this going for us."

He held her tighter. Of all times for this to be happening it had to be when he must go away, he thought.

What about her? Will she wait for him? Still feel the same way she does now? It might be months, maybe years, before he'll be through with his novel.

CHAPTER 22:

The Invitation

Very eagerly, Christine led Uncle Jess up the stairs to her studio. Opening the door and letting him in, she watched him looking at the different paintings on the walls and on the floor. She was relieved when his eyes at last caught the huge portrait placed against her studio desk.

"This it?" he asked, taking off his coat, loosening his tie, and stepping up closer.

"Yes," she said, swallowing hard. "That's it."

He took off his glasses, wiped them with his sleeve, then putting them back on, brushed his grayish mustache. In deep thought, he studied the portrait from different angles while Christine kept eying him suspensefully.

His semi-bald head went now up and down. He took off his glasses once again, put it back on and analyzed the portrait. This time his head went up and down emphatically.

She held a deep breath.

"Wonderful!" Uncle Jess said finally. "It's great," he added.

She let out a deep sigh. This was Uncle Jess, a brilliant architect and a famous painter, saying it.

"Oh, Uncle Jess!" she said. "I was afraid you wouldn't like it."

"Don't like it!?" he said. "You've captured the essence of this brave American soldier, his dedication, his devotion, his love of country. They're all there. Having been an old soldier myself. I know what I'm talking about."

"An old officer, you mean," said Christine.

"An old officer keeping up with the youngsters," he said.

"I knew you'd know how a young American hero looks like," she said.

"There's only a handful of Medal of Honor soldiers in this country," Uncle Jess went on. "This painting is a great tribute to one of them."

"He hasn't received all the honors he really deserves," she said.

"Did you get his parents' permission to display the painting at City Hall?" Uncle Jess asked.

"I wasn't really sure we could have it there."

"Who's going to object?" Uncle Jess said. "It'll be the demise of any councilman or supervisor not going along."

"But...City Hall!"

"Rudy Diaz is a great American war hero," Uncle Jess said. "Born and raised right here in LA."

"Still... City Hall!"

"I may be able to do even more," Uncle Jess said. "A City Councilman owes me a favor for designing a building in his district and a County Supervisor I gave a generous check in his last campaign haven't forgotten it. Naming a new road the Rudy Diaz Highway would go great in their districts."

Christine could not believe what she was hearing.

"Another possibility," Uncle Jess went on, "there's a park near Roosevelt High School, Rudy Diaz's alma mater, that isn't named yet. It could be called the Rudy Diaz Recreational Park."

"Oh, Uncle Jess!" She hugged Uncle Jess who returned the

hug as a father would to a loving daughter. She always regarded Uncle Jess as a man of great principles and vision, but had not expected him to use his influence, power and resources to immortalize a Mexican.

At the door downstairs, just before he left, Uncle Jess said, "By the way, Auntie Harriet wants to know if there's finally a man in your life."

Caught off guard, Christine tried to laugh it off. "Tell Auntie Harriet if there is she'd be the first to know."

"Not me?"

"You, of course. Then Auntie Harriet."

They both laughed.

"You're pretty close to thirty, aren't you?" Uncle Jess asked.

"Twenty-eight," she disclosed.

"Turn thirty and you're going to be even more particular."

Early this morning, Uncle Jess called and said the councilman and the supervisor thought it was a great idea to honor Rudy Diaz. They said they had thought about it when Rudy Diaz's parents were invited to Washington, D.C. to receive the Medal of Honor from the President.

Now that she knew her painting was not just okay, but "wonderful" and "great," she decided to get the best frame for it. She called Professor Wykoski, her painting instructor at LACC, and asked him to recommend someone who could do the painting justice. The professor was surprised and congratulatory when she revealed where the painting might be displayed. He recommended an expert who, though, expensive would do honors to her painting.

Excited, she called George at his office.

She could hear the secretary saying, "Oh, Georgie. Guess

who's on the phone?"

"Another taxpayer?" she could hear George's amused voice.

"Oh, sure," she could hear the secretary saying, "another of your beloved taxpayer."

George finally answered.

"Hi, George. And this is not one of your beloved taxpayers," Christine said.

"No?"

She told him what Uncle Jess had said about the portrait.

"Hey, that's great!" George said. "*Omedeto gozai masu.*"

"Domo arigato gozaimasu," she returned.

"Wanna go over to Kawamoto and celebrate?'

"Lets celebrate at home. Tomorrow night."

"Thought I'd save you the trouble of cooking."

"No trouble at all." And imitating George, said, "And I tell you what I'm gonna do. I gonna invite Shig and Armando."

"Hey, that's great.'

"It might be the first and last time we can get together before you leave."

CHAPTER 23:

Beyond Expectations

The parking lot was nearly packed, and Armando, having gone through his homework in his pickup, was now reading once again the short story he had written for his English class.

How you like that? An "A!" And a nice comment by the professor.

The story was about an up-and-coming professional boxer who had just won another fight. The next one would be a main event. At the Olympic Auditorium. And shortly thereafter who knows? A title fight!

Yeah, Armando thought. It could have been him. Fighting for the heavyweight title of California. Followed by a heavyweight title of the world.

A dream. Up to that moment in the trench. Just a dream. But it could've happened.

Rudy. Now there was a guy who really could have made it. He had everything going for him. Determination, skills, guts and a great style. Undefeated amateur champ. Ripe for the pros. Then suddenly it was gone. All gone. By a damn blast in the trench.

Armando now set aside his short story and began reading the LA Times.

He turned to the Arts Section. It wasn't long ago when he'd skip that section: plays, movies, books, critics' choices.

Whodahell cared about all that. Recently, however, ever since going to LACC and learning and appreciating the so-called finer things in life, he looked forward to reading them. Him, who hardly read a book or went to a play growing up at the orphanage, now enjoying reading books and interested in plays.

He now came to a movie review of the life of Vincent Van Gogh. Not too long ago, he thought Vincent Van Gogh was the name of a race horse. And he also thought Michelangelo was a name of a new beer.

Yeah. Going to college made him aware that life is more than boxing, drinking and raising hell. There was the finer things in life. And he was getting to be more aware of them reading, studying and listening to the professors at school. And he would appreciate them even more when he's accepted at UCLA.

He now came to an article about Pablo Picasso. Picasso's paintings were now exhibited at the county museum. Free. No charge. Maybe, he'd take that in. Being of Spanish descent, who knows, he might be related to Picasso.

He suddenly thought of Christine who was supposed to do a painting of Rudy. He hadn't seen nor heard from her ever since their visit to Mom's and Pop's two weeks ago. Has she started it? Still working on it? Finishing it? Gave up? She did say it would be hard to do a painting from a photo.

He didn't have her phone number. Nor her address. All he knew about her was she graduated from USC and is now taking an advance art course at LACC. According to the registration in her car her last name was Barrington. A pretty classy gringa name. Christine Barrington. She must have a pretty good job, being able to drive a brand new Chrysler; always dressed properly; always giving him generous tips for parking and washing her car, and gladly paying him, no questions asked, for the bouquet of roses, she bought from him on Mondays.

Once, when Ray asked if he knew an attractive girl who'd be willing to work as a part-time waitress at his bar, he immediately thought of Christine. Then, quickly brushed it off. She'd be too classy to be a waitress at a place like Ray's.

No sooner was he through with the Arts Section then Christine's Chrysler pulled in.

He jumped out of his pickup and rushed over.

"Hey, Christine," he greeted excitedly, opening the door, "where've you been?"

"I've been busy, Armando," she said, getting out. As always she was dressed sharply, this time in a crisp, starched, white blouse and a blue skirt.

"None of my business, hunh?"

"Yes. It is."

Stepping around to the trunk, she opened it. "Look inside."

There was a flat pinkish towel-wrapped bundle at the bottom of the trunk with a green ribbon around it.

"Take it out," she said.

"What is it?" he questioned.

"Go on."

He reached down. This can't be the painting, he told himself. It's too big and too heavy for a painting.

As he hesitated, Christine reached over and very delicately untied the ribbon. When she unwrapped the towel, he was jolted. Speechless. Holy!

It blew his mind. Tears flooded eyes. There was Rudy, his buddy, before him. Alive, breathing, smiling. He could hear Rudy greeting him. "Hey, Buddy, how's it going? Que pasa?"

"Hey, Compadre," he greeted back. "How're you doing?"

"So what do you think?" he heard Chistine asking distantly.

He turned to her, wiping his eyes. "You're the best," he said. "The greatest."

He hugged her. "I knew you was good--were good but not this good."

And they stood there studying the painting.

"I'm glad you like it," she finally said.

"Like it? Mom and Pop, they're not gonna get over it. Rudy there before them. Like he was there all the time. And never went away."

"Oh, I hope so, Armando. I hope so."

"Gonna go to class today?" he asked.

"No," she said. "Not today."

"I don' have a class until this afternoon," he said. "Let's go take the painting over to Mom and Pop."

"Right now?"

"Right now."

Just as they stepped into her car, she said, "Before I forget, you, Shig and George are invited for dinner at my home tomorrow night."

"Tomorrow night?"

"I'm cooking."

"Well, hell, yeah. --Yes. We'll be there."

"George will call you, and tell you how to get to my home."

"Sounds great."

Driving Christine's high-class Chrysler, Armando went all the way down Vermont, then headed to East LA. The wheels under him felt nice and smooth. Not like his noisy, bumpy pickup. You want luxury you've got to have dinero, he reminded himself. Mucho dinero.

He could tell that Christine beside him was a little nervous. Little? Mucho. An artist not sure how her work would be accepted. No different from how a paper he turned in for a class assignment would be accepted by the professor.

"Hey," he said, "stop worrying. It's gonna be beyond their expectations. Ain't that how you'd express it? Beyond Mom's and Pop's expectations?"

She nodded.

"Another thing," he went on, driving through heavy downtown traffic, "I know you ain't gonna charge 'em no hefty amount; I just hope they can afford it."

"Charge them?" she said, her voice rising. "What makes you think I'm going to charge them?"

"Ain't that—isn't that your business?"

"Armando. I am not charging them anything."

"Not charging for all the work you put in!"

"Painting is not my livelihood."

He glanced over at her. For real? She wasn't gonna charge Mom and Pop nothing for that great painting? Ain't that why she's taking painting courses at the college? To make some money?

How else could she afford a brand new Chrysler? Unless, she was in some kind of business, maybe, like selling real estate, door-to-door sales, or like selling one of those how-to-do books.

He glanced over at her again. Naw. She's no salesperson type. Too classy for that. And too nice to be conning someone to buy something from her.

"Armando," she finally said, "you know of any park, any gymnasium or any building in East LA that can use a new name?"

He glanced over at her. "New name?"

"Or even an old highway."

Oh, so that was her gimmick, he told himself. Renaming parks, gymnasiums and highways. And billing the communities, the cities, and the state for whatever names she came up with.

"No," he replied. "I sure don't know any place like that. Remember, I'm not from East LA. I'm a Valley boy."

"Oh, yes, of course," she said. "I forgot."

In a few more minutes, he parked in front of the Diaz home.

"Are you sure they're home?" Christine asked anxiously.

He looked at her. She was really going through it. "Hey," he said, "not'ing to worry about. I'm no connoisseur–that the right word? Connoisseur?"

She nodded.

"I don't know a Picasso from a Van Gogh," he went on "but I know a great painting when I see one. And your painting is the greatest. You've made my buddy alive. Y'know what I'm saying?"

She nodded again.

"Well," he said, "let's go in."

He turned off the engine and got out. Jesus', why am I nervous like her for? The painting's great. Mom and Pop, they're gonna go crazy over it.

He opened the trunk and checked the towel wrapped around the painting.

Christine checked the ribbon and helped him delicately carry the painting under his arm.

Mom, apparently having seen them walking up the steps, opened the door before they could knock.

"Armando!" Mom said, staring at the wrapping under his

arm. "I was wondering when you'd come back. And Christine," she said, hugging her. "So nice seeing you again."

Christine returned the hug.

"Mom," Armando said, "we brought you something."

"What is it?" said Mom, again staring at the wrapping.

"A surprise," he said. "A big surprise."

"Oh?"

"Is Pop home?" he asked.

"He's watching the morning news on TV. Come in. C'mon in. You, too, Christine. Please come in."

"Thank you," Christine said, stepping into the warm, cozy, family room.

Christine's nervousness was making him nervous.

Pop, in Levis and T-shirt, unshaven, his muscular body tight and brawny, rose from the TV chair and stepped up to them. "Armando!" he said, shaking. "I was on the road the last time you was here."

"Yeah. We missed you. --Oh, Pop. This here is Christine."

Pop eyed the tall and attractive gringa, very impressed.

"And she's not my girlfriend," he added. "Just a good friend."

"Aw, 'at's too bad," Pop said. "And here I thought you've got yourself a beautiful girlfriend."

"Too classy for me, Pop," he said.

"Oh, Armando," Christine dismissed.

"What's that you got there?" Pop said. "Don' look like no case of beer for me."

"No. Not'ing like that," Armando said.

He set the wrapping on the sofa near Christine and nodded for her to open it.

Carefully, very carefully, Christine drew the ribbons loose

and uncovered the portrait.

Mom's eyes suddenly popped open. She stepped closer, looked at the portrait, hypnotized. "Ohmygod!" Her hand jumped up to her mouth.

"Holy…!" Pop stared, not believing what he was seeing. "It's him! Rudy!"

When Christine placed the photo on the table beside the TV, Mom and Pop kept looking at the photo, back at the portrait, back at the photo.

Mom burst out sobbing, touching the portrait delicately. "Rudy… Rudy…" Pop stepped up to the portrait, speechless, choking, fighting himself.

Armando, watching Mom and Pop, rubbed his chin, biting his lips.

He glanced over at Christine. Her eyes were blinking off tears.

When Mom stepped up to her and put her arms around her, Christine eagerly returned the hug. Both of them suffering the loss of someone very close to them. Mom, her son, Rudy. Christine, someone who had become a part of her life while devoting herself to his portrait.

Mom and Pop kept studying the portrait, still painfully, still mournfully. Suddenly, Mom, unable to fight the pain any longer, rushed into Pop's arms.

Pop also broke. A big, brawny man, unashamedly crying over the loss of his son. "Rudy," he sobbed. "Rudy…"

Armando stepped over to the window and looked out. Cars were speeding by. Birds were flying low. Squirrels were jumping up and down the trees. And mourners in the cemetery across the street were placing flowers on the graves of their loved ones.

CHAPTER 24:

Fate

Earlier, right after she had prepared most of tonight's dinner, teriyaki steak, miso soup, sashimi raw fish and tako octopus, Christine had changed into a comfortable cotton dress, combed her hair, put on a touch of lipstick and sprayed on an almost unnoticeable bit of perfume on her throat. Ordinarily, she wouldn't care how she looked at home, but tonight was a special occasion.

She had met Armando and Shig months ago, but did not really know them. Oh, they have become good friends, as far as friendship goes, but they were still strangers. And they hardly knew her, either. She hoped to know more about them tonight. Not as just Armando, a student and a parking lot attendant; or, not just as Shig, a laundromat owner and also a student. She wanted to develop an intimate friendship with them, confiding each other, trusting each other and exchanging deep personal stories.

By really getting to know them, and they, her, she hoped they would let her do portraits of them. At the same time, she could probe into their lives and discover who they really are. Her life was, of course, no mystery to them. They both knew she grew up in Japan and that's why she could speak Japanese. On the other hand, there was something about Armando and Shig that she could not put her finger on. Armando, who grew up in an orphanage, seemed to want to put all that behind him and forget those days. And Shig, one of those Niseis who volunteered in the Army from a concentration camp, seemed reluctant to talk of why he had been willing to fight for a country that had treated him and his family as traitors.

They would both be wonderful, interesting models, she thought. There would be intriguing background stories tied in with their portraits. Armando, with that intriguing, and mysteriously handsome scar on his cheek, a story in itself, and Shig, with that narrowed, flashing eyes when remembering the horrors of the battles he had gone through.

Getting them together with George would let them relax and reveal what men who had gone through battles talked about when they were together. George, too, would be a wonderful model if and when he'd open up and not be so adamantly against posing for her.

The doorbell rang. Wiping her hands on the towel hanging on the refrigerator door, adjusting her dress and running her hand over her hair to make sure they were in place, she hurried over.

There stood George in his suit, apparently having arrived directly from his office. Without wasting any words, they were in each other's arms, kissing and hugging as though it was an everyday occurrence, a wife welcoming her husband home from work. And, in that moment, she realized she indeed loved George. Very much. It was an admission that she had always wanted to meet a Nihonjin man she could love, that a part of her since childhood in Kobe had transformed her into a Nihonjin.

She held his hand and led him into the dining room where she offered him a bottle of Kirin.

While she set the table, two to each side, she noticed George was preoccupied, watching her between sips of drinks, smiling warmly, but obviously much in his mind.

Finally, he said, "Funny how we met, huh?"

"It was fate, George," she said. "Fate."

"That I audit your tax return?"

"That things just happen sometimes. No planning, no warning. They just happen."

"Yeah," he said, "I guess so."

"You being a Nihonjin is what really made me interested in you."

"Even though I'm not that little boy in Kobe?"

"He was a young boy who was a dear friend."

He took another sip, then another.

"I've been thinking," she now said, "I could fly over to Indianapolis and meet you anytime you're free."

"Indianapolis?"

"It's the closest airport to Marshall, Illinois. I could drive over to Marshall or you could drive over to Indianapolis."

He said nothing.

"You don't think Lowney Handy would approve?"

"We'll see."

Again, their future seemed to hinge on Lowney Handy's approval or disapproval. How long will this go on? That lady seemed to have a strangling hold on him. Will she ever let go of him? Will he himself be able to unstrangle himself from her?

The doorbell rang.

George hurried over while she did the finishing touches to the plate settings and opened three bottles of beer.

She could hear Armando saying, "Wow, George! You mean

this is where she lives? Christine?"

Then Shig, saying, "What a mansion! Never thought I'd know anyone living in Remington Park."

"C'mon in," George said.

Shig and Armando followed George into the dining room, Armando with an extra big bouquet of carnations, Shig with a box of cookies.

"Hey, Christine," Armando marveled, "you never said you lived in Remington Park."

He offered her the bouquet.

"Thank you, Armando," she said. "They're beautiful."

Shig held out the box of cookies. "I had this shipped all the way from Japan."

"Domo arigato gozaimasu," she acknowledged. "Even though you bought them in Li'l Tokyo."

Laughing, Shig kept looking out the backdoor, the sunset already turned into early darkness.

"Go on out and see our Japanese garden," she said.

"That's a real Japanese garden you got back there?" Shig said, stepping out the back door.

"A real pond, too?" Armando asked, joining Shig.

"A real pond with koi fish in it," George informed.

Turning to Christine, he said, "They're sure surprised you're living in a mansion."

"Oh, George," she said, "it's just a home."

"Oh, sure," he said. "Just a home with big columns up front like a coliseum."

Shig stepped back into the dining room. "Never thought I'd ever see a Japanese garden in Remington Park," he said.

"Thanks to my dad," she said. *Kokoro wa Nihonjin deshita.* "He was a Japanese at heart," she translated for Armando.

"Yeah, he sure must have been," Shig said.

"Too bad your wife and daughter couldn't come," she said.

"They had to go to the little girl's birthday party, next door."

"I hope to meet them someday."

"My wife hopes to meet you, too," Shig said. "Especially when I told her of your Japanese background."

"Hey, c'mon," Armando said, impatiently, "I'm hungry."

"I smell teriyaki," Shig said.

"Wow!" Armando said, inhaling deeply, "Teriyaki steak. My favorite."

"Even better than tacos?" George teased.

"Hey, man," Armando said, "this Mexican loves all kinds of food."

As they all sat, Christine unfolded her napkin, bowed her head and gave a silent prayer, thanking the good lord for the opportunity to have her friends there at her home. When she recited, "Amen," the three of them, quite lost, repeated, "Amen."

"Hey, Christine," Armando said, "you're a regular church goer?"

"I try to be," she replied.

"Me," Armando said, "I was born Catholic, at least 'at's what I was told, but after I got out of the orphanage and went overseas, I stopped believing."

"Hey, you two," Shig said, "you're gonna keep talking about religion or we gonna eat?"

"Oh, please," she said. "Please start."

Her brief prayer had reminded her of last Sunday's service at Wilshire Methodist Church. She had started going back to church after meeting Reverend Richardson that day she received

Shoichi's letter. They had talked about Mom's and Dad's fatal accident and it was only then that she fully realized she had missed the comfort and solace of talking about Mom and Dad with someone from the church.

When she told the reverend that Shoichi was invited to attend the annual church conference in Los Angeles, the reverend asked if Shoichi would be interested in addressing his congregation.

Shoichi, his wife and two children arrived earlier that week and Christine had gone to the LA Airport to greet them. She would not have recognized Shoichi if he had not called out, "Christine-san!"

Instinctively, without further thought, so happy to see him, she very unJapanese-like, put her arms around him and let happy tears flow down her cheeks.

"Shoichi..." she cried, "it's been so long. It's so nice to see you."

Hugging her back, he said, "Hai. It's been a long time, neh, Christine-san?"

Shoichi had changed considerably since the last time she saw him. They were both just eleven then. Two innocent young children wishing their lives could go on forever as they were.

Shoichi's hair was sprinkled white at the edges and much shorter now, his waistline was a little bigger and wrinkles were beginning to settle beneath his eyes. If he had been wounded in the war, thank heaven there was no sign of it.

Shoichi quickly introduced his wife, Aiko, and his two children, a son, Hideki, five years old, and a daughter, Kazuko, three years old. Aiko-san, a little younger than Shoichi, and very pretty, bowed graciously then extended her hand in a warm American greeting. The children, hesitated, then extended their hands as their mother did. "How do you do?" they recited.

Shoichi and his family were, of course, guests at her home. There was so much to talk about, those intervening war years, the destruction of Kobe and other big cities in Japan, and the annihilation of Okinawan cities and villages by American bombers.

When Shoichi was asked if he'd be interested in addressing Reverend Richardson's congregation, he did not hesitate.

The Sunday morning service was packed with its usual devoted parishioners. Sitting in the first pew with Shoichi and his family, Christine was just as eager as everyone else to hear Shoichi's message.

When Reverend Richardson introduced Shoichi, all eyes followed Shoichi from the pew to the podium. They all waited eagerly to hear what a former enemy was going to say to them.

The war was nearing its end when he was drafted into the Japanese Army, he began. When his commanding officer, who had been to America, discovered his Christian upbringings, the commanding officer assigned him to the medical corps.

After a brief basic training in Japan, he said, he was sent to Okinawa to help defend the island against the impending invasion of the American forces. It was there during the horrible battles, he went on, when his faith in the Lord was tested. He was constantly surrounded by hundreds of Japanese soldiers wounded and dying in the care of the medical corps. It was a nightmare day after day. He, too, was wounded, but his wounds were minor compared to what most of the soldiers were enduring.

He and his fellow medics did everything possible to save the lives of the wounded, he went on. Many of them were dying and the medics could do nothing for them. He was determined not to hate the enemy who was causing all the destructions and deaths, he continued. His duty was to save; not to hate or kill.

There was an occasion when a gravely wounded American POW was brought into Japanese hospital cave. Having learned English from Christine, he was able to communicate with the American. The young soldier was from Utah. He had gone to school with Japanese children in Salt Lake City and they were his friends. His hatred for Japanese, he said, began when his fellow soldiers were killed in the Saipan battles.

Semi-conscious at times, he went on, the American soldier kept calling out, "Momma. Momma."

The soldier died a couple of days later. Shoichi had saved soldier's dogtag and when he himself became a POW, he handed the dogtag to an American officer and told the officer about the young American dying in his care. The officer promised to return the dogtag to his headquarters so that they could trace the soldier's family in Salt Lake City.

As Shoichi went on describing the terrible battles in Okinawa, the congregation, mostly mothers, listened to every word, some wiping their eyes, some smothering their mouths with their handkerchiefs. When Shoichi mentioned the last words of Japanese soldiers about to die and calling out to their mothers, "Okasan! Okasan!" several mothers in the front pew could not restrain themselves. They cried as Shoichi up on the podium paused to wipe his eyes.

Shoichi's message was relatively short, but electrifying and unforgettable. It was the first time many in the congregation had heard a former enemy sharing his experiences of caring for his fellow soldiers who were dying and calling out to their mothers.

When he finally finished, there wasn't a single dry eye in the church.   The mothers approached Shoichi, held his hand and expressed their sorrow for those who had perished in the war, both Japanese and Americans.

· · · · ·

Christine watched George, Shig and Armando finish their steaks and were now having the last of the sashimi, tako, and enjoying their beer.

"Hey, Armando," George said, "where'd you learn to eat sashimi?"

"And tako?" Shig joined.

"Taco?" Armand said. "I grew up on tacos."

"Not Mexican taco," Shig said. "Japanese octopus."

Everyone laughed.

"You always ate Japanese food" Shig asked Christine.

"Nothing but Japanese food when I was growing up."

"Just shows you, huh?" George said. "Not only slant eyes love Japanese food."

"Over in Italy," Shig said, "we used to buy black-market rice from the Italianos and cook it in our helmets."

"Turned out okay?" George asked.

"If you don't mind tasting sweat in your rice," Shig said.

After Christine served home-make apple pie with ice cream, they all sat quietly for a moment until Armando said, "I sure like to know if UCLA's gonna accept me."

"Oh, Armando," she said, "with your grades I can't see them not accepting you."

"And me," Shig said "I still don't know if I'm gonna be accepted at Cal Poly."

"They don't accept you," George said, "who they're gonna accept."

"Don't you have an announcement to make, George?" Christine said.

"Well, yeah," George said. "I've got some reverse good news."

"Reverse?" Armando said.

"I'm unemployed as of today."

"Oh, George," she said, "don't make it sound so dire."

George then told them why he had quit his job.

"You're a writer?" Armando was amazed. He leaned across the table and shook George's hand vigorously. "That's great, man. Great!"

Shig, on the other hand, knew of George's ambition. "So you're gonna go all out, hunh?"

Both Shig and Armando made George promise to give them an autographed copy of his book.

George now told them about the farewell luncheon his fellow IRS agents gave him at Brown's Restaurant on Hollywood and Vine. "When I'm selling pencils on Hollywood Boulevard," he said, "please remember I was once one of you."

· · · · ·

After Shig and Armando left, George helped Christine clearing the table and taking the dishes into the kitchen.

"They're happy for you," she said. "And they admire you."

"Admire?"

"How many of us are willing to quit a career job and do what we really want to do?"

George shrugged with a touch of uncertainty.

"I admire you, too, George," she added. "Very much."

He came over, wrapped his arms around her and they exchanged warm kisses. "Who can be more lucky than me?" he said in his Maui way.

Lucky, she thought. I'm the lucky one.

"How many guys like me know a *wahine* like you?" he said, taking a step back, arms still around her.

"How many girls like me know a man like you," she returned, pressing herself against him.

A long moment went by.

"George?"

"Hmmm…

"Take me with you."

"Would be great if I could."

"Lowney Handy?"

He nodded.

"You could ask her," she said.

He shook his head.

She let a moment go by. "We'll always be in touch, won't we?"

"Hai," he said, nodding emphatically.

"My life's been a dream ever since that night at Kawamoto's" she said.

"Mine, too."

"Please don't let that dream fade away."

"Never."

"Yakusoku?"

"Yakusoku desu," he promised.

CHAPTER 25:

The Colony

George got up at sunrise and gathered all the household goods he had accumulated the past eight years: a radio, a stereo set, phonograph records, pots, pans, dishes and a toaster. Next, he jammed his suits, dress shirts and ties into an old suitcase and placed it beside the household goods. He then called the Salvation Army to pick them up. All he kept for himself was a jacket, a sweater, two pairs of Levis, T-shirts and the pair of old shoes he was wearing. He felt free. Emancipated. No more worrying how he appeared before taxpayers, their business managers and their damn lawyers.

He had said goodbye to Christine last night, which had been a torture, and thought of leaving without calling her, then gave in.

"Hi," he said when she answered.

"Hi," she returned. "Are you dropping by?"

"I better not."

A pause.

"It was hard enough last night," he said. "I don't want to go through that again."

Another pause.

She finally said, "Will you call me as soon as you get there?"

"As soon as I can," he said.

He could hear her sniffling.

"Hey," he said, "I'm not going away forever."

More sniffling.

"I'll be back as soon as I can, okay?"

Another pause. then, *"Matte imasu."*

This was getting even harder than last night. A simple aloha or goodbye would have been adequate. But hearing her saying "I'll be waiting," suddenly brought tears to his eyes.

He took a deep breath. *"Sugu kaeri masu."* I'll be back soon.

"Kiyotsukete," she said. Take good care of yourself.

"Hai," he said, tempted to drive over.

That was the last call he would make on the phone that had been sitting there on his desk since moving into the apartment. He had thought of staying there just a few months and wait for jobs to open up on Maui. Then came *From Here To Eternity* and the long challenging correspondences with Lowney Handy.

There were times when he wanted to tell her to shove all her comments and criticisms up her okole. To hell with it all! There was, however, a warm attractiveness about that haole woman. Brutally honest, she did not give a shit what others thought. Her only interest was writing and those who wrote. "You can either keep sitting comfortably in your chair and watch the parade go by," she had said, "or you can get off your damn ass and be in the parade."

And so he decided to get off his damn ass.

The farthest he had driven out of Los Angeles was to San Francisco, a safe trip up and down the coast. Now, he'd be driving almost half way across the country. To a small dot on the map. Marshall, Illinois, 200 miles south of Chicago. Where the people most likely have never seen a Japanese.

He would take the southern route through Arizona, New

Mexico, across the panhandle of Texas, up to Oklahoma and Missouri, and finally across the Mississippi which would be only a few hours from Marshall.

He figured it would be three-and-half days of steady driving to get to Marshall, depending where he would spend the nights and keep on going early the following morning. He had once travelled to Mississippi and Minnesota, but the Army had furnished all the transportation and he had always been with other soldiers.

Gordon Wilks, a fellow IRS agent, had once told him about his adventure travelling across the country. A Negro, Gordon said he'd always have to map out where he would spend the night. Especially travelling through the South.

"Sorry, we don't have any rooms open," some had said politely, although the sign said, "Vacancy."   Several were outright angry that he had even stopped to ask. "We don't rent to you people!"

A pang sliced through him as he got behind the steering wheel. He wouldn't' be seeing Christine for God knows how long. He was already missing her soft, delicate voice, her warm laughter, her yasashi femininity, the closeness of her body, her lips, her perfume. Oh, Christ! Of all time to be going away.

Wait for me, Christine. Wait for me. I'll be back soon.

And he started on the longest journey of his life.

After driving through miles and miles of desert the first day, he made it through little towns, cities and to Flagstaff, Arizona. Early the following morning, he headed east through the Panhandle of Texas and continued on toward Missouri.

At mid-afternoon, tired and hungry, he pulled over at a roadside inn on the outskirts of Tulsa, Oklahoma, hoping to have more than just a hamburger or a hot dog. He stepped into the horseshoe-bar restaurant and flopped on one of the stools. Except for a single customer, the place was empty. He waited for the blonde waitress, who was talking to a customer. After a few minutes, he cleared his throat and called out, "Miss." She didn't even turn to look his way. Maybe she didn't hear him. "Miss," he called again.

The waitress snapped her head around, glared at him, then snapped her head back and continued talking.

Oh, Christ, he thought. One of those. Blaming him for the Pearl Harbor attack.

Not bothering to draw her attention any further, he rose, stepped over to the door and was tempted to slam it, then thought better of it. This was, after all, Oklahoma.

Reluctant to stop at any other country restaurant, he headed directly toward Springfield, Missouri, a big town. The waitress at the hotel restaurant was quite friendly. She even suggested that he visit some of the historical sites of her city. At the moment, after the long day's journey, all he could do was eat, take a shower and flop down in a comfortable bed.

Finally, the last leg. St. Louis. Then across the Mississippi into Southern Illinois. It was noon when he finally came up to a highway sign: Marshall. It seemed no different from the countless little towns he had gone through. Winter was fading and the trees were beginning to sprout green leaves.

He circled around the town square, noting all the businesses in the small town surrounded it. He stopped for a coke at a grocery store, hoping to get directions to the colony. The saleslady knew nothing about a writers' colony. When he mentioned Lowney Handy, the lady immediately knew that

Lowney was the sister of the County Clerk, Mr. Earl Tumner, and promptly drew him a sketch.

George drove out of the town square, went west for several blocks and finally came to a vast acreage of green lawn and tall trees surrounded by an endless circle of a white wooden fence. The ground was as big as a couple of football fields. He stopped at the gate which had a sign, *The Last Retreat*. Beyond the gate was a huge two-story white house, a mansion compared to the other homes in the area. Pushing the gate open, he speculated that the sign meant that once you left and came back, there was no other place to go.

He drove along a long winding dirt road that came to a small cabin with its chimney billowing a steady cloud of white smoke. Beside the road stood Lowney, tall, slim, her white hair, short and wavy. In wrinkled Levis and T-shirt, she was barefoot. She had somehow sensed when he'd be arriving and was waiting for him, another sign of her uncanny foresight and mental telepathy.

When he opened the car door, she stepped over and greeted him with open arms.

"Had a nice trip?" she asked.

"Yes," he said. "A great trip."

And he returned the hug.

"No problem getting here?" she asked.

He mentioned the incident at the roadside inn in Tulsa. "The waitress was pretty young," he went on. "I didn't think she'd know about Pearl Harbor."

"Pearl Harbor?" Lowney laughed. "You were in Oklahoma. They don't serve Indians."

"Indian?"

Lowney laughed again. "If I didn't know you, I'd have

thought you were an Indian, too."

Christ. He had been mistaken for Chinese, Mexican, even an Eskimo, but an Indian?

"C'mon in," she invited, laughing to herself and stepping toward a couple of steps leading to the small porch. "I just made a fresh pot of coffee."

She had an accent which he could not pinpoint. Southern Illinois? Kentucky? Tennessee?

When she caught him looking at the big white home in front of her cabin, she said, "That's Jim's home. He's in Paris now. Too big and too famous to be here in Marshall anymore."

George said nothing, surprised that she seemed to harbor a grudge against Jones.

When he followed her in through the unsteady, squeaky screen door, he noticed immediately that the confined, spare cabin was filled with books on shelves, table, chairs and on the floor. There was no TV, no radio, no newspapers. In the right front corner was an old typewriter with a piece of paper dangling out of it. Lowney apparently was typing something when she heard him driving up.

She poured him a steaming cup of coffee, motioned him to sit on the old couch, and she sat across from him in a wooden chair. The fireplace was crackling with new wood and it was nice and warm, the hot coffee tasting great.

"So..." she said, "you're ready to start writing?"

"Yes," he replied, surprised that the greeting was already over.

"Your cabin is that one on the far end," she pointed to a cabin isolated from many others. "I once had twenty writers here," she went on. "I'm too old to handle that many now.

"Over there," she indicated a rather large rectangular brown building nearby, "that's the Ramada. The cafeteria. You can cook your meals there if you want to."

Suddenly, there was a man's vague pleading voice outside.

"Lowney," the man called out again, "the birds on my roof, they're makin' too much noise. I can't concentrate no more."

Another southern accent?

Lowney stepped over to the window. "Now, Eddie," she said, "you go back to your cabin and keep working on that chapter."

"Okay, Lowney," Eddie said. "I'll try."

"Good."

"But, Lowney, what if the birds keep on makin' all that noise?"

"Now, Eddie, you tell those birds to stop disturbin' you."

"All righ', Lowney. I'll tell 'em if they don't, Lowney's gonna get mighty angry."

"Yes, Eddie, you tell 'em that."

"Okay, Lowney." A few seconds later, he went on, "But Lowney, what if they don' listen to me?"

Lowney suddenly reached for a BB shotgun beside her typewriter and raced out the door.

"Eddie!" George could hear Lowney's loud, menacing voice. "You get back to your cabin and finish that chapter or I'll shoot your damn black ass full of holes!"

There was a round of laughter from Eddie. "Okay, Lowney. Okay. I'll tell those naughty birds to leave me alone or Lowney's comin' over with her shotgun."

Lowney returned, muttering, "Always playacting. Always playacting. If it's not the birds it's the damn squirrels on his roof."

George, barely over the exchange, had to keep from laughing.

"That's Eddie for you," Lowney muttered. "Gotta keep after him day after day. Or he'll keep drinkin' his supply of vermouth and stop writin'."

"How long has he been here?" George asked.

"This time, a couple of months. He drifts in and out whenever he feels like it."

"Had anything published?"

"First one did pretty good," she said. "The second one is due any day."

"He's written two books?"

"He's working on his third one."

"Yeah?"

"A very gifted writer, Eddie," she said. "His trouble is discipline. Right now, he's sitting on pins and needles waiting for his second book to come out."

"Wow," he said. "A Second book."

"He grew up in St. Louis, then moved to New York. Where he thinks, all writers should be."

"New York?"

"That's full of shit," she said. "You can write anywhere if you've got it in you. How about you?" she questioned.

"Me?"

"Where do you plan to live after you become famous?"

She was assuming he'd be famous!

"You'll be moving to New York, too?"

"Me? Naw. My home is Los Angeles and Hawaii."

"Good," she said. "You'll be able to write about what you know best. Like Jim did about his Army days in Honolulu."

"Ever been there, Honolulu?"

"Only in spirit," she said. "While helping Jim with *Eternity*."

He looked over at the bookcase full of books. Alongside Eternity was Hemingway's *Farewell To Arms* and *For Whom The Bell Tolls*.

"I still don't understand why Hemingway didn't like Eternity," he said.

She rushed over to the bookcase and, grabbing Hemingway's books, shouted, "That has-been old fart!" and threw the books on the floor. "He couldn't stand Eternity being better than any of his books. So he refused to endorse it. Jealousy! Plain jealousy!

"Now don't tell me you're reading Hemingway!"

"You told me to read all the great writers."

"The great writers, yes!" she screamed. "Not a has-been." She picked up one of the books on the floor and flung it at him. "I don't want you to ever mention his name around here. You hear me. Never!"

She flung the other Hemingway books at him.

"If you don't think you can write better than that old fart I won't waste my time on you!"

He remained silent.

"Hemingway! Hemingway! Every would-be writer thinks his books are the bible."

Jesus. What trigged her off?

"Get out of here!" she pointed to the door. "Go to your cabin. And stay there until you know you can write better than anyone else in this fiddlefucking world!"

Oh, Christ! He got up, headed outside, and drove to the end of the grounds to the last cabin, still puzzled.

He carried his belongings into the small cabin which consisted of a tiny kitchen, a combination bedroom/living room and a small bathroom.

Still exhausted from the last leg of the long trip to Marshall, he lay on the bed wondering what he'd gotten himself into. He had quit a career, travelled nearly two thousand miles and now his life was in the hands of a high-strung, nutty woman who was as unpredictable as an earthquake. He wished he had someone to talk to. Christine. He missed her even more now.

In a minute or so, there was a knock on the door.

It was Lowney.

"I'm sorry, George," she said, tearfully. "Here you've travelled all the way from California and I treated you like you're the plague. I'm not really myself lately," she continued. "As you know, Harry died last month. We were married for nearly forty years. And suddenly he's gone. I didn't realize how much I depended on him." She wiped her eyes.

George, of course, knew her husband Harry had died. Having felt sorry for himself over the incident in her cabin a moment ago, he now felt like an okole. He reached over, put his arms around her and shared her loss. She clung for a moment, fought back sobs, then quickly recovered. "Now, we're both feeling sorry for ourselves," she said, forcing a smile. "I want you to get up early tomorrow morning and start working on your novel. Always believe in yourself; let nothing come between you and your book."

He stood there watching her retreat to her cabin at the other end of the colony. His admiration for her was even greater now. He was fortified even more by her belief and her dedication to writers.

Later that evening, after he had hanged whatever clothing he had brought with him, there was a soft knock on his door.

It was Eddie, who looked cautiously toward Lowney's cabin and stepped in quietly. George was surprised how young he was. Probably in his early or mid-twenties.

"So," Eddie said, nodding to George's Ford parked nearby, "you're from California." He had a distinct Negro accent and a warm smile that was between playacting and a laughter.

"And you're from St. Louis," George said.

"Now a New Yorker," Eddie emphasized.

"I hear your second novel's coming out."

"Any day now."

"Must feel great."

"This third one I'm working on, it's gonna be better. Helluva lot better.

What about you? Anything published?"

"Not yet."

"You're here," Eddie said. "Lowney's gonna see to it that you get published."

"I hope so."

"Hey, wanna go over to Terre Haute and have a few?" Eddie said wishfully.

"I better not," George said. "Don't want to forget why I'm here."

"Shit, man. Relax. It'll come to you."

"Well," he said, "I'm not a published writer like you."

"You'll get there, man. You'll get there. Hey, man, you're sure you don' wanna go over to Terre Haute?"

"I better not."

"Well, I better finish that bottle of vermouth I just opened," Eddie said. "One thing Lowney won't stand is any of us going into town here and hanging around the bars.

"Catch you later," Eddie said, and disappeared out the screen door.

George stepped over to the desk and, hoping that some of the greatness of James Jones would rub off on him, he rubbed his finger over the initials JJ carved on its surface. He could picture Jones sitting at the desk day after day writing his great novel *From Here To Eternity*.

Later, he drove out of the colony, went into town, and looked for a public telephone booth. He found one at the far wall of the Greyhound bus depot. He held his breath, inserted a couple of quarters into the slot, dialed and waited excitedly, hoping that Christine would be equally excited to hear from him.

After a few rings, she answered.

"Did you just get there?" Her lilting voice thrilled him.

"A couple of hours ago."

"How is she, Lowney Handy?"

"She's great. Tough as nails, but honest and holds no punches. The colony's out of town," he explained. "Quiet, peaceful, isolated, a country atmosphere."

"It sounds like a beautiful place, George. You should be able to finish your novel in no time."

"It's not gonna be that easy," he said. "I have a strict schedule to follow."

"Have you met him?" she said excitedly. "James Jones?"

"He's not here.

"--Listen, I'm calling from a noisy bus depot. Kids shouting at each other, their folks screaming at them."

"Can't you call from the colony?"

"There's not even newspapers or magazines there."

"I was hoping I could call you whenever I want to."

He said nothing.

Then, "Look, my quarters are running out. I have to go."

"Next time you call, reverse the charges."

"Yeah, okay."

A pause again.

"Christine?"

"I'm still here, George."

"Oh. I thought we were cut off. I'll call again. Soon. Okay?"

"Yes, please, George. There's so much to talk about. Especially about the Rudy Diaz Medal of Honor event."

The phone in his hand clicked off. Damn it!

· · · · ·

He pushed himself day after day. He would finish a chapter, place it under Lowney's cabin door, and would get it back under his door the following morning with corrections, comments and analysis. There still would be harsh criticisms, but also encouraging words about how much his writing have improved.

He and Eddie would meet at the Ramada, prepare their simple meals, and Eddie would fill him in about the old days at the colony. Eddie said he had corresponded with Lowney for several months, always waiting to be invited. One day, when one of the writers left, Lowney invited him to fill the opening.

Laughing, Eddie said he had never told Lowney he was a Negro. When he arrived and walked up to the steps of her cabin, she stared at him through the screen door.

"'So you're Eddie,'" she finally got hold of herself.

"'At's me,'" he told her. "'Eddie Hopkins from St. Louis.'"

Eddie continued, "I was scared shitless one of the writers gonna come over and kick me outa the place."

Laughing, George waited for Eddie to go on.

"She didn't kick me out; she didn't invite me in," Eddie said. "She stepped out and really gave me the onceover."

"Nothing more about you being a Negro?"

"Uh huh. Surprised the shit outa me."

Although Eddie had stayed only a few more days while high on vermouth, George was glad to learn from him about the rough, tough, younger Lowney who not only controlled the writers harshly, unrelentingly, but sometimes carried a baseball bat and pounded the cabin doors to keep reminding them to cut out the bullshit and keep writing.

Thank heaven Lowney has mellowed somewhat since those days, George thought. No need for a baseball bat to keep reminding him why he's there. One day soon, he told himself, he'd be a published writer like Eddie Hopkins. And he'd be a great celebrity in Hawaii. At least, in his hometown, Maui.

CHAPTER 26:

The Maui Room

George would write continuously for a couple of weeks then Lowney would encourage him to get out of the colony and forget about writing for a few days. Go to St. Louis, Indianapolis, Chicago, just get out of Marshall, she would suggest. Get drunk, raise hell, get laid and be ready to start writing when you return.

Getting laid was the last thing on his mind.

He had always managed to stop himself from demanding more than passionate kisses from Christine and he could not see himself going to bed with anyone now. In moments of awful loneliness and cravings for Christine, he pictured himself going all the way with her. Then was glad he had not. She was someone special. Not to be trifled with. The right moment would come when they were both ready for it.

On his first trip to Chicago, he drove up to Clark and Division Streets where he remembered was Japanese Town. He had been stationed at Camp Savage in Minnesota at the Army's Japanese language school when he and his Hawaiian buddies would take the bus to Chicago. The war, of course, was still on and Chicago was a wide-open town. Gambling, women, drinking and raising hell. They all knew they'd be shipped off overseas soon and might be their last chance for good times.

Walking down Clark Street now, he noticed that the Japanese markets and restaurants were no longer there. Most of the owners, he guessed, had gone back to California, Oregon or Washington to start new lives. The downstairs pool hall was still there, so was the Sea Isle Bar, the Mikado Hotel and the Aloha Grill where gambling used to go on in the backroom.

At the corner of Clark and Division was a new Chinese restaurant with a bright colorful neon sign: MAN FOOK LOW. Craving for chow mein, roast pork, chicken soup and rice, he stepped into the restaurant and was quickly overwhelmed by the salivating aroma.

There were several patrons at the rows of booths enjoying various Chinese dishes.

A trim, young, haole waitress in sweater and skirt sat him at the corner booth and was taking his order when she asked, "You're from Hawaii?"

"Yeah," he said. "How could you tell?" And he chuckled, knowing that his pronunciation was unmistakable.

"My husband's from Kauai," she said.

"Oh, yeah," he said, surprised, "he speaks pidgin to you?"

"Him," she said, "no can be more Buddhahead."

He laughed.

"The manager here, he's from Maui," she said, indicating an Oriental man at the last booth reading a newspaper.

George glanced over at the profile of the man wearing a white long-sleeved shirt.

"Jimmy," she added. "Jimmy Ota."

"Jimmy Ota!"

"You know him?"

George was on his feet, rushing over to the last booth in a second.

"Jimmy!"

Jimmy looked up from the newspaper, and stared. "George?"

"Yeah. Me."

Jimmy jumped up from his chair and rushed around the table with opened arms. "Whattahell you doing here in Chicago?"

"Whattahell you doing here," George returned.

For the next few minutes they tried to catch up with what happened to them during the intervening twelve years.

They had both volunteered in the Army back in 1943 and had joined the 442nd Regimental Combat made up of Japanese-American boys from Hawaii and the Mainland. They were going through basic training in Camp Shelby, Mississippi, when George was transferred to Minnesota. Jimmy, on the other hand, kept training at Camp Shelby and was later shipped to the European front.

George suddenly noticed Jimmy's missing fingers on his left hand. "Got hit?"

"Yeah," Jimmy said, rolling up his left sleeve, and showing a hideous scar from the elbow down to his hand. "Fuckin' shrapnel."

"No shit."

"Heard it was pretty rough over there in the Pacific, too."

"Naw. Not half as bad as what you guys had to go through over there in Germany."

After a passing moment, Jimmy said, "Remember Mr. Watanabe from Baldwin?"

"The Ag teacher?"

"He was our company commander."

"Mr. Watanabe?"

"He never made it back."

"Oh, Christ."

"Lotsa guts, him. He was right there up front with da rest of us."

"Yeah. He was the type to be right there with the boys."

Jimmy told the waitress, Joyce, to sit George at the front booth which he occupied.

"...And you never went back home after the hospital days?" George asked, sitting, sipping water from a fresh glass.

"No more nobody to go back to," Jimmy said. "Y'know..."

"Everybody's gone, eh?"

Nodding, Jimmy said, "And you. What happened to you after da Army days?"

George filled Jimmy in about his LA days and what he was doing down in Marshall.

"No kidding," Jimmy said. "You're trying to write a book?"

"Trying to."

Again, George filled Jimmy in. This time, about his novel which was taking place on Maui and the Pacific front.

Jimmy laughed out loud when George told him about his old-fart Okinawan characters brewing extra sake to offer the Japanese soldiers when they landed on Maui.

"How're you gonna end da story?" Jimmy wanted to know.

"Aw, I don't know yet."

They let a moment go by after Joyce brought George his plates and he started devouring the food.

"Real ono pah-ke kau kau," George said, enjoying the Chinese dishes. "Where I'm at, not one Oriental restaurant."

While George was still busy eating, a rather short, crew-cut Japanese man of about thirty stepped over to the table and sat down. When Jimmy introduced Sam to George and mentioned that George was a former IRS agent Sam bolted up.

"You one of 'em fuckin' treasury agents!" he said bitterly.

"Hey, Sam," Jimmy said. "Me and George we grew up together from kid days. No worry about him."

"You're not one 'em treasury agents always putting the screws on us?" Sam said to George.

"His IRS days, dey over," Jimmy explained. "He no give a shit you owe the government money."

Sam sized George up and sat back down. "So what're you doing here in Chicago?"

When Jimmy filled Sam in about George's ambition, Sam admiringly said, "You wannna write a great book, write about Chicago."

"He's writing about our days on Maui and his experience fighting the Buddaheads, "Jimmy explained.

"You can write about the fighting that goes around the gang here," Sam said. "Ever'body wanting a piece of the action."

'I don't want the gang to get after me," George said.

"They ain't gonna hold it against you," Sam said. "The gang they wanna be written up. Y'know, become famous."

"Maybe someday," George said. "When Jimmy fills me in."

"Jimmy?" Sam said. "He don't know shit."

"And 'at's da way I want it to be," Jimmy said.

Laughing, Sam stood up and shook George's hand. "You're Jimmy's friend; you're my friend, too."

As he walked away, he said to Joyce, "The table's on me."

Jimmy told George that Sam was of the few non-Italians in the mob. Sam had learned the numbers racket while living in New York and had introduced it to the Chicago gang which became a money maker.

"He's so far in da mob he no can get out now," Jimmy said.

"What about you?"

"Me? You heard Sam. I don' know shit."

"You can get out?"

"I not even in. I just manage this joint. Sam, he wanna get out, he's gonna get out feet first."

Finally, eagerly, George asked, "You married?"

"Was. Once."

"Never worked out, eh?"

Jimmy revealed reluctantly, but openly, that he had met a pretty redhead working in one of the nightclubs at Rush Street. Rosalie. A young kid. Had a rough life back home in the Kentucky hills. Was sending money back home. Him, he felt sorry for her. Before he knew it, he was helping her sending money to Kentucky. When Rosalie wanted to get married, he thought why not? They already living together.

Jimmy laughed bitterly. More to himself. What're you gonna do? he expressed. Him, just a Maui boy. Howdahell he gonna know a pretty girl like her was conning him. She was from Kentucky all right. But not from the hills. She one big city girl. Louisville. Where they have da derby.

"And you kept helping her send money home?" George inquired.

"She was my wife," Jimmy said. "Trying to help her family. Y'know us guys from Hawaii. Do anything for family."

"What's wrong with that?"

"I find out from one of the girls at Rush Street night club she was sending the money to her ex-husband to support their kid back home."

George waited for Jimmy to go on.

"I can see her helping support her kid," George went on,

"nothing wrong with dat. But conning me to think she was helping her family up in the hills of Kentucky! Dat was too much. Especially when she had me crying with her how poor she grew up."

"No problem with the divorce?" George asked.

"She never wanted to. Then when I told her I know guys who know how to take care girls like her…"

"You really meant it?"

"Naw," Jimmy said. "I never really know anybody gonna hurt her. But it worked."

"Boy, oh, boy," George said. "You sure meet 'em all."

"Yeah. Maui boy living da fast life. And you?" Jimmy asked.

For a moment, just for a moment, he thought of telling him how lucky he was that he had met someone as wonderful and beautiful like Christine, then let it go. After Jimmy's account of his Rosalie, he couldn't do it.

"Hey," Jimmy now said, "where're you staying?"

"No place yet. The Paris Hotel still there?"

"Naw. Pau right after da war. Go over to Supreme Hotel coupla blocks down from here. It's not da Waldorf, but it's okay. Tell da night clerk, Vic, send a girl to your room."

"Those days they gone," George said.

"What, you no like girls no more?"

"Yeah. Sure. But not just any girl."

"You change your mind, tell Vic you and me we're old friends. Some of dem girls dey really beauties. Young and stacked."

How could any girl be more beautiful than Christine? he thought. He felt he was betraying her just listening to Jimmy talking about whores.

Across the aisle, several haole customers came in and Joyce took them to their table. George was surprised that haoles were beginning to like Chinese food. There was a time when only Asians enjoyed Chinese food.

Joyce took their orders, placed the orders with the kitchen help, then stepped over to George's table. "Want more rice?" she asked.

"No. No thanks."

"How about desert? Ice cream? Cake? Pudding?"

"You gotta to be kidding," he said, patting his belly.

As she walked away, he said to Jimmy, "Nice kid."

"Helping her husband through De Paul Law School," Jimmy said.

"Not a hilly-billy from Kentucky, eh?" he teased.

"Aw, Christ!" Jimmy said, "no remind me of her. Worst two years of my life. More worse than fighting the Germans."

Laughing, he patted Jimmy's good hand.

The phone at the counter rang.

"Jimmy," Joyce called.

Jimmy rose from his chair and, stepping away, said, "Stick 'round. Still got lotsa talk 'bout.

"Hey, Joyce," he called out. "Bring George some fresh tea. And whatever else he wants."

Joyce was back at the table with another cup of tea.

"You've got to excuse Jimmy," she said. "Bettors gonna keep calling all afternoon and he's gotta catch the race results on the radio."

"Race results?"

Joyce explained that a steady stream of bettors would be calling all afternoon to make bets. She was glad the numbers people didn't call. They'd be calling all day.

"You sure know what's going on here."

"Can't help but catch on this place is more than just a restaurant."

"How come you don't have a Chicago accent."

"People here say I have a farm accent. When I go back home to Peoria my friends there say I have a Chicago accent."

"And Hawaiian accent, too." He laughed.

Jimmy returned to the table.

"What lies Joyce been telling you," he said, placing his arm around her.

"Lies?" Joyce said, slapping Jimmy's arm away, stepping away to serve new patrons walking in.

"Christ," Jimmy said, "tough 'nough running this place, I gotta take bets, too."

"Boy," George said, "you sure live a fast life. Not like the good ol' Maui days, huh?"

"Sometimes I wish I was back there," said jimmy. "Y'know, nice and peaceful. Lying in the sand..."

"And watching the clouds go sailing by."

They laughed.

"Boy, dem days," Jimmy said. "wonder if they'd ever come back."

"Go back," George suggested.

"To what?"

"I guess for guys like you and me, it's too late," George said. "We've seen too much, went through too much."

A moment went by and Jimmy said, "You wanna hear something crazy. Real crazy."

And Jimmy told of an incident involving a horse race at

Arlington Park. He had heard that the syndicate was fixing a race. He told all his Hawaiian friends about it and they all chipped in to make a big bet. When that day came, he went up to Arlington Park. It was the third race. A claiming race. Their horse, Harry's Girl, was dropped way down in class and was training really good. The syndicate wanted insurance. They paid off the groom to needle the horse.

When George asked what that meant, Jimmy explained that the groom was supposed to inject the horse with some powerful chemical to make it run faster.

When George asked if it worked, Jimmy told him there was big favorite in the race, Dynamic Girl. An odds on. The jockey, Jimmy said, was paid off to be left in the gate. Their horse is on the rail. A front runner.

George, having been to the races at Hollywood Park, was barely following Jimmy who, according to the incident, was at the stands with five hundred bucks of tickets in his hand. When the gate flew open, Harry's Girl, their horse, was left in the gate and Dynamic Girl, the favorite, jumped ahead of all the other horses.

Whattahell's going on, Jimmy thought. The favorite was supposed to be left in the gate and Harry's Girl was supposed to be up front. The jockey on Dynamic Girl couldn't pull his horse any longer. It would look too obvious. And so he kept running ahead.

"There went our five hundred bucks," Jimmy said, shaking his head, laughing painfully. "Fuckin' stupid jockey forgot he's not su'pose to win. And da stupid groom forgot to needle da horse.

"Da jockey," Jimmy went on, "he's still riding. The groom, he knows better than to stick 'round. He's back in Mexico."

George sipping tea, fascinated with Jimmy horse-race story, kept shaking his head. Boy oh boy, here's Jimmy his boyhood friend, getting involved in a fixed race at one of the biggest race tracks in the country.

Laughing, Jimmy shook his head. "What're you gonna do. You win some; you lose some.:

Joyce came over and wanted to know what was so funny.

"Aw, you don' wanna know," Jimmy said.

"How do you know what I want to know and what I don't want to know?" Joyce said, placing her arm around Jimmy.

"Hey, go get us coupla beers," Jimmy said.

"This early?" Joyce said, walking off.

"You still drink, huh?" Jimmy asked George.

"Not as much as I used to." George said.

"Boy, those days in the Army. Sure drank a lot."

"Us guys in the Pacific, we had no choice. The water wasn't safe."

"Same with us in Europe. Muddy water or beer."

"Makes you wonder how you went through all that."

"Here we are today," he said.

"Hey, I sure glad you dropped in. Y'know, talk story like da ol' days."

Joyce placed couple of Budweisers on the table. "Tell him about the judges disqualifying that horse," Joyce said, holding Jimmy's arm.

"At's her favorite," Jimmy said.

"Go on tell him."

"Why don' you tell him," Jimmy said to her.

After a moment of recollection, Joyce explained: "When a

race pau," she used the Hawaiian word for 'finish', "the laboratory analyzes the horses' urine. They have to make sure the horses don't have any foreign chemicals in their system.

"This one time," she went on, "the laboratory reported to the judges that they can't figure out how one of the horses had marijuana in its system. The judges investigated the stable workers and finally pinpointed to a hot walker. The hot walker, a wetback, finally confessed. "'I wait and wait,'" he said, "'da horse he no wanna piss. I no can wait no longer. So I piss in bottle and give it to the laboratory.'"

Joyce, barely finishing her story, laughed out loud. George joined, more so that it was Joyce who told it than Jimmy who joined them in laughter.

The phone rang. Jimmy went over to answer it.

"You're good for him," Joyce said. "I've never seen him so free and laughing so much. You made his day."

"Aw, us Hawaiians," George said. "Laugh at anything. Fall on your okole, we laugh."

"My husband," Joyce said, "I went to a funeral with him once. He was listening to the eulogy when he found out we were at the wrong funeral. He couldn't stop laughing."

"What can you expect? He's a Buddhahead."

"Us Buddhaheads," Joyce said, "we're all pupule."

"Ya, we're all a little crazy" Jimmy said returned to the table, quite somber. "Da call, it was from one of da boys," he said. "Da Senate Investigation Committee from D.C., they're gonna investigate mob activities in Chicago."

"Why now?" Joyce said. "It's been going on forever."

"Da chairman, he's trying to make a name for himself," Jimmy said. "Wanna run for president."

"They might shut down all the night clubs on Rush Street?" Joyce asked.

"Who knows?"

"This place, too?" George asked.

"This joint?" Jimmy said. "It's owned by a Japanese. Who's gonna connect it with da mob?"

CHAPTER 27:

Chicago

Rather than going back up to Chicago, George began spending his breaks in the cities closer to Marshall: St. Louis, Indianapolis and Springfield. He would call Christine as soon as he checked in at a hotel and would have a warm longing conversation with her uninterrupted by the noisy bus riders in Marshall. He told her of his visit to Abraham Lincoln's home in Springfield which was historical but not as impressive as it would have been had she been there with him. He said that without her it was like looking at the Grand Canyon and seeing not the spectacular, picturesque canyons but a deep insignificant hole in the ground.

He said he had enjoyed visiting Jimmy up in Chicago, but the two-hundred-mile drive had been long, boring and tiresome, and it had cost him a full day of regrouping his thoughts before he was able to start writing again.

Spring, he said, was in full bloom in Marshall and the trees were sprouting healthy green leaves. The squirrels, he said, were playing up in the trees, the birds flying wherever they pleased and the grass was growing rapidly in the colony and needed mowing.

The hardest part of talking to Christine was the goodbyes. After hanging up, he would sit there staring at the phone, picturing her beside him, smelling her fragrance, wanting desperately to reach out and feel the warmth of her comforting body. Christine, oh, Christine...

Getting back to his writing schedule, wanting desperately to finish his novel as soon as he could, he was always careful not to mention Hemingway again to Lowney during their brief conversations. Wanting to know more about his favorite writer, James Jones, he went, one day, down to Robinson thirty miles south of Marshall where Jones was born and raised.

He drove around the town and quickly noticed that like Marshall, Robinson also had a town square but a little bigger and busier. It also had a theatre, a big library and a shopping center. Having learned that Jones' home was near the library, he drove around it and pictured a young boy riding his tricycle to the library where he spent most of his time.

George also searched and found the Handy home before they had moved to Marshall to start the colony. It was in a corner lot as described and photographed in a magazine article. George parked and stood looking at the house, especially at an additional backroom where the Handys had built for Jones to do his writing. Standing there, George could hear Jones' typewriter banging away page after page of his great novel.

He parked in the heart of the town and went into a bar, hoping to meet someone who knew Jones before he became famous.

When he stepped into the long, narrow, semi-dark bar, he quickly noticed that the only one in there was the burly, thirtyish bartender, who was wiping glasses and rearranging them on the shelf. The bartender looked up curiously at him. George, of course, realized that he was one of few, if any, Asians to step into the place.

"Hi, there," the bartender greeted friendly.

"Hi," George returned and sat at one of the stools across the bar.

"Passing through town?"

"Kinda," George said.

"Anything I can do for you?"

"Well, I can go for a Bud right now."

"Coming up," the bartender said, reaching into the refrigerator, taking out a Bud and placing it and a glass before George.

After a few sips and warming up to the bartender, George asked him if he ever knew James Jones.

"Jim?" the bartender said. "Hell, yeah, I knew him. We were classmates from grade school right on to high school."

That's a good start, George thought.

"What kind of a guy was he?" the bartender repeated. "He was no different from the rest of us. Well, a little. His father was a dentist here in Robinson and so he had advantages most of us didn't have.

"Y'know, come to think of it," the bartender went on with no further encouragement, "he was a whole lot smarter than most of us. Either that or most of us were stupid. He was one of those guys with a curious mind. A'ways reading. A'ways talkin' about going off to far-away places."

"Ever saw him when he came back from the Army?" George asked.

"Yeah. From time to time."

"He changed?"

'Well, he was little older and more worldly."

"And after his book came out?"

"And he became famous?" the bartender said. "You're bound to change. After all, the whole world read his book. Whenever he was here in town, though, he'd drop by. Y'know. Just to say hello. Be a regular guy."

George ordered another Bud and kept prompting the bartender to keep talking. Whatever additional information the bartender offered was now no different from what he already knew from magazine and newspaper articles.

Driving back to Marshall, he was glad that Jones remained a regular hometown boy. Jones did not seem to be a someone who felt he must live in Paris to be famous.

Would you change if you became famous? George asked himself. Not as famous as Jones, of course, but famous in Hawaii.

Next day, after his writing session was over, he mowed the lawn, took a shower to cool off, then went into the Ramada kitchen to make himself a peanut butter and jelly sandwich. Unexpectedly, Lowney walked in with a bulky paper bag. She was, as usual, in her baggy T-shirt and Levi's, mud-stained rubber shoes, her short white hair dangling loosely over her ears.

She looked around the spacious Ramada and seemed satisfied that George was keeping the cafeteria spotless. The concrete floor was swept and mopped clean and the wooden counter over the galvanized sink was cleared of cups and dishes. The benches were in place, the long tables wiped clean and there were no cigarette butts in the ash trays.

"Ever had fried mushrooms?" Lowney asked, going over to the counter with the bag.

"I've had shitake," George replied. "Japanese mushrooms."

"These are fresh mushrooms," she said. "Just picked them. Right here in our yard."

"Never had fresh mushrooms," he said, watching Lowney emptying the bag on the counter.

"Well," she said, "you're going to have some now."

He watched her washing the mushrooms and soaking them in a big bowl. Then, placing a frying pan over the stove, she mixed a batter of eggs, flour and some of kind of seasoning in the bowl and stirred them expertly.

"I used to cook for all twenty of our writers," she said, glancing around the huge room nostalgically, stirring the batter. "Don't know how I did it."

She then told him about some of the writers who were published while still at the colony and some after they had left. Eddie, she said, was the only one she tolerated drifting in and out.

"And The Last Retreat?" he asked.

"Jim's doing," she replied. "No other place left once you return."

The frying plan was now hot.

Stepping over to the stove, Lowney placed oil in the frying pan and waited for it to start sizzling.

"Fried mushrooms were Jim's favorite," she said. "Like the way I'm preparing for you."

"He cooked, Jim?"

"He could do anything once he put his mind to do it. One thing he couldn't do was quit drinking. He'd drink martinis right after he was through writing for the day. Sometimes too much. But early next morning, there he was at his typewriter. Couldn't tell whether he was hungover or not."

"From the magazine articles I've read," George said, "he used to travel to Florida, Arizona, New Mexico and California."

"We did it so he wouldn't be bored," she said. "Going from place to place resuscitated him."

She had said, "We." So there was a closer relationship than a mentor/writer between them, he told himself. What about Harry? Didn't he mind?

Hey, he warned himself. It's none of your damn business if she was going to bed with Jim. As for himself, his attraction for her was, of course, not sexual. She was like a mother to him, whom he respected and looked up to.

"I don't know whatever got into him," Lowney now said. "He actually brought his wife, Gloria, to live here. Why, she was one of those sophisticated big-city New York girls. Used to the bright lights. Theatres. Night clubs. Society. Celebrities. What on earth would she do here?"

This was the first time Lowney had mentioned Jim's wife.

"Surprised she lasted as long as she did," Lowney said.

"She went back to New York?" he asked.

"To all her big-shot celebrity socialites.

"Bunch of phony New Yorkers!" she went on, stepping over to the stove. "All they're interested is getting in bed with you. I once went there with a novel of mine," she continued. "No sooner did I settle in the office than the damn publisher was propositioning me. I stepped out of the office, swearing I'll show that bastard someday we country pumpkins can outwrite any one of them sonsofbitches."

She placed the mushrooms into the sizzling frying pan, waited for it to cook before pouring the batter into the pan.

For no apparent reason, she laughed to herself. "Did I tell you?" she said. "I once scared the hell outta Gloria.

"She had brought that cat of hers," she went on, fighting off laughter. "One of those elegant cats New Yorkers have. Well, cats and me, we don't get along. One day, that cat came into my kitchen while I was cutting some tomatoes. I chased it out. Just then, Gloria stepped out of their mansion. She saw me waving the knife at her precious cat and thought I was going to scalp it."

Lowney burst out laughing.

"Gloria was about to have a fit," she said. "She held her cat away from me and screamed, "'Don't you dare!'

"I waved the knife like I was ready to use it."

"'Get away from me you crazy bitch!'" she cried out.

"You don't want me butchering your damn alley cat?" I yelled at her, "keep it outta my cabin!"

"'You mean old witch!'" she yelled back, babying the cat in her arms.

"Go back where you came from!" I screamed at her. "Whattahell you doing here!"

Lowney could not keep from laughing again.

"Next day," she went on, "she packed up and was going to leave. Poor Jim, of course, could not let his precious wife leave him. Why, he'd die without her."

Listening, George shared Lowney's pain. Her laughter was actually her crying bitterly.

"--Well, your mushrooms are done," she now said and scooped a good portion of it into a plate and placed it at the table before him.

"Smells good," he said, inhaling deeply.

"Good ol' Southern Illinois mushrooms," she said. "Nothing like it."

And it was great. Nothing like he had ever eaten before. Much better than shitake.

Lowney sat across the table from him and watched him enjoying the mushrooms. "You've got a good appetite," she said. "Good. You need all the energy you can store to keep you writing."

While he kept eating, she said, "Writing is no different from digging ditches or working out in the fields. Instead of using your hands, you use our mind.

Actually, writing is much harder. Much more exhausting. That's why after writing for three long hours your gas tank is empty, You don't know where you are, who you are, what time it is.

"Stretching and prolonging your emotions can be merciless at times," she went on. "That's why a writer drinks so much. He had become lost in his characters. He is no longer himself. The only way for him to return to himself is to get drunk."

Although he did not fully understand what she was saying, he knew what she was driving at.

"All great writers were drunkards. They could not cope with the power of their empathy. Of getting out of their characters. You understand what I'm saying?"

He nodded again, not quite getting it.

"Empathy. Empathy. Empathy," she continued. "The greatest power a writer can have. But there is a price that goes with it. If you don't know how to handle the precious gift it'd destroy you.

"Jim's greatest quality was his talent for projecting himself into his characters. Each and everyone of them. You either got it or you don't. If you do you should go down on your knees and thank God for it. You are one of the chosen few.

"Once," she went on, "Jim and I came out of a restaurant in

Terre Houte, and there was this man helplessly tapping his way with a cane. He was about to cross the street. We just stood there, not wanting to interfere. I looked over at Jim. He had become that helpless blind man. Not able to take it any longer, he stepped over, held the man's hand and helped him cross the street. When he came back, there were tears in his eyes."

Lowney was now blinking away her own tears.

"If you didn't have a strong empathy," she said, "I wouldn't be bothering with you. From the drafts you've written so far, you do have it. You must develop it. Utilize it. Become that great writer you can be."

Humbled by her teachings again, he placed his fork on the empty plate and nodded gratefully.

"Now," she said, "you've got yourself a wonderful story. All the elements of a great novel. You've written about that family on Maui. The war is on. One of the boys is in the American Army willing to fight the country of his father and mother. A wonderful situation. You must show us, not tell us, show us the boy going into battle against the Japanese. There must have been incidents, episodes, experiences when that boy went through inner conflicts. After all, the Japanese were his own people, uncles, cousins, grandfathers and grandmothers.

"Write it," she went on. "Take us away from Maui. Take us to the shores where the Americans landed and were confronted by the enemy. Jim, in his own way, respected the Japanese soldiers. They were dedicated. Willing to die for what they believed in. Someday, God willing, Jim's going to write a great novel about the battles he went through in the Pacific. You could go one step further. Your character speaks, reads, understands Japanese. And his counterparts are fanatic Japanese soldiers ready and willing to die for their Emperor."

She was right, George thought. His character is in a unique situation. Is he willing to kill a Japanese soldier who might be his own relative?

"The utter uselessness of wars," Lowney continued. "It's senselessness. Just ten years after battling each other we're now allies. Helping each other to overcome a common enemy. Ten years from now we'll be fighting another common enemy. When will all this end?"

Hell, yeah, George thought, he should be able to come up with a battle situation depicting what she's driving at. In fact, while she was talking, he recalled an experience that took place shortly before and after they landed in Okinawa.

How could he have forgotten it?

Thanking Lowney for the delicious lunch, he returned to his cabin to take a nap. With his eyes riveted on the ceiling above him his thoughts floated back to Okinawa, late Spring and early Summer of 1945, when the mopping up battles were taking place.

He could write the episode as it actually happened.

Kazuo and his buddy, Walt, both twenty-years-old stocky Japanese-American interpreters, were on a troopship heading toward the next battlefront. They had just finished off the Japanese soldiers on Saipan and were in for a bigger battle. Intelligence had reported that Okinawa, the first battleground on the Japanese home ground, was heavily fortified with tens of thousands of Japanese soldiers prepared to die for the Emperor.

Standing on the deck, they could see under the moonlight hundreds of troopships, carriers, battleships and heading northward away from Saipan. Like all the weary American soldiers, Marines and Sailor, they hoped the war would end soon so they could all return home.

Kazuo from Maui, Hawaii, couldn't imagine they would be engaged in another battle as vicious and costly as the Saipan battle had been. He hoped Japan would throw in the towel and consider ending the war.

"Whattahell did you tell those people in the cave that made them surrender?" Walt asked.

"I remembered a few Okinawan words my father and mother used to say to each other," Kazuo said

"No shit," Walt said, "you're Okinawan?"

"Okinawan, Japanese, what's the difference?"

"Different culture; different language."

"But the same loyalty to the Emperor."

"So what did you tell them?"

"Minasan, watashi mo Uchinanchu desue."

"That did it? You're an Okinawan, too?"

"There I was," Kazuo said. "One of 'em in an American Army uniform. Pleading with them not to commit suicide. They will be treated well."

"They could've shot you or bayoneted you."

"They could see I was unarmed."

"Still…"

"They were desperate. It never took much to convince 'em. Why not take my word?"

"Hell, man," Walt said, "you talked dozens of 'em to surrender. Civilians and soldiers. You should've gotten the Distinguished Service Cross. Not a lousy Bronze Star."

"Better than a Purple Heart," Kazuo said. "I never got wounded."

"I hope our luck holds up."

"After Okinawa I guess it's gonna be the mainland. Kyushu or Honshu."

"If we survive Okinawa," Walt said. "I just hope my name's not on any of the damn bullets."

At sunup next morning, the troopships began unloading their cargos, Marines, soldiers, tanks, trucks and heavy artilleries.

"It's April first," Kazuo said, jumping down on a landing craft alongside Walt with his backpack and weapons, "but it ain't no April fool."

"Not when them sonofabitches are waiting to mow us down," Walt said.

"So far so good," Kazuo said. "They haven't fired a single shot yet."

"Oh, sure," Walt said. "They're gonna surrender the whole island without putting up a fight."

When the tens of hundreds of landing crafts began landing their cargoes ashore, there still was no retaliation.

Next day, however, when the troops were less tense and enjoying their cigarettes and coffee, all hell broke loose.

The enemy, hiding in deep trenches and behind concrete bunkers, made their banzai charges. Hundreds of thousands of them came charging with fixed bayonets, hand grenades, small and big weapons. They were like ants dashing forward, going down, getting up, dying as though they were enjoying sacrificing themselves for their emperor.

"Stupid bastards!" Walt yelled out to Kazuo, lying on the sand firing his rifle, "they don't stand a chance. Why don't they retreat or throw their weapons down."

"It ain't April Fools day!" Kazuo yelled back, also firing his rifle, "It's us or them."

"You heard the Lieutenant," Walt said. "Headquarters wants us to get information from the wounded POWs."

"Just like that," Kazuo returned. "They're gonna tell us how well the island is fortified."

The chargings went on until they were all mowed down or regrouping for more banzai charges.

"We must've gotten most of 'em," Kazuo said.

"Don't bet on it," Walt said. "Intelligence reported that General Ushijima of the Tenth Japanese Army's got over 100,000 troops waiting for us."

"Sonsofbitch!" Kazuo said. "If we can get hold of him, we'd end the fighting.""

"Surrender? General Ushijima?" Walt said. "He'll kill himself before even thinking about it."

The mopping up battles on the western shore continued for days. Finally, the enemy was all killed or was regrouping and waiting for the next move by American forces.

After helping exterminate the enemy defending Shuri Castle, Kazuo and Walt, led by tall, broadshouldered, light-haired Lt. Chuck MacKinzie, headed south toward the last Japanese stronghold in Mabune.

All over the hills and mountain sides were hundreds of Okinawan turtle-back tombs. The Japanese were hiding behind some of the thick, well-fortified, concrete graves, using them as their fortresses.

Kazuo, a few feet ahead of Lt. MacKenzie, led the platoon up the dense forest, his eyes searching for Japanese soldiers who might be ready to fire on them from behind the tombs.

Suddenly, unexpectedly, a machine gun burst out and a hail of bullets came screaming their direction.

Kazuo dove into a ditch, his eyes racing forward toward the source of the bullets.

The rest of the platoon were hugging the ground, digging their heads into the mud, unable to retaliate. When the Lieutenant rose and fired his rifle into the tomb, the rest of the platoon also rose and began firing desperately in the same direction.

The machine gun was suddenly silent.

The platoon stopped firing.

Kazuo, rising from the ditch, looked for Walt.

"Walt!" he cried out. "Walt!"

Lt. Mackinzie was now beside him. "Where's Walt?" he asked the Lieutenant. "Where's Walt?"

The Lieutenant avoided his eyes.

"Lieutenant!" he cried out.

Finally, the Lieutenant shook his head. "He got hit," he said. "Got hit! Walt?"

"The first round," the Lieutenant said. "Never had a chance."

"Oh, God!"

"C'mon, Sergeant," the Lieutenant said, "we gotta get rid of those bastards."

"Sonofabitchs!" he cried out, aiming his rifle at where the sound of the machine gun was coming from. "Motherfuckas!" He fired randomly.

"Hold your fire!" the Lieutenant ordered.

After another moment of silence, the Lieutenant turned toward Kazuo. "Maybe they're out of bullets.".

"Don't count on it, Lieutenant," he said. "That's what they want us to think."

They let the silence go on for a moment longer.

He now crept closer to the tomb.

"See them?" the Lieutenant asked, crawling on his elbow and knees beside him. "How many of them?"

He crept closer. He could see several Japanese soldiers lying dead on the sandbags inside the wall.

"Any of them alive?" the Lieutenant asked.

"They all look dead," he replied.

"Be careful," the Lieutenant said. "Damn Japs! They might be up to no good!"

The platoon seemed to have done a good job annihilating the machine gun nest.

When he and the Lieutenant, now on their feet, approached the machine gun, they quickly counted three dead bodies. There was, however, a lone enemy soldier, bleeding from a head wound, barely holding on.

The Lieutenant ordered the rest of the platoon to stay back and take a break. They'd soon be encountering more Japs.

Kasuo stepped over to the wounded enemy soldier who was lying on his back. The soldier was in his mid-twenties, unshaven, his dirty and smelly mud-stained uniform shredded, his face gaunt from near starvation.

"Get his name and rank," the Lieutenant ordered.

"Oi, namae wa nan dai?" Kazuo asked the prisoner. What's your name?

The prisoner turned his head away, stoically.

"He won't give it to you, get his dog tag," the Lieutenant ordered.

He questioned the prisoner again. When the prisoner ignored him, he reached over for the dog tag around his neck. The prisoner pulled the dog tag away.

Kazuo struggled and finally got the dog tag. He looked at the name in Japanese and stuck it into his shirt pocket.

"Get all the information you can out of him," the Lieutenant ordered. "We gotta move on." The Lieutenant stepped away, and took a sip of water from his canteen.

"Oi," he addressed the soldier, "koko ni takusan Nipponjin heitai ga oru ka?" Are there many Japanese soldiers here?

The wounded enemy turned his head away again.

"Oi!" Kazuo screamed, "Henji shiro!" Answer me.

The soldier looked up at him.

"Henji shiro!"

The soldier spat into his face.

Kazuo's head snapped back. He unsnapped his holster, yanked out his pistol and pressed it into the prisoner's head. "You damn sonofabitch!"

"Go ahead! Shoot!" the prisoner screamed.

The damn prisoner spoke English!

"What're you? A Kibei? A Nisei went to school in Japan?"

The prisoner sneered.

He placed his pistol back into its holster, not bothering to snap it shut.

Unsuspectingly, the prisoner's hand gradually maneuvered towards the holster. In a flash! the prisoner reached for the pistol, and was holding it against Kazuo's chest.

"Whatta!" he stared at the pistol.

"Get back!" the prisoner ordered. "Get back!"

He backed away from the prisoner who was not wounded as severely as first suspected.

"Put that away," he said. "How far d'ya think you can go?"

"Call the Lieutenant," the prisoner ordered.

"You won't get away with this," he warned.

"Call him!"

"Lieutenant!" Kazuo complied.

The Lieutenant stepped over tentatively.

The prisoner suddenly raised the pistol and aimed it at the Lieutenant. "Don't get any closer!"

The Lieutenant stared at the pistol, his eyes shifting over to Kazuo. "Whattahells going on!"

Kazuo shrugged helplessly, shaking his head.

"Put that away," the Lieutenant ordered the prisoner. "You kill us you won't get more than a few feet away from here."

"Where are you from?" Kazuo asked the prisoner.

The prisoner sneered, his lips tightening.

"Your name's Nagata?" Kazuo questioned.

The prisoner neither confirmed now denied it.

"Your family's still in the States?" the Lieutenant asked.

"Yeah," the prisoner said bitterly. "In one of those concentration camps where you put all the Japanese from California."

"Where in California you're from?" Kazuo questioned.

"Fresno," the prisoner informed, grudgingly.

"Nagata from Fresno?" He pulled out the dog tag from his shirt pocket and looked at it.

"You know my family?" the prisoner asked, pleadingly.

"You had a young brother?" he inquired.

"Yeah. Mitsuo."

"His English name?"

"Walter," said the prisoner.

Shocked, Kazuo exchanged grim stares with the Lieutenant.

"You know him?" the prisoner asked.

"It...can't be the same person."

"Where is he?!"

Finally, "Walt, he was with us just a few minutes ago."

"Here!" the prisoner said. "In Okinawa?"

Kazuo and the Lieutenant stared at each other, avoiding the prisoner's eyes.

"Where is he?" the prisoner asked.

Kazuo and the Lieutenant said nothing.

"Where's Mitsuo?!"

"Look," Kazuo said, "we're not talking about the same person."

"There was only one Nagata family in Fresno," the prisoner said.

Kazuo and the Lieutenant remained silent.

"Where is he!?" The prisoner was now desperate.

"You guys just killed him," Kazuo finally said.

"What!"

"When you guys opened fire on us, he was first one..."

"No!" the prisoner cried out. "No!"

Kazuo dug the dogtag out from his shirt pocket. He looked at it then tossed it to the Lieutenant who, in turn, tossed it over to the prisoner.

The prisoner reached for it. He glanced at it.

"Mitsuo!" he cried out, pushing the dog tag away. "Mitsuo!"

The prisoner aimed the pistol at his head.

"Nagata!" Kazuo cried out. "Don't!"

The shot echoed throughout the tomb.

The Lieutenant and Kazuo rushed forward.

The prisoner was dead.

"Jeesus..." Kazuo muttered.

He retrieved the dog tag and handed it back to the Lieutenant.

"Wasn't Walt's name 'Nakata?'" the Lieutenant questioned.

"Yes, sir," Kazuo said. "Not 'Nagata'"

"Then...?"

"Walt wasn't even from Fresno, Sir. From LA."

"Nice work, Sergeant," the Lieutenant complimented. "Quick thinking."

Kazuo glanced over toward where Walt's body was lying.

"Sorry, Sergeant," the Lieutenant said, also looking toward Walt's body. "Sorry about your buddy."

"Fucking war," Kazuo said, wiping his eyes. "This stinking no-good fucking war."

"C'mon, Sergeant, "the Lieutenant said, placing his hand on Kazuo's shoulder. "We've got to move on."

· · · · ·

On his bed in his cabin, George's eyes shifted away from the ceiling. He could still hear, however, machinegun bullets screaming over his head. One of them having Walt's name.

CHAPTER 28:

The Spirit Lives On

George finished the next chapter, placed it under Lowney's cabin door and went into the warehouse where he changed into a sweat-stained T-shirt and wrinkled Levis. He poured gas into the lawn mower and pushed it to the spot he had stopped yesterday. He then spent the next hour going back and forth until the lawn mower ran out of gas.

Sweating, exhausted and hungry, but quite happy that he had completed the week's mowing, he took a quick shower, changed, got into his Ford and headed for Terre Haute.

A thirty-minute drive from Marshall, Terre Haute, a town but much bigger than Marshall, was the home of Indiana State University. He had driven around the campus once to feel how it was to be a college student again. It had been refreshing to see the students eagerly walking to class and jabbering away with their classmates.

He parked on Main, picked up the *Terre Haute Express* at a corner newspaper stand and stepped into the Blue Bird Cafe, not yet reading the headline. The sweet-smelling aroma of spaghetti sauce and hamburgers greeted him. The bar stools were unoccupied, but the tables with checkered red and white table cloths were packed with the usual loud lunch crowd, a couple of young waitresses rushing in and out of the kitchen with orders.

He had been there a couple of times and Lou Pastrano, the

owner/bartender, a stout bulky dark-haired man in early thirties, recognized him immediately. Well, why wouldn't he? How many Japanese are there in Terre Haute?

"Same thing?" Lou remembered.

"Right," George said, "and a tuna sandwich."

Lou called into the kitchen, picked up a bottle of Bud and placed it before George with a glass and napkin.

George glanced at the headline of the *Terre Haute Express* and was shocked. **CHICAGO GANGSTER TURNS GOVERNMENT INFORMANT!** Holy shit! It was Sam Sato, Jimmy's boss at Man Fook Low restaurant. The article said that a mob family was being investigated by the Senate Investigation Committee and had subpoenaed Sam Sato as a material witness. Sam was free on a $50,000 bail when the mob, afraid that he would "talk", had put a contract on his head.

According to the article, a couple of men had picked Sam up on Clark Street and were presumably taking him to their family's boss. As they went through Lake Shore Park, the man sitting in the back shot Sam up front, and the driver stopped to dump Sam's body. The newspaper said that Sam had miraculously survived the assassination when the bullet had only grazed his head.

"If that's what they think of me," the article quoted Sam, "I'll really squeal on 'em." And he became an informant for the government.

The article revealed that the bodies of the two contract men were later discovered in an Indiana cornfield.

George remembered Jimmy telling him that the only way Sam would ever get out of the syndicate was feet first. He hoped Jimmy knew more about the screwed-up attempt on Sam than the newspaper did, and would tell him all about it on his next trip up to Chicago.

"How you like that?" Lou said, indicating the paper, "a Japanese in the mafia."

"Really something, huh?" George said, and let it go at that.

"You've been out there in Marshall how long now?"

"Five months, going on six."

"Wasn't too long ago when writers from Marshall used to hang out here," Lou said. "They couldn't drink back there according to 'em."

"Lowney Handy's rules."

"Your novel, another *From Here To Eternity*?"

"It's a great book, *Eternity*," George said, evasively. "My favorite."

"All takes place where you're from, right?"

George nodded.

"Like I told you," Lou said, "me and my brother, Frankie, we was stationed there before shipped out. A great tour, '43 and '44. Then all hell breaks lose. My Army outfit we're sent to the Philippines. Frankie and his Marine outfit, they're eventually off to Iwo. "

"Iwo Jima must've been tough."

"Tough!" Lou said. "A nightmare according to Frankie. Never thought he'd make it."

Lou called out to the kitchen. "How's the sandwich coming?"

"In a minute," a woman's voice returned.

"Remember Harry, I told you about?" Lou said to George.

"Your interpreter buddy?"

"Harry and me, we was like to two flies stuck together on a fly paper. Orders from headquarters.

"When we landed at Leyte in the Philippines it was worse than the other landings," Lou went on. "We had to worry about them Flips. Them Filipino scouts. They hated every last one of 'em Japs. I had to make sure they knew Harry was one of us. If they tried to shoot him, they'd have to shoot me first."

George remembered that's the way it was with his bodyguard in Okinawa.

"Just after we landed, here comes MacArthur," Lou continued. "Remember his speech? 'I said I will return?'" There we was, already landed, the whole beach secured, and he wades in through the water. Like he was the first one there.

"Sure looked real in the newsreel," George said, still waiting for his sandwich.

"Phony bastard," Lou said. "Made me wanna puke."

"He did a pretty good job ending the war," George said, recalling the ceremony on the SS Missouri where General MacArthur formally accepted the unconditional surrender of Japan.

"Then he got his ass kicked in Korea for acting like he was president of the United States."

The waitress, a slim light-haired lady in late twenties, finally brought the sandwich.

"This here's my wife, Sylvia" Lou introduced. "George," he said to Sylvia, "is one of 'em Japanese-Americans who fought on our side."

"Hi, George," Sylvia said with a friendly smile. "From California?"

"Hawaii."

"Hawaii!" said Sylvia. "Beautiful place, from what Lou tells me. He promised to take me and our kids there someday."

"Someday," Lou said.

"I'm still holding you to it, Lou."

"Yeah, sure," Lou said. "Just close up shop and fly away."

"You promised."

"And I'm still promising," Lou said, slapping his wife's butt and pushing her toward the kitchen.

"Lou!" Sylvia cried out. "Stop it."

"Nice meeting you, George" Sylvia said, disappearing.

"Sandwich okay?" Lou asked.

Nodding, George took another bite. "Great."

"It ain't, I'll send it back."

After another bite and another sip of beer, George asked, "It was from Hawaii your brother and his outfit went to Iwo?"

"After Tarawa and some other island," Lou said.

"What about you guys in the Philippines?"

"Them Japs there, they was getting meaner as hell," Lou said. "They knew they'd be dying soon. So they started slaughtering thousands of Filipino civilians. And the Filipino soldiers, they couldn't wait to get their hands on them Japs. And there was Harry, poor Harry, them Flips didn't give a damn he was one of us."

"They still couldn't tell the difference between him and the enemy?"

"They just wanted to kill anyone who was Japanese. I always made sure Harry was behind me."

"Sure glad I was in Okinawa; not there."

"You had the same problem over there? The Okinawans hating your guts?"

"Not the Okinawans," he said. "The GIs."

"They must've known you was one of 'em."

"Didn't make any difference. Not when they're been shot at from people looking like me."

"Ain't that the shits," Lou said.

After a moment, Lou said, "Over in Iwo, according to Frankie, dem Japs were ordered to fight to the last man. Even the general."

"From what I heard," George said, "they never found the general's body."

"Could be he was buried deep down in the volcano ashes, according to Frankie. He said it wasn't the ashes that was holding the Marines back. It was the damn mountain looking down on 'em."

"Mt. Suribachi?"

One of the middle-aged waitresses approached the bar. "A bottle of Miller, Lou," she ordered, looking at herself in the mirror behind Lou and brushing back a strand of blonde hair. She glanced over at George and nodded friendlily.

Lou placed the bottle on her tray.

"Hey, Lou," the waitress said softly, "just heard a good one."

"Later, Pattie."

"This cowboy is captured by a bunch of Indians," Pattie went on, "and the chief gives him a chance to live if he comes up with three good reasons…"

"Later, Pattie! Later."

"Lou! You never ever wanna hear my latest."

"Your customers, they're waiting,"

"Well, you ain't gonna hear this one," Pattie said, and walked away with her tray.

"I always gotta listen to her latest," Lou complained to George.

George chuckled.

"Like I was telling you," Lou said, "that mountain…"

"Suribachi."

"Yeah. Su-ru-ba-chi. Frankie said, dem tunnels was so deep their artilleries could do nothin' to 'em. Below, the Marines was sitting ducks, advancing inch by inch, shells exploding all around 'em."

George took another bite of his sandwich. "He at least made it back."

"Not like a whole bunch of 'em who din't."

Listening to Lou, George thought what he had gone through in Okinawa was nothing compared to Iwo Jima.

"Frankie, he was one of 'em lucky ones," Lou continued. "Guys 'round him they're getting banged up by the artilleries and there he was just nicked on his leg. Not 'nough for the hospital ship, but 'nough for the medics to sew him up and get him a purple heart.

"All this time," Lou went on, "Frankie and his buddies, they're down below the mountain, watching them guys up there struggling to plant the red, white and blue."

"He really saw those guys putting up the flag?"

"They all did. They're at the bottom, those guys up at the top. When the flag went up they jumped up shouting, yelling and firing their rifles in the air. Never saw nothing so beautiful, Frankie said. The red, white and blue waving in the wind up there. Ever since, whenever he sees our flag it takes him back to that moment in Iwo."

Lou blinked, his eyes moist, his voice cracking.

They said nothing for a moment.

Finally, George asked, "What ever happened to your buddy, Harry?"

"Harry? We're still in touch. He got married, got coupla kids. He went to the University of Oregon, got a degree in engineering and doing real good."

"And you? You opened this place after your discharge?"

"With the help of the GI Bill," Lou said. "Not getting rich. Can't complain though. My own business. A nice home. Three kids, all good and healthy."

"Gonna tell them what you went through in the war?"

"Why have them go through all that?"

George finished his beer.

Lou reached down into the refrigerator and brought out another Bud.

"On me," he said.

"Thanks."

As George sipped, Lou asked, "Hey, how 'bout you? Married? Kids?"

George took another sip.

"Divorced? Don' wanna talk about it, eh?"

"Never got married," George said.

"Any girlfriend?"

Christine's face flashed before him. She was smiling that quiet beautiful smile of hers, her red full lips parted slightly, He swallowed hard.

He took another sip.

"You left her back in Hawaii?" Lou asked.

George shook his head. What could he tell him? That there is a girl named Christine Barrington he left back in California, and hoped to be with her soon?

"Harry's a winner?" Lou said. "A nice girl from a hardworking Japanese family. Well educated. Good mother for his kids."

"Life turned out good for him, huh?"

"After what him and his family went through during the war days," they deserve it.

What if I told him about Christine? George wondered. He'd most likely think I met her in a bar. Or walking the streets. Or worst, in a whore joint. How could a decent a white girl love a slant-eyed Jap? Would he be like other white men protecting white girls from non-white men?

Lou, of course, wouldn't understand that Christine was like him, a Japanese. In fact, more of a Japanese than he. Would he have to explain about Christine to every white man objecting to a white girl going out with a Japanese?

"Japanese, they're like us Italianos," Lou said. "Marry your own kind."

George said nothing.

He took the last drop

"Going?" Lou asked.

"Yeah, I better. Don't want the cops stopping me for drunk-driving."

"Aw, just tell 'em you're a friend of mine."

"I'll remember that," George said, getting off his stool, heading for the door.

CHAPTER 29:

The Telegram

Christine, at her desk up in her studio, was going over the schedule and the events that would take place in the Rudy Diaz Medal of Honor gala. She was grateful and relieved that Uncle Jess was guiding her through the countless details: the streets where the parade would go through, the park where the solemn dedication would take place, the discovery of a singer, preferably from the East LA area, to sing the national anthem, and the selection of a guest speaker from East LA.

Good heavens, was she biting off more than she could chew?

If only George were there to help her! He had called several more times from the bus depot in Marshall and it was again as though he was making a speech to the noisy bus riders around him. There were moments when he had to yell into the phone.

The first time they were able to speak privately was when he went to Chicago and called from his hotel room. He said life at the colony was getting better, Lowney Handy was still strict and demanding but seemed satisfied with his progress.

One day, he discovered a phone booth in the corner of a drug store in Marshall and managed to make collect calls from there. It was, however, a public phone and he couldn't speak as long as he wanted to.

He had been calling at least once a week, but had not called for over a month now. Was he all right? Was he still at the colony? Has he moved to Chicago after meeting his Maui friend?

When he did call, it was usually at four p.m. California time. Lately, she found herself staring at the phone in her studio at about four, wishing and expecting a call.

She had answered the phone several times with: "Moshi, moshi." and the caller had hung up.

She looked at the clock above her head several times this afternoon commanding it to ring. It went past four and still no ring. At about 4:15, it suddenly rang.

"Hello," she answered, expecting a salesman or a census solicitor to reply.

"Moshi moshi."

It was George!

"Bar-ring-ton, Chris-teen-san desu ka?"

"Hai. So desu," she replied playfully. "Tsu-ka-ya-ma, Geo-gie-san desu ka?"

"Hai. So desu."

After a brief playful conversation, his tone changed. "When was the first time we met?" he asked.

"Let's see," she said. "When did the IRS agent first come to my home?"

"Three more months and it'll be a year ago.'

"That long ago?" she said. "Never thought I could ever thank an IRS agent for examining my tax return.'

He laughed.

"My life's changed ever since," she said.

"Mine, too."

"George," she went on, "is it all right if I flew to Indianapolis?"

Silence.

"George?"

"I don't think it's a good idea," he finally said.

"Lowney Handy?"

"She has rules."

"Why would she object us getting together?"

"Christine," he said, patiently, "she's going through a rough period. Her husband died not too long ago. There's no one else here except me. She's very protective of herself. I don't want her to doubt my devotion to her."

A pause. Then, "George, is there something going on between you and her?"

"Christine! She's like a mother to me."

She sighed.

"Besides," he went on, "aren't we planning to get married?"

"Is that a proposal?"

"Of course."

"Thought you'd never ask."

"You're willing even though I'm Japanese and you're a haole?" he injected.

"I'm Nihon-jin, too," she told him.

"Well," he said, after another moment of silence, "That's settled."

"We'll be happy together, George. Very happy."

After they hanged up, she let out a great big sigh.

He did ask her to marry him! Oh, Tsu-ka-yama, Geor-gie-san!

She could understand his concern about a marriage between a so-called haole and a Japanese. But she really meant it when she said she, too, was a Nihonjin. Perhaps, more so than he. She grew up in Japan; he grew up in America. Her Nihongo is a natural Nihonjin; his is a learned and bookish Nihongo.

The wedding. It should take place as soon as he returned. A

Japanese-American wedding. Yes, that's what it would be. She would invite Shoichi and his family. Shoichi would perform the ceremony in both Nihongo and in English. For the background music she would invite the popular Japanese-American band. The Rising Sons. They would play both American and Japanese songs. Also Kei Kali Nei Au, the Hawaiian Wedding song.

As for the guests, she'd have to ask George who'd he like to invite. One of them, she knew, would be his IRS agent friend, Mark Irving. Then his friends from Little Tokyo. As for her guests, there, of course, was Uncle Jess and Auntie Harriet and the only neighborhood friend, Mr. and Mrs. Harold Upland. There's Carole and her professor boyfriend, Hanson Goodlane. And, of course, Amando, Shig and his family, and Mom and Pop. Oh, goodness, the list can go on and on. She'd have to talk to George about it. –And, oh. Lowney Handy. She might be willing to come from Florida.

Next day, Christine was at Grand Crystal in downtown LA shopping for her wedding dress. Nothing elaborate or fanciful. Just a form-fitting white dress she had once seen in Grand Crystal's display window.

After scheduling for measurement, she thought she'd drop by Uncle Jess's office building on Spring Street close by. Won't he be surprised? She has "finally found a man in her life."

Knowing Christine, Helen, the friendly, middle-aged Latina receptionist in the high-ceilinged, ornate front office, told her to go right into Uncle Jess's office.

"Christine," Uncle Jess welcomed, "so nice to see you."

She instinctively gave Uncle Jess a kiss on his cheek. "I was passing by and I thought I'd drop in," she said.

"Like you used," Uncle Jess said.

Behind the high desk was a large painting of Auntie Harriet, Uncle Jess's wife, beside it a large photograph of Uncle Jess and Dad, partners in the architectural business.

After a few more minutes of a warm family conversation and the upcoming Rudy Diaz Memorial, Christine finally announced the surprise.

"You are!" Uncle Jess said. "You're finally getting married?" He reached for her hand and squeezed it warmly. "And who's this lucky man?'

"His name is George Tsukayama."

"Sounds like a nice Polish name. He's an American though."

"Yes, he is."

"And where is the wedding taking place?"

"In our backyard."

"The Japanese garden?"

When she explained that the minister was going to be Reverend Shoichi Murata from Japan, Uncle Jess seemed puzzled.

"Why a Japanese minister?" he asked.

"George and I are both Japanese," she announced.

Uncle Jess looked at her, apparently not quite sure he had heard her right.

"He's Japanese?"

"Not Polish," she said, trying to laugh it off.

Uncle Jess kept eyeing her. "You're marrying a Japanese?"

"A Japanese-American."

"Christine. You think your father would have approved?" Uncle Jess questioned.

"Mom would, too."

"You're aware, of course, that the attitude of people here in

California toward the Chinese, the Filipinos and most recently the Japanese is nothing to be proud of."

"I'm aware of all that, Uncle Jess."

"You still want to marry this… ?"

"George Hiroshi Tsukayama."

"Who is a Japanese."

"Uncle Jess, Mom and Dad spent many years in Japan. They loved the Japanese people."

"But to have you, their daughter, marry one of them!"

"They would have been very happy for me, Uncle Jess." She found herself raising her voice to a man she loved and respected. Has she been wrong about him all these years?

"This boy, is he aware of people's attitude about interracial marriages?"

"He's very aware of it." Is this the Uncle Jess she has known all her life?

Uncle Jess shut his eyes, his head going from side to side.

Tears came to her eyes.

Dad and Mom would not be at her wedding. Uncle Jess would not be there, either?

"Christine," Uncle Jess said, taking a step closer, "you can't really be serious…"

Wiping her eyes, she stepped away, turned and rushed out of the office.

Next morning, still not having gotten over Uncle Jess's objection and still not wanting to believe that Uncle Jess was no different from other bigots, she kept herself busy restoring the upstairs garage apartment for George's homecoming. It would be his studio/office. Where he could do all his writings.

She had already installed new carpets, repainted the garage

inside and outside a few weeks ago and had replaced the old desk with a new oak desk. She had also purchased an automatic electric coffee pot and stocked several packages of George's favorite Kona coffee. Reluctanly but resolutely, she took down Dad's architectural paintings from the walls and replaced them with paintings of Mt. Haleakala, Iao Valley and the winding Hana road all of which she had painted from photographs taken on Maui many years ago.

At the top of the apartment door, she painted, THE MAUI ROOM.

She knew George would be happy. She just hoped that his Nihonjin pride wouldn't make him feel he was being kept.

He had said he might be able to finish his novel in six months. He had left in mid-spring which meant he would be coming home sometime in October or November.

That would be perfect.

Or is it? Uncle Jess. Would he still be interested in going through with the Rudy Diaz Memorial on Veterans Day after yesterday's encounter? Would he still go through with the plans of inviting his dignitary friends, especially the politicians seeking votes in the next election? He said he would send invitations to several prominent figures in the movie industry who would love to have their pictures in the newspapers. He would also send an invitation to President Eisenhower who always golfed at nearby Palm Springs.

She thought she heard the doorbell ringing at the front door.

She looked out the window. It was Uncle Jess, his shiny Cadillac parked at the front steps. She would have been thrilled to have Uncle Jess visit her. But not after yesterday. Not after discovering he is no different from others.

The doorbell rang again. She wished he would go away. When the doorbell rang persistently, she could no longer ignore it.

She went downstairs, went out of the garage and approached the front steps where Uncle Jess was waiting patiently.

"Oh, there you are," Uncle Jess said, not opening his arms as he usually did. "I was wondering if you were out."

"Hello, Uncle Jess," she said politely.

"Christine," Uncle Jess began, his voice rather soft, not confidently as usual, "you didn't give me a chance to know more about this boy, George Tsu-ka…"

"George Tsukayama."

"Yes. George Tsu-ka-yama." Uncle Jess looked down at his shoes for moment, then looked back up. "You didn't tell me of his background," he went on.

"Like?" she said, challengingly.

"Well, like he was in our Army during the war. Received several medals for bravely in the Pacific fighting against Japan."

She looked up at him.

"Now, you know I have certain connections and resources to find out about people in this town," Uncle Jess went on. "I also found out that this George Tsu-ka-yama worked for the U.S. Treasury Department."

"He was an Internal Revenue Agent," she said.

"Yes, he was," Uncle Jess said. "And he resigned his position to become a writer."

So far, Uncle Jess had not tried to discourage her.

"Very admirable," Uncle Jess went on. "After all, how many of us are willing to walk away from a career and to do whatever we really want to do?"

She could feel a warmth resurging for Uncle Jess.

"Well, anyway," he continued, "I should have given you a chance to tell me more about George than he was Japanese."

"Then, you approve, Uncle Jess?"

"Yes. Of course. Now that I know about him." And he opened his arms to her.

Tears flooded her eyes. Not tears of pain and hurt of yesterday, but of happiness and joy."

"Oh, Uncle Jess..." She hugged him warmly. "I should've known better than to even think of you being..."

"A bigot?"

"Oh, no. Not you. Not my Uncle Jess."

And they embraced a moment longer.

"Then, you and Auntie Harriet will come to our wedding?"

"Of course, we will. Not even a cavalry of wild horses is going to keep us away.

By the way," Uncle Jess added, "you haven't asked me to give you away."

"You will, Uncle Jess?"

"I'd be terribly hurt if you didn't ask me to."

"Oh, Uncle Jess. Dad and Mom would be so happy."

And she hugged him again.

"This might not apply today," Uncle said after letting a moment of silence go by, "there was a law in California forbidding interracial marriages."

"Forbidding?"

"It goes back to when whites did not want their daughters marrying a Negro, Chinese or a Japanese."

"You mean George and I cannot get married!"

"It might not be in the books anymore," he said.

Ohmygoodness! Here, she thought everything was going along fine.

"It if is," he said, "there's ways to get around it. Get married in Tijuana."

"Across the border?"

"The marriage might be recognized here."

"Might be?!"

CHAPTER 30:

Kicking A Dead Horse

George was busy washing his Ford with a bucket of soap water near the Ramada when Lowney sped her Chrysler through the Last Retreat gate and came to a screeching halt beside him. Getting out, slamming the door hard, she stepped up to him, a crumpled envelope in her hand.

"I just picked this up at the post office," she announced.

George stopped washing, the sponge in his hand dripping, and stared at the envelope.

"Remember I mentioned our agent, Ted Agnew?"

He kept staring at the envelope.

"Ted liked the early chapters I sent him," she said. "Really liked them. Now, he's saying the chapters I sent him this past month are losing their focus; not preparing for the closure."

The sponge dropped into the bucket.

"Damn bunch of know-it-all New Yorkers," she went on, shaking the letter in her hand. "Just because they've placed stories with publishers, they think they can tell a writer how to write."

Oh, Christ.

"Fiddlefucking agents," she continued, "they can't tell good writing if it flashed before their eyes."

He reached down, picked up the sponge from the bucket, and squeezed it hard.

Still agitated, she took the letter out of the envelope and stood there going through it again.

Calmed down a bit, she said, "All the chapters we sent him, they're good. Very good. The storyline couldn't be any better. Every one of 'em. 'Losing focus' my ass! 'Not preparing for the closure!' bull shit."

George gritted his teeth.

"We'll show him how focused we are," she said. "Leave those chapters alone. Nothing's wrong with them. When we come to the closure it'll flow naturally."

He let out a deep sigh. He won't have to rewrite those chapters!

"Ted's a good agent," she went on. "Sold many stories. Well known in the publishing business. Look what he did with Jim's story. Like most frustrated would-be writers, though, he gets his kicks out of rewriting somebody else's. Your story is uplifting, enlightening, and it's going to be even better when you're done with the closure."

George found himself breathing easier.

"In the last chapter I sent Ted," she went on, "when George, your central character, comes back from the Pacific war, he has to deal with his father who can't articulate his thoughts, so you need to fix that."

"Let Kazuo's father ask him about the war?" he asked.

"His father is a paradox," she said. "He is uneducated, but he is wise. He is not worldly, but he is insightful. He understands people, but people don't understand him. Got that?"

George thought of his own father, and was astonished that Lowney had described him exactly how he was. Otosan was now Kazuo's father, adamant, dogged, reluctant to let go old traditions and beliefs.

"You must digest Otosan very carefully," she instructed. "Understand him fully. Become him. Don't make him a fool and don't ridicule him. He is a simple man trying to cope with a complex world that does not understand him."

She handed him the agent's letter and told him to read it carefully and try to read between the lines. "One thing you have to say about agents," she said, "they may not be creative, but they know what sells and what don't.

"Now, I don't want you to lose any sleep over it," she said, turning toward her cabin. "It'll come to you. From your subconscious to your conscious mind."

He glanced at the letter, stuck it into his back pocket, and decided to read it later. Greatly relieved he did not have to rewrite the whole book, he splashed the Ford with a bucket of fresh water and wiped the windshield.

Early next morning, he got up from a sleepless night, sat at his desk and started rewriting the last chapter. He became Kazuo and began writing Kazuo's homecoming from the war.

• • • • •

Kazuo was stationed in Tokyo for a few months after Japan's surrender and had come home in early 1946. Like Naha, Okinawa, Tokyo was spared nothing by America's B-29s. People were starving, lacking shelter and staggering around in a daze with just the clothing on their backs.

Otosan, his father, and Okasan, his mother, when told what had happened in Okinawa, were reluctant to listen to him. Realizing he was kicking a dead horse, Kazuo backed off. He told them instead of meeting some of the family clan in Ginoza. By mitigating the clan's misery and suffering, he said he did whatever he could for them, offering them food and medicine and whatever clothing he could forage from the Army camps.

Otosan, after a second, asked, "Were there many Japanese soldiers from Ginoza?"

"A few were from that area," he said.

"Were they brave? Willing to die for their country?"

Wanting to close the subject about the Okinawan battles, Kazuo said they were all brave. He could not tell Otosan that they died for a lost cause.

On the second day home, he was out in the front yard eating mangos, and Otosan and Okasan were sitting on the goza mat beside him, enjoying the sunny tropical day, when Kaneshiro Obasan came dashing across the Kapuna Bridge. Obasan, a fortish widow and a life-long family friend, had learned from the local Okinawan grapevine that Kazuo had returned home from the war.

Unlike the customary Japanese tradition of bowing, Obasan wrapped her arms around Kazuo, hugged him and cried. "You came home, Kazuo," she said in Nihongo. "You came home. One of you returned home."

Otosan and Okasan, apparently familiar with Obasan's plight sat silently, their eyes on the goza.

Knowing what Obasan was going through, Kazuo hugged her back, tears flowing down his cheeks. Unable to say express himself, he could only hope that Obasan understood he was sharing her grief.

The news had been shocking and wrenching when Okasan told him what had happened to Hitoshi, Obasan's only son. A couple of years older than he, Hitoshi was always someone he had looked up to. They were in the boy scouts together, Hitoshi, an Eagle Scout.

Okasan had told him that just before the war in Europe ended, two haole soldiers came to Obasan's home. The soldiers, unable to express themselves, told Obasan verbally and in sign language that the carefully folded American flag they carried was now hers. Obasan finally understood. Bowing to the soldiers and fighting back sobs, she accepted the flag. Moments later, she had come rushing across the bridge to let Otosan and Okasan know about Hitoshi.

After telling Kazuo that Hitoshi was buried somewhere in Europe, Okasan had told him to call on Obasan and offer his condolences. Still shocked over the news, he could not bring himself to call on Obasan. It would be too painful. He himself had not fully recovered from the Okinawan battle and could not handle the death of his "older brother."

Obasan now joined everyone on the goza, still weeping, her eyes red and swollen. Otosan and Okasan comforted her and offered her solace by speaking in their native Okinawan dialect which Kazuo could understand but unable to speak it.

Obasan now asked Kazuo about the people in Kana Village, near Ginoza Village, where she was from. Again, Kazuo mitigated the battle of Okinawa and said that the Okinawans in central and the northern villages were spared the ravages of the war.

"The Okinawan soldiers must have been all very brave," Otosan said. "They were brought up to believe in the Emperor and be willing to die for him."

"Why did they have to die for him?" Kazuo asked, recalling the senseless banzai charges.

"You were born and raised here," Otosan said. "It's only proper that you were willing to die for America. No different from an Okinawan soldier willing to die for his country. Nihon."

"But you, Otosan, you have lived here most of your life. Why can't you appreciate a country that has given you all you have enjoyed?"

"What about pride?" Otosan said. "Pride in who I am."

Oh, God, not that again. And yet, Kazuo realized that he, too, was proud to be who he was. A Japanese. A Japanese born and raised in the United States. Proud of himself and the values he has learned from childhood.

"Someday you'll understand," Otosan went on. "Someday you will understand why I feel the way I do. You will understand how it feels to be made a fool because I don't know the ways of this country. Because I cannot speak proper English. You will understand how it feels to be laughed at. Teased at. Always reminded that all I'm good for is to work in the sugar cane fields and pineapple fields. Or as a houseboy, a yard boy, a chauffeur... a servant."

"That is what Hitoshi's father used to always tell him," Obasan joined. "What his father had to go through those early days here."

Kazuo, of course, knew what they were talking about. He, too, had worked in the sugar cane fields, hoeing, planting and harvesting. For a measly twenty-five cents an hour.

"It's not easy to forget those days," Okasan said. "I had to work in the sugar cane fields, too. We were always scolded by the Portuguese luna boss on a horse. 'Work fast; work fast. Hana hana, hana hana.'"

Again, Kazuo was familiar with what they were saying.

Nihonjins were always considered inferior by the haoles and the Portuguese. They were at the bottom of the totem pole. But all that would change now. The Niseis have proven their loyalty. They will be respected and accepted as fellow Americans.

It's education, he wanted to say to Otosan, Okasan and Obasan. Education that they themselves did not have the opportunity to have. They had made sacrifices for their children. Kodomo no tame ni--for the sake of their children. Their children would now show their gratitude by seeking higher education and improving the lives of their parents.

"You keep saying Nihon lost the war," Otosan went on. "The picture of Tenno Heika and Mac-u-Arthur Taisho you brought home shows they are friends who respect each other."

Oh, boy, Kazuo thought. It was a photo of the Emperor and General MacArthur standing next to each other. MacArthur, in his casual, tie-less shirt and khaki trousers, was a head taller than the Emperor, and the Emperor in his long, dark, formal tuxedo, was a humbled, humiliated man.

"Mac-u-Arthur is a great general," Otosan said. "Very smart. Very brave. He knows if he has the cooperation of the Emperor, America and Japan could be strong allies. Together they will be able to defeat the threatening nations, China, Korea and Russia."

Otosan was right about that, Kazuo thought. America now needed Japan's cooperation to fight off the communist threats.

"Japan never lost the war," Otosan went on, his head high, his eyes moist, his voice trembling with great yamato-damashi pride. "Japan stopped the war for humanitarian reasons."

Wow, Kazuo thought. For an uneducated, almost illiterate man Otosan was using big classy Japanese words. "For humanitarian reasons."

"Take a good look of the picture you showed us," Otosan added. "Take a good look at the Emperor's eyes. Are they the eyes of a defeated man? Of someone who lost the war? No, Kazuo, they are the eyes of a wise leader. Of Kami-sama."

Oh, Christ. He'd brought the photo home to show Otosan and Okasan that the Emperor was not God. He went to the bathroom like everyone else.

"You understand what I'm saying, Boy?" Otosan lectured.

Oh, let the old man think whatever he wants. The war was over. That's all that really mattered.

· · · · ·

Coming to the end of the chapter, George hoped that it was what Lowney wanted. It not, he'd have to rewrite the whole damn chapter.

CHAPTER 31:

The Painting

Right after Uncle Jess told Christine that all the people he had invited to the Rudy Diaz memorial were willing to participate in the program, she hurried over to Armando's parking lot.

"They're all coming to East LA!" Armando couldn't believe it.

"All of them," she said, "the mayor, the councilmen, the supervisors and get this, maybe President Eisenhower, too."

"The President! Wow!"

"Let's hope he's golfing at Palm Springs that weekend."

When she assured Armando that Uncle Jess was doing all he can to make the memorial a colossal event, Armando chocked up. "What can I tell you? You, you're the greatest…"

She looked around the parking lot and noticed that there were no open space. "Why don't we drive over to Mom's and Pop's and tell them the good news?"

. . . . .

Shig was proud and honored that Christine had sent him a special invitation to the Rudy Diaz Memorial. [He and his family would be sitting among the dignitaries.] He had received a Silver Star for his gallantry in the Texas Lost Battalion rescue and a Purple Heart for his wound. But wanting to forget what he went through that hellish day, he had tossed the medals in his trunk, swearing never to look at them again.

Christine's invitation gave him second thoughts. From what Armando said about his buddy, Rudy was a great warrior. Gutsy, fearless and willing to die for what he believed in.

Hell, yeah. He'd be glad to go to the memorial. He'd also be glad to wear his Silver Star and his Purple Heart medals.

And, he told himself, he'd finally get to meet Hiroshi Miyamura who had been invited to the memorial. Miyamura, a one-man army in the Korean trench the day of his heroism, was the only surviving Japanese-American to receive the Medal of Honor. After his release from a POW camp, he was invited to the White House to receive the medal from President Eisenhower. Rudy Diaz, unfortunately, received his posthumously.

$$\cdot\ \cdot\ \cdot\ \cdot\ \cdot$$

Christine parked her Chrysler across the street from the Evergreen Cemetery, and she and Armando headed up the concrete steps to Mom's and Pop's home. As before, Mom looked out the window and, seeing them, quickly opened the door.

"Armando, Christine," she quickly greeted, wiping her hands on her colorful apron and opening her arms. "I was thinking of you two. And here you are."

The door opened wider, and Pop, in his usual T-shirt and Levis stepped out.

"Hey," he greeted, "look who's here? C'mon in. Don' keep standing out here. C'mon in."

Pop turned off the TV in the warm comfortable living room. "C'mon here, Christine," he invited. "Sit. Be comfortable."

She sat at the soft, upholstered chair opposite the silent TV,

Armando sitting next to her.

"Hey, Marie," Pop said in mock anger, "how come you're sitting there when you're supposed to be serving coffee or beer or something?"

"Oh, no, Pop," Christine quickly intervened. "We're fine."

"Just had some coffee," Armando interjected.

"Well, okay, then," Pop said, "This is your home. Just ask. For anything. –Unless it's for a million bucks," he added, and burst out laughing.

"Hey, Pop, Mom," Armando forced the opening. "Christine here, she's got something great to tell you."

"Oh?" Mom looked at Christine.

"Go on," Armando encouraged. "Tell 'em."

"Well," Christine began, "remember I was going to have a nice frame for Rudy's portrait?"

"You've got it finished?" Mom said excitedly.

"You'll be able to see it soon." She was glad she was finally breaking the news. "At City Hall."

"City Hall?" Mom was puzzled.

"Yeah. At LA City Hall," Armando announced triumphantly.

"Los Angeles City Hall?" Pop questioned.

"But how can that be?" Mom said.

"Christine, she's got great connections," Armando said. "She knows big shots there."

"Not me," she said. "Someone I've known all my life."

"Whattahell all this got to do with Rudy's painting!"

"Tony!"

"This guy," Armando went on, "when he saw the painting, he was, y'know, speechless. Like he told Christine, he wants everybody in LA, in the whole state, to see it. It's almost alive, he said. What's the word he used, Christine?

"Three dimensional."

"Yeah, it's got depth," he said. "You can almost see Rudy like he was right there before you."

Mom's hand went up to her cheek. "I thought you were giving us the painting."

"It is yours and Pop's," Christine said.

"But you said…"

"It'll be there just for a short while," she explained.

"Until the memorial is over," Armando announced.

"Memorial?" Mom was even more confused. "What memorial?"

"The Rudy Diaz Memorial," Armando said. "On Veteran's Day. Right here in East LA. All the big shots gonna be here."

Mom and Pop looked at each other. Finally, Mom, blinking away tears, said, "Rudy's already been honored. When we went to Washington, D.C."

"And got the medal from President Eisenhower," Pop added.

Christine had envisioned Mom and Pop hugging her and Armando with great joy. Why wasn't the revelation a wonderful surprise? Their son's portrait in the sacred hall of City Hall!

"Tony and I, we're thankful for what you're trying to do," Mom told her. "But we don't want to go through all that."

"This gonna be a great honor," Armando said. "A parade with floats, Rudy's high school band playing, everyone in East LA listening to speeches by the governor, the mayor, councilmen and…"

"And possibly President Eisenhower," Christine added.

Again, Mom and Pop looked at each other, Mom fighting tears, Pop rubbing his chin silently.

"When we returned from Washington, D.C.," Pop now said, "and the newspapers and the magazines wrote about us, our old friends and neighbors, they started treating us like we was... Y'know.

"We was no longer old friends like we used to be," he went on. "We had shook hands with the President of the United States. We're not the Tony and Marie they'd known all their lives. Made us feel ever'thing went up our heads.

Even our neighbor's dog stopped barking at us. And our postman, it used to be 'Hey, Tony.' Suddenly, it's 'Hello', Mr. Diaz.'"

Christine was stunned. Shocked. Why in the world didn't it occur to her? Mom and Pop did not want their world changed. Others may have welcomed the fame and attention. Not them.

"It took us a while to make our old friends know that we're the same people they'd know all their lives," Mom said.

And Pop explained that after their trip to Washington and all the newspaper articles about them and Rudy, people had kept away. As though they were somebody special who did not want to be bothered by old friends.

"Now," he said, "we're old friends again. I'm back picking up our neighbor's waste can and putting 'em in their backyard like I used to. And when I'm busy they put our waste can in our backyard.

"Y'know what I'm saying? We're nobody special."

"Rudy, he was somebody special," Armando said. And, tearfully, haltingly, he finally revealed what had happened that day in the trench in Korea up to the moment Rudy jumped on the grenade. No longer able to contain himself, he cried.

Mom stepped over tearfully and hugged him. She told

Armando that Rudy had written them about him and felt like he was his brother. Whatever happened in the trench that day, she was sure Armando would have done the same for him.

"I don' know," Armando said. "I don' know if I've got that kinda guts."

"You and Rudy," Pop said, "you was soldiers. Looked after each other. Rudy's gone now. But you came into our lives and took his place."

"And we're very grateful," said Mom.

"People should remember him," Armando said, wiping his eyes. "What he stood for."

Christine could see Armando contemplating. He finally opened up. He suggested that Pop make a speech at the memorial.

Pop looked at him. Startled. Not quite sure he had heard him.

When Armando went on, suggesting a short, but a deep and warm speech, Pop shook his head vigorously.

"Just a short one," Armando said. "Coming from your heart."

"Long one, short one, I ain't no speaker."

"You'd be speaking to everyone like you're speaking to us right now," Christine said. "Telling your neighbors, your friends, that you and Mom are honored they had all come to celebrate Rudy's memory."

"He's never made a speech in his whole life," Mom said.

"And I ain't gonna break that record now," Pop emphasized.

Christine looked over at Armando, at Mom and Pop, tempted to throw up her hands.

"Everyone expects you to say something," she said as a last resort. "What made Rudy turn out to be what he was."

"Rudy was always a East LA boy," Pop said. "Nothing

changed him.   Not even when he won the Golden Gloves championship."

"He was far better than a boxing champ," Armando said. "He put his life on the line for his country."

Finally realizing that nothing would change Mom's and Pop's mind, Christine thought of Uncle Jess. How will she explain to him that all they had planned and worked for will have to be cancelled? How will he notify all those he got involved, his business associates, his political friends and his workers, about the cancellation?

And George! Will he ever trust her judgment again?

Pop, his voice soft, but firm said, "You gotta forget what happened that day, Armando."

"Remember Rudy for what he was," Mom said. "He did what was expected of him."

"All the memorials, they ain't gonna bring him back," Pop went on. "Let Rudy lie in peace. He did his duty; you did yours. It's now time to go forward."

When Pop reached over, placed his arm around Mom and hugged her, Christine choked on a deep breath and swallowed hard.

CHAPTER 32:

Uncle Jess

The painful eye opener lingered on until next morning and Christine knew the gate was not yet closed.

Driving downtown after an early-morning call from Grand Crystal to come in for a fitting of her wedding gown, she thought now is as good a time as any to break the awful news to Uncle Jess.

She tried on the wedding gown, requested that the waistline be a little tighter and the sleeves a little longer, then walked over to Uncle Jess's office.

Helen, the receptionist in the front office, told her to go right in.

Uncle Jess quickly rose from his chair when she stepped into his office. In addition to the large painting of Aunt Harriet and the photo of Dad and Uncle Jess behind the high desk, there was now a photo of Uncle Jess in his Army officer's uniform.

"Christine," he greeted, "I was just thinking of you."

As always, she kissed him on his cheek and squeezed his hand.

"Coffee?" He stepped over to the long guests' table.

"No thanks." She kept standing there, wanting to get it over with.

"Well," he said, "everything's going smoothly so far. All the guests are looking forward to the memorial and the dedication. I spoke to the Mayor yesterday and he's prepared to make his grand speech. So is the councilman representing East LA. How's your end coming along?"

"Ah, Uncle Jess…"

"You're having difficulty lining up your people?"

"Well…"

"You've gotten everyone lined up?"

She shook her head. "Uncle Jess," she began again, "Armando and I--he's a close friend of Mr. and Mrs. Diaz—we went to break the news to them."

"They're excited?"

She shook her head.

"They're not?"

She shook her head again.

"They're not looking forward to the grand event?"

She finally told him what had happened yesterday.

"But… I don't understand," said Uncle Jess. "They're not happy their son being honored?"

She struggled to make Uncle Jess understand that the Diaz's are humble, but very proud people. They cherish their privacy and do not want their lives to be an open book.

"They live a quiet, peaceful life," she went on. "So do all their friends and neighbors. They want to go living as they have all their lives and not have outsiders interfere with their ways."

"And the dedication and memorial will?"

She nodded.

"Christine," he said, "here's a chance for them to have a great hero among them. To have the whole country recognize someone among them who is the recipient of the country's highest medal."

She nodded. "I told them that."

"And...?"

She shook her head.

After a moment of bewildered silence, Uncle Jess, his voice suddenly harsh and stern, unlike his usual calm and controlled self, boomed out, "Do these people know all the trouble I've gone through!"

She could say nothing.

"Do they know how I've obligated myself to get the leaders of our city, our state, to include this event in their busy schedule!"

"Uncle Jess..."

"How am I going to explain to them that I've made a terrible mistake."

"Perhaps, I should explain to them that it was I who made the mistake."

"It would be simple, just so darn simple, if the Diaz's would go along. I can't understand why they are against it."

She struggled to make Uncle Jess understand that the Diaz's cherish their privacy and do not want their lives be interrupted.

He stepped up to the phone. "I'll make them understand they can't back out.

"What's their number?"

"Uncle Jess, please."

"Christine! We can't just call off everything. All the people I've contacted... It's the biggest moment in LA. In the whole state!"

What else could she say? All the words she had memorized finally came down to, "It won't do any good, Uncle Jess. Armando and I tried to convince them that...what an honor it would be, not only for Rudy, for all the Mexican Americans."

Uncle Jess would not budge.

"Like you," she said, "I couldn't understand at first."

"What's their number!"

"Uncle Jess, please."

"They'd listen to me."

"Uncle Jess, if you were there with us yesterday, you'd understand what they have gone through since... Rudy was killed. They don't want to be reminded of it."

She wiped the tears brimming her eyes.

Silence.

Finally, "You know how many of our soldiers have received the Medal of Honor?" Uncle Jess finally said. "Just a few. A select few who were willing to sacrifice themselves for their fellow soldier. When one of our presidents placed the Medal around a hero's neck, he said, 'I would rather have one of these than be the President of the United States.'"

"Mom and Pop Diaz still have not gotten over..." She could not go on.

She let a moment pass until the pain eased.

Then, "The death of Rudy, their only child," she said, "was somewhat eased, but not completely, when they received the medal from President Eisenhower..."

"They met the President?"

She nodded.

"Then our event would be even more significant."

She shook her head. And explained what they had gone through with their friends and neighbors. They did not want to go through all that again. Like themselves, their friends and neighbors are regular, hard-working people. They don't want their lives disrupted by outsiders.

"By being honored?"

She let the moment go by longer.

"Christine!"

"Uncle Jess. I can't let them go through another painful moment."

"I'll explain to them…"

"It won't do any good. They've been through so much since…

"All they want now is to remember how Rudy lived; not how he died."

Uncle Jess looked at her. Digesting it, his eyes now downcast.

He finally placed the phone back in its cradle.

"I know what you've gone through, Uncle Jess, calling all the people, all your friends. I'm sorry. So awfully sorry. I should have spoken to Mom and Pop before starting the crusade."

Uncle Jess sat at his desk, his chin resting on his open hand, silently, contemplatively.

"It's rare when people don't want to be recognized," he said, finally. "Even more rare when the recognition is for such a great honor."

She stood there looking at him silently. Poor Uncle Jess. Always so loving. So supportive. And she's causing him all this agony.

She stepped over to his chair behind the desk.

She kissed his cheek. Lovingly. Warmly.

"Thank you, Uncle Jess. Thank you for always being so good to me."

He reached for her hand and squeezed it.

"Are you still going to give me away?"

"Of course. All this have nothing to do with your wedding."

As she headed for the door, Uncle Jess lifted the phone. "Helen," he said, "please write to all the people we got involved in the Rudy Diaz memorial. Tell them, due to unexpected and unforeseen circumstances the event has been cancelled. I'll sign the letters as soon as you're done."

CHAPTER 33:

Flip a coin

George had arrived at the Handy Writers Colony back in April, nearly eight months ago, and it was now time to return to sunny California as Autumn in Southern Illinois was rapidly turning into Winter, the night air already frosty, chilly and biting cold.

He repacked all his belongings in his suitcase and was ready to bid aloha to his adopted home. He cleaned the bathroom, the kitchen and the bedroom, and was already missing the cabin which had provided him the privacy, the sanctuary and the drive to finish his novel. Unlike his spare, drab and uninspiring apartment back in California where he had started the novel three years ago, his adopted home had become his spiritual and faithful companion, guiding him day after day.

Rather dramatically, he took a long, deep breath, the familiar odor of the cabin's knotted pine wood passing through his nostrils and settling in his lungs. He suddenly found himself blinking away tears as he took another deep breath, knowing he'd miss the cabin and the entire surroundings as much as he had missed Christine all these months. Christine! Oh, how he had missed her. Just a few more days, Christine, just a few more days and they'd be together again.

For a second, he wondered if he was abandoning Lowney like Jones had, leaving her for the fast New York and the Paris life.

But Lowney left him no choice. She was leaving, too. He can't go with her, and he couldn't stay alone at the colony.

Guiltily, he was elated he was returning to California. Lowney, of course, knew nothing about Christine. He was always careful not to mention Christen to her. She had once gone off into a tirade about girlfriends and marriages; how they had ruined the lives of artists and writers, and how they had kept writers and artists from achieving their full potential. "You want to be a great writer," she had said, "don't ever get married. Shack up, have affairs, get laid, then walk away before you're trapped."

This was one time he wasn't going to go along with her, he told himself. Christine was an inspiration who believed in him, someone who wanted him to succeed, someone who wanted to share his aspirations. She was not someone trapping him.

He gave the cabin a last farewell look, stepped out, and drove over to Lowney's cabin.

Lowney was at her porch waiting for him. He parked nearby and stepped out of his Ford.

"Ready to leave?" she asked.

"Ready," he replied, approaching her, a strong fondness gripping him. She had become not only his devoted teacher, his mentor and his second mother; she had become a part of his life.

"I'll be leaving for Florida tomorrow," she said. "Will be gone until Spring. You want to, you can return and keep working on your next novel."

"That'd be great," he said.

She sat on the step and made room for him.

"I've had many writers here," she said. "You've been the most dedicated and most disciplined. Thank heaven. At my age, I can't go through any more hell raisers and drunkards."

"I'm not as young as some of the others were," he said.

"And you weren't here on a picnic.

"Readers will love your novel," she went on. "Jim wrote about Hawaii from the soldiers' point of view and it was great. You wrote yours from the Hawaiians' point of view and it's just as great. Both novels have historical and social values.

"You may think I helped you," she continued. "Don't believe that. Without your faith and belief in yourself, no one could have helped you."

He thanked her for believing in him, his words not quite adequately expressing his true gratefulness. Without her where would he have been? Most likely in LA's skid row, a drunkard staggering and living with the denizens there.

"I love the title, 'LUCKY COME HAWAII,'" she said. And paraphrased it, "'We were lucky to have come to a beautiful place like Hawaii.' Very original."

He let out a deep sigh. Nothing, absolutely nothing, could be more precious than Lowney's praises. He had endured long periods of harsh criticisms, painful ordeals, and sometimes even condemnations, and now the rewards.

He wished Christine was there listening to Lowney.

"Now, don't expect the agent to place your novel with a publisher right away," she warned. "Publishers are very reluctant to publish first novels. It's a gamble when they do. Just have faith," she encouraged. "And the rewards will follow."

He nodded, hoping he wouldn't have to go through a long waiting period like many beginning writers.

"Don't ever be smug and content over your first book," she warned. "The second one is just as important, if not more so. You don't want to be a one-book writer. That would be a curse."

Christ, he thought. What he'd give to be a one-book writer right now. It wouldn't be a curse; it would be a blessing. Him at last a writer!

When he had told her a few days ago that he'd like to write a sequel to Lucky Come Hawaii she had been against it. Vehemently. "You had a unique experience in Okinawa," she had said. "Write about it through the eyes of your principal character. He almost killed his father's brother, his own uncle. And his father's brother almost killed him.

"There must have been other encounters in Okinawa that you've blanked out," she continued. "Now, open them up. Share what you went through with your readers"

He had agreed. Rather than sitting on pins and needles waiting to hear from the agent, he had gone ahead and had written the first two chapters which Lowney thought was a good start. He would send her the other chapters from California.

Sitting there at her doorsteps ready to leave, he said he was dedicating Lucky Come Hawaii to her. She was against it. She had played no part in it. "Dedicate it to the memory of your father and mother," she suggested. "They've played an important part in your story."

When he told her how deeply she had changed his life and possibly saved him from a frustrated, self-destructive alcoholic life, she compromised. "Flip a coin," she said. "Head, your father and mother."

He dug out a quarter from his pocket and flipped it. Tail!

He wrapped his arms around her and gave her a warm, farewell hug. "Thank you," he expressed, his eyes filling. "Thank you for all you've done for me."

"You deserve it, Dear," she said, returning the hug. "I believe in you. You must keep believing in yourself. We'll always be together. If not here in this life, in the garden beyond."

CHAPTER 34:

Medal of Honor

While George was driving out of the, The Last Retreat gate, Shig in Pomona received a call from Christine.

She said the Rudy Diaz memorial was cancelled. Not postponed; cancelled. She'd explain everything when he and Armando came over for George's homecoming celebration.

Shig was shocked, angry and pissed. He had to stop himself from cursing over the phone. How can they do that? Whattahell's going on!

It, of course, wasn't Christine's fault. Her hands were tied. It's those damn politicians! They must have realized that having a memorial for Rudy Diaz, a Mexican, wouldn't do their political life any good. If anything, it might ruin their political life.

Damn gringos! he cursed. They can't stomach a Mexican being honored.

It was the same with the Niseis in the 442nd. Many of them received the second highest medal, the Distinguished Service Cross. Why wasn't some of them recommended the Medal of Honor? The only one receiving it was Sadao Munemori who got it posthumously after someone who knew a U.S. senator complained that with all the DSCs, why wasn't one of them presented the highest medal?

Words were rampant among the 442nd troops that if the Medal of Honor were presented to every Nisei who made the supreme sacrifice or had distinguished himself in the front lines, there would be too many Japs receiving the country's highest medal.

A Nisei lieutenant, despite losing an arm, had kept spearheading his men against German forces and had saved his men from annihilation. For his extraordinary bravely and exemplary leadership he was recommended the Medal of Honor, but received a lower commendation. Had he been a haole would he have received the Medal of Honor? Damn right!

Shig had polished his Silver Star and his Purple Heart medals and had pinned them on his *VFW Veterans of Foreign War* cap for the Rudy Diaz memorial.

After Christine's call, he dumped all the damn medals and his cap into a garbage can.

CHAPTER 35:

Rumors

As much as he missed Christine and yearned to be with her, George decided to go up to Chicago. God knows when he'd be able to see Jimmy Ota again.

After reading about Sam Sato, Jimmy's boss, George was obsessed to find out what had happened to Sam. Is there still a contract on his head? Is the FBI still protecting him? Is he hiding? Jimmy would surely know and would fill in the missing gap.

Driving farther away from Marshall, he glanced up into the rearview mirror and could see the small, quiet town receding and blending with the rolling hills and the corn fields. Someday, if not next year, he'd like to come back, enjoy the idyllic surroundings and finish his next novel with less pressure from Lowney.

Winter, spring and summer sure went by fast, he thought. Now, as the leaves were turning autumn yellow and orange, they brought back the lonely, uncertain days when he first arrived at the colony. Days when he was tempted to pack up and go back to California and be with Christine. There was always Lowney, however, the driving force that kept encouraging him, reminding him anything worth achieving is worth the sacrifice.

He had always been a dreamer, many times dreaming of vague events with no beginnings nor any endings. Recently, his dreams involved Otosan and Okasan. They could not believe that their son, Georgie, was a writer. When they themselves could barely read or write.

And who was his *sensei* teacher? A haole. He had never even spoken freely to a haole growing up on Maui. They were the elite, the big shots, the rich who lived on the hillsides and the mountain tops. Their children went to private schools, belonged to exclusive country clubs and associated only with their own people.

It was hard to believe that Lowney, a haole, was not only his caring sensei; she was his close friend as well. When his book comes out he hoped it would show the difference between the Maui haoles, who were always imposing their ways, from their counterparts on the Mainland.

Like that day at Baldwin High School. Without any warning the principal, a haole, of course, announced over the public address system that *"as of tomorrow everyone must start wearing shoes to school. Those who did not would be sent home."* The carefree barefoot days suddenly came to an end. A sad day for everyone. Except for the shoe stores.

Now, passing a high school along the highway, the rearview mirror no longer reflecting Marshall, he wiggled his toes in his shoes. Weeks had gone by at Baldwin before his feet were comfortable, the blisters mercifully gone and he could walk around the campus no longer carrying his shoes.

Boy, those topsy-turvy pupule high school days. Those black-out nights after Pearl Harbor. Those curfew hours, sundown to sunup. Only four days of school, the fifth day a victory-corps day, working in the sugar cane fields or in the pineapple fields. For him and Jimmy Ota, those were great days. Whodahell cared about studies. Someday, when the President changed his mind and started drafting Niseis again, they would be going into the Army and off to war.

It wasn't until early 1943 that the tide of the Pacific war began changing and the Japanese forces were stopped from taking over more islands. In Hawaii, the blackout and curfew hours were lifted; people were no longer arrested for failing to carry gas masks and the food and gasoline rations were eased.

It was then that President Roosevelt tested the loyalty of the Niseis. He asked for 1,000 volunteers to join the army. The President and the Army generals were astounded when 10,000 volunteers showed up the next day at the various armories in Hawaii. In the Mainland, though they were incarcerated in relocation camps, hundreds of Niseis stepped forward to show their loyalty.

He and Jimmy were the first to step into the Wailuku armory. They would at last be going to Mainland U.S.A. A dream comes true.

Those young pupule days, he thought. They had volunteered not only for patriotic reasons; it was a chance to go to the good ol' U.S. of A and to experience the Mainland life they had heard all their lives.

What they experienced wasn't what they heard or read. Like the Negro troops, the 442nd was a segregated outfit. They trained in separate camps in the South and were thought to be foreigners by the Southerners. Some even thought they were Jap POWs now fighting for America.

And the rest was history.

It was noon when he finally pulled into Chicago. He drove directly to the corner of Clark and Division Streets, parked and went into the Man Fook Low restaurant. Only, it was no longer

Man Fook Low. It was now New China House.

Stepping into the newly decorated restaurant, the walls adorned with colorful Chinese paintings, the showcases filled with intricate dolls and figurines, he spoke to the head waiter. Chuckling amiably, the head waiter explained that Sam Sato no longer owned the restaurant and Jimmy Ota was no longer working there. If he wanted to see Jimmy he'd have to go to Joe's Pool Hall down the block.

Glad that Jimmy had not skipped town after the Senate investigation, he walked across the street, and went down a block to the pool hall.

As expected, and as he remembered, Joe's was one of those rundown basement hangouts, the stairway dank and dark, the doorway narrow and dilapidated. The entrance was open and he could hear the cracking of pool balls.

Stepping in, he immediately noticed that there were four pool tables, all occupied by Japanese players who were either shooting or standing around the tables with pool sticks and chalks in their hands. Jimmy was not one of them.

In the far back corner was a low wooden desk, a bare, uncovered light bulb hanging over it. Sitting at the desk was someone he could not make out until he stepped up closer. It was Jimmy, a cap covering his long, uncut hair, a cigarette between his fingers.

"Hey, Jimmy."

Jimmy looked up through the dense cigarette smoke, and stared.

"What? You forgot me?"

"Hey, George!" Jimmy rose, extending his good right hand. "Wheredahell you been? Thought you went back home."

He shook Jimmy's hand heartily.

The phone on the desk rang.

Picking up the receiver, Jimmy spoke softly. "…Yeah, okay. The Fifth at Golden Gate. Ten on Social Theme."

Hanging up, Jimmy, indicating the phone, said, "'At's what I do now. Take bets for the syndicate."

George, of course, understood. The Senate investigation had tightened up actions in Chicago. No more open gambling. Just phone calls with established bettors.

"So. How long you gonna be in town?" Jimmy wanted to know.

"Just overnight."

"Just overnight?" Jimmy was disappointed.

"Gotta head back to California."

"Well, you least dropped by."

"Had to. Don' know when I gonna see you again."

He finally asked the impending question.

"Aw, nobody know what happened to him," Jimmy said. "Maybe he mah-ke."

"Rubbed out?"

"The syndicate, dey wanna know if Sam ever contacted me," Jimmy said. "'Hell no, I told 'em. Me, da last guy he's gonna contact. He knows you guys keeping an eye on me, I told 'em.'

"Shit man, even his wife don' know what happened to him. Da word on the street, da FBI gave him plastic surgery."

There goes my novel, George thought.

"All kinda stories 'round town," Jimmy went on. "Y'know. Who set up the contract on Sam's head? Who took care those two hit men dat screwed up? Da word on da street, it's Angelo Trimaka. One of those guys tryin' to get in good with da big boss.

From what we hear, Angelo's the next one gonna be found in da cornfield."

Wow! George thought. Killings among the mob themselves. What a great story. If he can get the details.

"Da word, Angelo was jealous Sam rising up fast in the syndicate," Jimmy continued. "Y'know. Him, a Japanee. 'Nother talk. Da syndicate no wanna fool 'round with drugs. Dey t'ink Sam was getting into it."

"He was?"

"Aw, just rumors. Me, I t'ink Sam too smart to go against the syndicate. He had it made. Whattafuck go against 'em. But, whattahell I know. Dat way, they leave me alone."

He wanted to take Jimmy out for to a farewell dinner, but Jimmy said he was going to be busy with his weekend poker game. Along with booking for the syndicate and his poker games, he said he was doing pretty good. Soon, he'd have enough for a long vacation to Maui. Who knows? He might run into Sam."

"What makes you think he's on Maui?" George asked.

"Aw, just a hunch," Jimmy said. "He used to a'ways like go fishing there."

He told Jimmy he'd drop by in the morning before leaving, and walked back to his Ford. He drove over to a parking space at Supreme Hotel where he had stayed on his first trip, then went over to Kyoto Restaurant across the street for a sukiyaki dinner.

Returning to the hotel, the desk clerk asked if he wanted a girl sent up to his room. In the old days, he and his GI buddies would have jumped at the chance. That, of course, was those reckless Army days.

After a quick shower, he made himself a cup of hotel-room

coffee, sat on the comfortable sofa, and picked up the phone.

It was the usual time when he called Christine and she answered right away.

"Moshi moshi." An overflowing warmth surged through him at the sound of her warm yasashi voice.

"Moshi moshi," he returned.

"You're calling from Chicago?"

"Hai. Ima sugu kimashita. Just arrived.

"Jimmy wa yoroshiku?"

"Hai. He's fine. Was nice seeing him again."

A pause.

"Christine? You still there?"

"Hai."

Another pause.

"What's wrong?"

Very reluctantly, she told him about the Rudy Diaz memorial fiasco.

"The whole thing's cancelled?"

Her voice faded for a moment. He could see her wiping her eyes. "I shouldn't have assumed anything," she finally said.

"Hey," he said, "It was a great idea. I'm sure Rudy's mom and dad appreciate very much what you and Armando planned."

After another pause, she asked, "*Itsu kaeri masu?*"

"I should be back in three days."

"Honto? Yakusoku?"

"Hai. Yakusoku."

"Oh, George! I can't believe it. You'll finally be back."

Next morning, he dropped over at the pool hall. Unlike their usual long Hawaiian aloha, he and Jimmy made it short.

"We'll see ya, okay?" Jimmy said.

"Yeah. Okay," he said, thrusting out his hand.

Instead of shaking his hand, Jimmy gave him a warm aloha hug. "Take care," he said. "You got a long drive. No forget now. Me, I'm waiting for your book come out," and he handed him a match box with the poolhall's address.

"You'll get the first copy," George said, tearing away.

He headed out of Chicago and decided to take the northern route, Nebraska, Wyoming, Utah, Nevada and finally good old California.

Eager to be with Christine, he was speeding through a wide open Nebraska highway when a patrol car flashed its lights.

Oh, Christ!

The tall, blond, blue-eyed cop, about his age, got out of his patrol car and marched over stoically.

"In a hurry?" the cop said, taking out his note pad from his shirt pocket, a pencil in his hand.

Remembering his IRS days, George warned himself to be humble and not say any more than necessary. "Was I really going fast?" he said innocently.

"Eighty in a sixty-five mile zone."

"Yeah?"

"Your driver's license," the cop requested.

He took out his wallet from his back pocket and handed his license.

The cop studied it, looked at him, back at it. "Someone waiting for you back in California?"

Smiling, he nodded.

"Born and raised there?"

He shook his head. "Hawaii."

"Hawaii, hunh? Japanese?"

Nodding, he hoped the damn cop wasn't one of those who's gonna blame him for the Pearl Harbor attack.

"My cousin, he was once stationed in the islands."

"Oh, yeah. You, too?"

"Me? Naw. I was in the Italian front."

"In General Mark Clark's Fifth Army?"

'Hey," the cop said, "you weren't with that Japanese outfit that fought along us, were you?"

"Me? Like your cousin I was in the Pacific."

"Boy, that Japanese outfit over there Europe," the cop said. "What a bunch of fighters. Best fighting outfit in the whole damn Army."

"A friend of mine was in it," he said. "Italy, France, Germany."

"I was there when they were recognized for their bravery and valor by General Clark. Right there at the front."

"Yeah. I heard about that."

"What a small world," the cop said, sticking his pad and pen back into his shirt pocket. "--Hey," he went on, "you're in a hurry to get back to California, you better get going. Watch out for patrol cars behind them signs."

"I'll stay within the speed limit," he said.

"Just don't keep your girlfriend waiting." The cop winked.

Chuckling, he got his license back, shook the cop's hand warmly, and started his Ford.

Driving off within the speed limit, he thought the cop was like himself during his IRS days. If the taxpayer was humble and sincere he was inclined to give the taxpayer a break.

He had thought of driving up to Heart Mountain near

Yellowstone National Park where one of the ten relocation camps for Japanese during the war was located. Going there meant he'd lose a day and so he turned south toward Utah. There was another relocation camp in Utah which was on his way to California. His army buddy, Tak Enomoto, and his family was incarcerated there. It'd be interesting to see from where Tak had volunteered in the army.

Making it to Salt Lake City before nightfall, he located the city's Japanese town which was only a few blocks away from the Mormon Tabernacle. He drove around the brightly lit tabernacle square, surprised that bus loads of tourists were still going in and out of the square at sundown. Along with Heart Mountain in Wyoming, he would have wanted to visit the Mormon headquarters, then again, it would take another extra day before heading home.

He had never heard of a Little Tokyo in Salt Lake City and was surprised that it occupied several blocks. Near it was the Mormon headquarters with hundreds of blond, blue-eyed haoles intermingling with dark-haired, dark-eyed Japanese.

He checked in at an old, red-bricked Japanese hotel, Colonial Inn, and was happy when he was able to order a teriyaki fish dinner with miso soup there. He could understand Japanese pioneers settling in the West Coast. What made them settle here in Salt Lake City miles away from the Coast?

Eager to get going, he got up quite early, did not have breakfast, and headed south.

At sunup, a few hours out of Salt Lake City, he came across a highway sign, Delta. He veered right, away from the main highway, and came to a Mormon farming community.

While waiting for the young boy to fill his tank, he stepped into the café adjoining the station, and had a light breakfast.

He asked the boy for the direction to Topaz relocation camp. The boy seemed confused. All he knew was that there was once a Japanese community nearby. "There's no one living there now," the boy said. "If you want to know more about it go over and talk to Mrs. Wills who lives just a block from here. She knows everything about Delta Valley."

If he's going to make it to Los Angeles in 10 hours, he told himself, he can spend just a a few minutes there in the valley.

Topaz, as the boy said, was nothing more than open desert with wind-swept sage brushes and weeds tumbling everywhere.

He parked at the entrance of the vast isolated open space where a huge sign said it was once the location for Japanese evacuees. It never mentioned nor did it explain why the evacuees had been there.

The sign, he quickly noticed, was full of bullet holes. Holes that covered every inch of open space. Adjacent to the sign was a warning that anyone using the sign for target practice would be promptly arrested and prosecuted.

As he stepped out of the Ford and stood there, the chilly wind whipping across his face, his eyes blinking against the sand storm, he could hear Tak describing the camp days. There were times, Tak had said, when the wind was so strong no one could leave their tar-papered barracks. And during the winters the mountains and the flat lands would be covered with blankets of snow which seemed beautiful until the freezing, biting cold got to you.

Tak had also talked about him and his buddies working for farmers in central Utah picking strawberries. They were trucked from Topaz to the farms and back to the camp. The Mormon farmers, Tak had said, were quite friendly. Not so the non-Mormon agitators who used to take potshots at them out in the fields.

Looking around, George could hardly imagine that over ten thousand Nihonjins had survived in the barren desert throughout the duration of the war. That was more than the entire population of Delta. And guys like Tak had volunteered in the Army after being treated like traitors!

Stepping back into his Ford, he took a last look at the harsh, isolated desert around him. Would he have volunteered in the Army had the damn government abandoned him in a place like this?

CHAPTER 36:

Typical Japanese

When Uncle Jess warned her that the state of California might not allow marriages between whites and non-whites, Christine, of course, was shocked. How could marriages be dictated by bigoted, prejudiced politicians? People got married because they loved each other. Not because they were white, black or Asians. It was absurd and ridiculous that a state could dictate whom one could marry.

She hurried over to SC's law library and, with the help of one of the law librarian students, looked up the statute. The law student, a young girl, was also shocked that there could be a statute dictating marriages.

The girl thumbed through pages of California statutes before coming to what they were looking for. Yes, indeed, there was such a law. It was associated with laws passed many years ago during the slavery days in the South. A Negro could not marry a white. The restriction was eventually passed on to other states, including California, not only between a Negro and a white, but between all non-whites and whites.

Checking further, they discovered, much to Christine's relief, that the law in California was repealed in 1948.

Christine wondered if George knew there was once such a statute. When she'd mention it to him she was sure he'd deem the redemption a good omen for them.

George would be home any day now and she waited for another call before he finally arrived.

The call had come earlier this morning.

After exchanging warm, happy greetings and feeling he was there beside her, she pleaded, "Don't ever leave me alone again, George."

"We'll always be together from now on," he said.

"*Honto?*"

"Hai. Honto desu."

"*Anata ga ano tokore itta hi kara tottemo sabishi katta.* I've been awfully lonely ever since you went away that day.

"Watashi demo tottemo sabishi katta."

"*Do shi-te?*" She wanted to hear him to say it.

"Because…"

Although he's an American, she thought, he's still a typical Japanese.

All right, she'll say it. "You know why I missed you so much, George?"

"Why?"

"Because I love you. Very much."

There was a silence.

"Did you hear me, George?"

"Yeah. I feel the same way."

Well, she supposed that was as close as she'd hear him say it, she thought.

During her young Kobe days, she used to wonder how did Japanese couples manage to have so many babies when they never showed any affection for each other. Well, maybe under the futon.

Around mid-morning, a car came speeding into the driveway.

Looking out the window, she saw a teenage boy getting out and hurrying up to the front door.

What's he up to? she wondered.

She waited, hoping he'd go away.

After another round of urgent knocking, she finally opened the door.

"Yes?" she said, studying the young, blond, blue-eyed boy.

"Does George Tsuk-yam live here?" the boy asked.

She looked at the brown envelope in his hand.

"Does he?"

"Well, yes."

"Will you sign here, please"

"What is it?"

"This?" The carrier looked at the envelope in his hand; back at her. "It's a telegram."

"A telegram? From whom?"

"Please," the carrier said impatiently, indicating the dotted line, "will you sign here."

As she took the pen and the envelope, she was reminded of that dreadful day when the highway patrol officers came to inform her of Mom and Dad's horrible auto accident.

She let out a deep sigh when she discovered that the message was not from the police department. It was from Florida. George had told her that Lowney was driving there for the winter. Did something happen to her?

She signed the envelope.

As the carrier drove off the driveway she kept staring at the envelope in her hand, over at the retreating car, back at the envelope, tempted to open it. She'd better not, she warned herself. It was George's, a private matter.

She placed the envelope on the lamp table close to the door, her eyes riveted to it. If it's from Lowney, she hoped nothing has happened to her. George would be devastated if she was suddenly ill or got involved in an accident.

CHAPTER 37:

The Novel

It was almost two in the afternoon when George, anxious and with great expectations, drove up the Hollywood Freeway and sped up the Santa Monica Boulevard off ramp. Although he had been on the road for nearly ten hours, stopping once in St. George, Utah, for a sandwich and a cup of coffee and once more in Las Vegas to gas up, the 750-mile long drag surprisingly had not tired him as much as he thought it would.

Heading west on Santa Monica, he finally approached Remington Park.

Parking at Christine's driveway, he rushed out of his Ford and dashed up the front steps. Before he could knock, the door flew open.

Christine, in her usual, casual Levis and a T-shirt rushed into his arms. "George, oh, George. You're home! You're home!"

He wrapped his arms around her, the moment not a dream anymore. "God, I missed you," he said. "Never thought I could miss anyone so much."

They stepped into the house, shut the door behind them, their arms still around each other, the sweet fragrance of her perfume arousing him, her slender body pressing against him, her lips so soft, so delicate, so maddening.

Then, gradually, as an afterthought, her arms dropped to her sides.

"What's wrong?" he said, looking at her, puzzled.

She reached for an envelope at the lamp table.

"This came this morning," she said, her fingers unsteady.

He looked at her, at the envelope, back at her, finally reaching for it. It reminded him of the Western Union message he got from Lowney when Harry, her husband, had died.

Reluctantly, he opened the envelope.

He glanced at the message, looked over at Christine, back at the message. Startled, unbelieving, he could hear Christine saying in an alarmed, tremulous voice, "Something's happened to Lowney? Is she all right?"

It finally sunk in.

"George!"

The envelope dropped out his hand.

"George! Is she all right?"

In a vibrant, jubilant voice, he screamed, "He Sold It! Ted Agnew, the agent, sold my story!"

Christine reached down and picked up the envelope.

"Ohmygosh!" she cried out, and read it again. "Oh, George!"

"Holy…! My novel, it's gonna be published!"

As Christine read the message again, George added, "Ted Agnew must've called her."

He hugged Christine again, his eyes blinking away joyful tears.

"Oh, how I love her! How I love that woman!"

He squeezed Christine in his arms again, not wanting the glorious moment to end. "And I love you, too, Christine! I love you, too!"

"Oh, George!" He could feel her arms wrapping tighter around him.

Backing away a moment, still breathless, he cried out, "Let's celebrate!"

"Go over to Kawamoto?"

"I mean really celebrate."

She looked at him.

"Let's get married."

"What?!"

"Let's get married!"

"Today?" she questioned.

"Right now," he said. "We'll drive over to Las Vegas, get married and celebrate at one of the hotels."

"George," she said, "we can't get married in Nevada."

"Why not?"

And, she explained that while at the USC law library she discovered that there were many neighboring states that had anti-miscegenation laws.

"You mean, because I'm Japanese I can't marry you!" he said, his voice rising. "Whattahell kind law is that?!"

Then, she explained the history of the law. That it was originally meant to prevent Negroes from marrying whites and it was extended to include Asians.

He couldn't believe that Nevada, of all states, would have such a law. It allowed gambling of all types, permitted girls walking the streets, even permitted prostitution in the hotels. And it wouldn't allow a Japanese to marry a haole!

When Christine said Utah was another state that had an anti-miscegenation law, he was even more shocked. Utah, a Mormon state that had missionaries all over the world, including Japan, preaching brotherhood, equality and spiritual guidance would not allow one of their own kind to marry a Japanese. What a bunch of…!

He caught himself and stopped from condemning the Mormon church. Or any church. He and Christine had never discussed religion or politics and he warned himself not to. Besides, who was he to condemn any religion when he never went to church.

When Christine mentioned that California had repealed its anti-miscegenation law, he was surprised.   California hated Japanese more than any other state. It had suspected Japanese, without exception, as spies, saboteurs and traitors during the war, and had swept them off to race horse stables before abandoning them at godforsaken, windswept deserts throughout the western states.

"You mean you and I can get married in California?"

"Since 1948," she said.

"What, Japanese are no longer spies and traitors?" he said spitefully.

"Attitudes have changed, George."

Still spiteful, he said, "Good to know we're finally Americans."

"And finally accepted," she said.

Accepted? Japs accepted by haoles?

He let a moment go by.

"Well," he finally said, "let's do it then. Kekon shi masho."

"Today?"

"Right now."

"But.."

"Don't you wanna?"

"Yes. Of course. But…"

He did not give her a chance to reason why they should wait.

They could drive downtown, get a marriage license and go over to one of those marriage shops near Little Tokyo and have a preacher perform the ceremony.

"Don't you want some of our friends there?" she said, pleadingly.

"We don't have time," he said. "The window gonna be closed in couple of hours."

"Don't you want me to at least change?"

"We'll get married as we are."

She looked at him, glanced down at her Levis and T-shirt.

"You're looking fine."

"George!"

"Who said you gotta wear a wedding dress or me wear a suit to get married," he said, and headed for the door. "C'mon."

Finally, throwing protocols out the window, she joined him at the door.

"No more time talking story," he urged.

"All right," she said, just as determined. "No more time talking story."

THE END

Source:

Wikipedia.org Japanese-American service in World War II
World War II Nisei vet

During the early years of World War II, Japanese Americans were forcibly relocated from their homes in the West Coast because military leaders and public opinion combined to fan unproven fears of sabotage. As the war progressed, many of the young Nisei, Japanese immigrants' children who were born with American citizenship, volunteered or were drafted to serve in the United States military. Japanese Americans Nisei served in all the branches of the United States Armed Forces, including the United States Merchant Marine. An estimated 33,000 Japanese Americans served in the U.S. military during World War II, of which 20,000 joined the Army. Approximately 800 were killed in action.

The 100th/442nd Infantry Regiment became the most decorated unit in U.S. military history. The related 522nd Field Artillery Battalion liberated one or more subcamps of the infamous Dachau concentration camp. Other Japanese-American units also included the 100th Infantry Battalion, the Varsity Victory Volunteers, and the Military Intelligence Service.

The Nisei Soldiers of World War II Congressional Gold Medal
By US Mint design:
Obverse-Joel Iskowitz Reverse-Don Everhart

Other Titles by Jon Shirota

Title: Voices from Okinawa: Featuring Three Illustrated Plays

- Author: Jon Shirota
- Publisher: University of Hawaii Press
- Paper Back: ISBN: 9780824833916
- Number of pages: 224
- Publication Date: January 2009

Despite Okinawa's long and close relationship with the United States, most Americans know little about the rich and remarkable culture of Japan's southernmost islands. And they know even less about the Okinawan immigrants who brought their heritage to the U.S. over one hundred years ago. In this landmark publication the first literary anthology showcasing Okinawan Americans their voices are heard in plays, essays, and memoirs.

Title: Lucky Come Hawaii

- Author: Jon Shirota
- Publisher: Univ of Hawaii Pr; 1 edition
- Paper Back: ISBN: 9780824834487
- Number of pages: 240
- Publication Date: January 2010

In the opening chapter of this classic novel set in Hawai'i, news of the attack on Pearl Harbor has just reached rural Maui. Miscommunication, confusion, and rumors of war aggravate the already tense relations among the diverse immigrant communities, Native Hawaiians, and the American military.

Title: The Chronicles of Ojii-Chan

- Author: Jon Shirota
- Publisher: TotalRecall Publications
- Paper Back: ISBN: 9781590954614
- eBook: ISBN: 9781590954621
- Number of pages: 256
- Publication Date: 2016

Ernie Pyle, America's greatest war correspondent, covered the battle fronts in Africa, Italy, France and Germany. Then, during his last assignment, he was killed on tiny Ie Jima off the coast of Okinawa.

There have been speculations who shot Ernie Pyle. Grandpa Ojii-chan who was in the battle of Ie Jima fighting for Japan alarmingly discovers that he could have been the one who had killed the famous non-combatant war correspondent.

Title: A Navajo Love Story

- Author: Jon Shirota
- Publisher: TotalRecall Publications
- Paper Back: ISBN: 9781590951231
- eBook: ISBN: 9781590951217
- Number of pages: 160
- Publication Date: 2017

Andrea Begayee, an attractive part-Navajo girl, is about to venture out to the world of life. She hasn't decided what college to attend until she meets Mark Kimball, a missionary, who convinces her to attend college with him.

When the young couple meet and they had no intention of getting to know each other. Despite their vast differences in race, religion and beliefs they are helplessly pulled together.

Would they have continued their friendly relationship had they known that love does not conquer all, and that the past of one of them will eventually destroy their life.

www.ingramcontent.com/pod-product-compliance
Lightning Source LLC
Chambersburg PA
CBHW021501110726
47899CB00001BA/249